THE BLUE TATAR

L. N. GRUER

UNION SQUARE
PUBLISHING

Published by
Union Square Publishing
301 E. 57th Street, 4th floor
New York, NY 10022
www.unionsquarepublishing.com

Manufactured in the United States of America, or in the United Kingdom when distributed elsewhere.

Gruer, L. N.
    The Blue Tatar
    LCCN: 2019917425
    ISBN: 978-1-946928-25-2
    eBook: 978-1-946928-47-4

Cover illustration by: Alyson Carpenter
Cover design by: Natasha Clawson
Cover photo by: Monique Feil
Editing and Interior design by: Claudia Volkman
Proofreading by: Carolyn Olson

Disclaimer: This is a work of fiction. All names, characters, organizations, and events are fictional. Any resemblance to actual persons, living or dead, or actual events is purely coincidental.

www.lngruer.com

FOR SHUROCHKA

Miss you every day

CONTENTS

LIST OF CHARACTERS

Prologue

Sergei Vladimirovich Kanevsky—a low-level NKVD commissar from Tver, Russia sent to Ukraine to "deal with the enemies of the Soviet state"

Zina—a young woman from Vinnytsia, Ukraine, a survivor of the Vinnytsia massacre

Azrael—the Angel of Death and transformation in Abrahamic religions. In Islam he is often called "Malak al-Maut." In Hebrew, *Azrael* translates as "The Helper of God," "Help from God," or "One Whom God Helps."

Dr. Bella (Isabella) Ginzburg

Yuri Novikov—Dr. Bella's husband

Polina (Lina)—Yuri and Bella's college age daughter, their only child

Sasha (formally Alexandra)—owner of a flower shop, originally from Kiev, Ukraine

Papa Victor—adoptive father of Sasha, a Soviet WWII veteran

Klavdia Petrovna—adoptive mother of Sasha, now deceased

Dr. Sonya—Papa Victor's first wife

Gary—Papa and Dr. Sonya's natural son; Papa lost contact with him when he signed away his parental rights

Lee—Sasha's husband

Jason—only son of Lee and Sasha

Alla Markovna Novikova—Yuri's mother, a retired physician

Bozena—the Polish caregiver

Oksana—Yuri's baby sister

Slava (formally Stanislav)—Oksana's husband

Avi—Israeli neighbor to Victor and Alla Markovna, who taught Krav Mag. Oksana considers him her lifeline and BFF.

Maya—Slava's sister and Oksana's sister-in-law, works at day spa

Svetlana (Sveta)—owns the day spa where Maya works

Zina—Maya's grandmother

Vlad (formally Vladimir) Kanevsky—Maya's husband and descendant of Soviet commissar Sergei Kanevsky

Vera Stepanovna—nanny to Slava and Maya

Comrade Schevchenko—widower and neighbor of grandmother Zina

Uncle Alec, Uncle Lev—worked for Zina as protection (not real uncles)

Flora—Maya's client

Ken—Flora's American second husband, Vlad's business partner

Zack—Ken's son and Flora's stepson

Dora Osipovna Ginzburg—Bella's mother

Anna Sergeevna Kanevskaya—Vlad's mother

Steve—Bella's horse trainer and lover

PROLOGUE

Vinnytsia, Ukraine, 1937

THE SOVIET COMMISSAR, wearing a sweat and bloodstained NKVD uniform and muddy regulation boots, sat under a young linden tree on the banks of the Southern Bug River, legs spread wide, shaved head hanging low, his bent arms behind his head. He'd seen plenty of horror and carnage in his nearly thirty years on earth, but what he witnessed in the last few days had burned his soul, causing him as much, if not more, physical pain than the bullet he took as a teenage Bolshevik soldier, fighting the treacherous counterrevolution bandits during the Civil War.

His name was Sergei Vladimirovich Kanevsky, and he hailed from the medieval city of Tver, northwest of Moscow, where the holy mother Volga meets her little sister, the River Tvertsa. Although the rich soil he now sat upon wasn't his own, he felt no inherent hatred toward its people; after all, Ukrainians weren't immoral foreigners, like the Germans or the Christ-killing Jews—they were good Slavs, just like him. Unlike some of the old-guard Bolsheviks, the now-purged Internationalists, Sergei was a simple man, a patriot, loyal to Comrade Stalin's vision of building Communism in his homeland.

In all the harsh years of fighting for the Great Socialist Revolution, Sergei never questioned his commitment to the party or his commanding officers. When the orders to liquidate "without mercy" first arrived directly from the NKVD (People's Commissariat for Internal Affairs), Sergei expected that the executions would be strictly limited to a few convicted "Enemies of the People," either serving life sentences or about to be detained. He knew only too well that the Revolution was still vulnerable and needed to be protected from her enemies, both external and more dangerously, internal; but now he was questioning not only his own part in the mass murders of Vinnytsia's civilian population, but his faith in the entire system.

Nothing had prepared him for the hundreds of shots, screams, curses, and finally the desolate silence as piles and piles of freshly excavated ground covered the dead bodies, some of them young women stripped bare. That wasn't the worst of it, however. Some weren't dead at all, and still his comrades didn't stop, suffocating the victims without mercy by burying them alive. He saw the atrocities with his own eyes. His job was to check the site for any leftover evidence and execute anyone who refused to follow orders or attempted to save lives. To Sergei's relief, no one did either: the orders were followed to a "t," and the mass grave sites looked as if nothing sinister had transpired.

No matter how hard he tried to justify the mass executions of the state's enemies, he simply could not swallow the fact that he just stood by and saw evil on such a grand scale perpetrated against the innocent. No rational person could believe in the guilt of all of the citizens. The grand cover-up spoke volumes as well. Sergei had killed in battle, but never like this; he had mercifully finished off two gravely wounded but still alive Ukrainian men—a father and a son—with his own gun, unable to see them struggling for each breath. He shook his head and rubbed his raw, sleep-deprived, tear-stained eyes. It was time to go, but he couldn't make his body do what his mind said it must.

The weary commissar decided to take a swim; maybe the cool, murky river water would clear his head, if not his conscience. He took off his khaki tunic, undershirt, and trousers, leaving his long johns on—one thing he learned during the numerous military campaigns was that you never wanted to be caught bare-assed, especially in enemy territory. Just removing the uniform made him breathe easier. Looking down at his hairless chest, he remembered wearing a small silver cross as a boy, before he joined the Revolution. For some reason, he reached for it, finding his neck bare. Just for a moment, he considered hiding the holster holding the single-action semiautomatic Korovin behind, but on second thought took it with him.

Entering the water in one swift movement, Sergei didn't flinch, being well accustomed to the smell and the feel of the river. The water was chilly but refreshing to his skin. He began to increase his speed, using the powerful freestyle stroke he had learned swimming as a young boy in the

Volga, enjoying the resistance of the current against his tense muscles. He figured he'd swim for a few minutes and then walk back to his belongings. The river did its magic, and he was starting to feel more like himself when he thought he saw something odd on the bank. Deciding to investigate, Sergei swam ashore and exited the water slowly, his gun at the ready.

At first, he thought it was a wounded animal because of the birds circling above, but when he approached, he realized it was a nude human body, lying face down and covered with dirt, twigs, and leaves. By the look of the well-developed backside and long, thick black hair, the body was that of a young woman, barely past her teen years. Sergei got on his knees and checked for any signs of life; he found she was still breathing, though barely. He turned the girl over on her back as gently as he could to check for injuries. He couldn't see anything obvious except for a gorgeous pair of breasts; in fact, the rest of her was so exquisitely formed, his heart skipped a beat.

Then he saw it: caked blood on the side of her temple, right above the ear, the bullet just grazing her head. Oh, Lord help him. The girl was one of the executed Ukrainians! Somehow, she had managed to find a pocket of air, wait out the executioners, and escape. Moved by an uncontrollable urge to see her face, the commissar moved the tangle of her hair to the side, gasping in shock: she was a rare beauty, perfect in every way—as if nature decided to collect pleasing-to-the-eye features from different women and arrange them together in a most unique way. Her generously lashed eyes were closed; her face looked oddly peaceful considering the circumstances.

Conflicted about what to do, Sergei knew he should either finish the job himself (which would be the most merciful option) or bring her in for someone else to finish her off for good. He sat there, almost paralyzed by internal turmoil. The longer he sat without killing her, staring at God's perfect creation, the less inclined he was to take another sin upon his soul, if there was such a thing.

The day was nearing its end as the pleasant afternoon breeze morphed into a cold wind, causing Sergei to shiver in his still damp bottoms. He took them off, hanging them on the branch of a bush facing the sun. He placed his gun on the ground by his side and lay down next to the girl, trying to get both of them warm. He draped his arm around her shoulders, placing her head inside the crook of his arm. She was quiet, but her breathing began to change; in his head, it was getting stronger.

Whatever possessed him to kiss her lips, he didn't know, but he did. Her pale, agate-smooth skin smelled of forest mushrooms, rich cream, and wild strawberries—and suddenly he was lost. There and then he decided to save her, binding her to him, waking her up with a kiss as if she was not the Enemy of the People, but Sleeping Beauty from a long-forgotten fairy tale.

One kiss turned into many. Blood rushed into his head as he continued to caress her now-warm skin, waiting for her to open her eyes, expecting her to scream and stop him. Sergei wasn't a rapist; he had his own little girl, a newborn he had named after his mother Anya back in Tver. He used to abhor his comrades who used war as an excuse to hurt the innocent, but here he was doing something he knew was wrong, unable to control his own lust. Maybe it was his way of erasing the memories of death, or maybe he had lost his mind and the young woman was a forest witch who trapped him with her beauty, but God help him, he was desperate to mate. Slowly and as gently as he could, he took his pleasure; still she didn't open her eyes. He prayed she wouldn't remember the assault and one day would forgive him, provided he saved her, provided they both survived the wrath of the NKVD.

—◆◆◆—

Azrael, the Angel of Death, his giant soft wings tinted silver and azure blue to match the sky, soared above the killing fields, making sure those in need of his assistance received it without delay. It had been a busy few days, although for him, time did not exist. Making a turn toward the river, he saw her—a young woman, more of a girl— standing near two bodies, both nude, the man on top. She was attired modestly in a long white linen skirt and matching wide-sleeved blouse, common to these parts of Ukraine. The dress was embroidered with white birds and red roses around the neck, along the cuffs and the hem, and the black apron, decorated with metallic thread, was tied neatly around her tiny waist. The red and white colors signified her purity, and the uncovered head, her single status. She was playing with strands of large red beads, looking down at the nude couple, her shiny black hair interwoven with silk roses tightly braided around her small head, making a crown. There was nothing unusual about her appearance, except that she was neither dead nor alive. Azrael was intrigued, a rare occurrence that demanded investigation. He folded his wings and drifted down, landing next to the young woman, careful not to give her a fright.

"Don't be afraid, *ditina*," Azrael said gently in her language, his voice rich and melodic, akin to a shepherd boy's lyre, putting his hand on the girl's shoulder. "I'm not here to hurt you, child."

"I'm not afraid of you, and I am not a child," she answered without a hint of emotion, turning toward him. Rendered speechless by her unearthly beauty, so similar to his own and his kind, God's Special Helper shook his head in sheer amazement. In her face, Azrael recognized the striking bone structure found among the daughters of the windswept steps of Central Asia, covered with the porcelain skin of the Kiev Rus Slavs, framed by the midnight silken Romany hair, but most curiously, he responded to the call of her blood, the blood of the children of Canaan.

"Good, you are as brave as you are comely." Azrael smiled his most consoling smile, the one he reserved for infants and martyrs. "I'm here to take you home, where you will find peace and see your loved ones, those I accompanied before you." When the girl ignored his invitation, once more turning her head toward the two bodies on the ground, he repeated, using an ancient Aramaic word for *love*, this time extending his hand. "Come, it's your time, *khuba*."

"No! It's not my time. It wasn't time for any of us! I will decide if and when I come with you!" she answered with absolute conviction, shocking Azrael with an ice-cold look that turned her stormy sea eyes violet, just like his own, "but do stay and watch. I promise, you will have someone to accompany after all," she offered, once again surprising Death himself by jumping back into her lifeless body.

Within a few moments, her rapist finished and rolled off her, falling into a deep, almost paralytic slumber. Slowly and methodically the girl, completely nude, got up on her knees, keeping a watchful eye on her assailant, who was still sound asleep. With agility and grace, she straddled his body, spreading her bloodied thighs wide as she reached for his weapon, her hair blowing in the wind behind her like a black cloud.

Sergei made a growling, satisfied sound and opened his eyes. At first, he didn't register the danger, enthralled by her wild splendor and the instant sexual reaction from his own body.

"Ah, you are awake and safe," he said, sighing with pleasure and suddenly feeling more alive and hopeful than he had in years.

"Ah, I am awake, but it is you who are not safe," she echoed, with a smile so malevolent that Azrael, who had seen armies of demons, felt cold shivers run up his spine. Before Sergei could react, he felt a searing, unimaginable pain as the girl put a bullet into one of his testicles. He howled, going into shock, but he didn't pass out.

"Feeling satisfied? Had enough?" the vengeful girl asked, pressing the cold tip of the man's own Korovin this time into his forehead. Fighting for his life, Sergei began to cry, the words of his mother's prayer on his lips: "God save me and have mercy on my sinful soul."

Feebly, he tried once more, seeing his death reflected in her eyes, the color of the lilac bushes back home in Tver. "Please, let me go. I have a little girl, a newborn I haven't seen, and a wife. If I didn't follow orders, they would shoot me too. I could have killed you, but I risked everything to save your life."

"And that was your mistake," the girl hissed, cocking the trigger, pressing the tip into Sergei's brow. "An eye for an eye, as the scripture says. I believe this is how you murdered my father and my brother."

"At least promise you will say a prayer for my soul," the dying man whispered, resigned, suddenly remembering shooting the older of two men in the eye.

"I thought you Communists were a godless lot, but sure, why not?" she said, chuckling bitterly. "Here's my prayer: May you never find peace. May all your descendants ten generations forward find no peace. May you burn in hell, and when you get there, tell them Zina sent you. Remember my name: Zina." With those words, the girl pulled the trigger.

Azrael, the Angel of Death, felt uncommon tears well up in his now scarlet eyes. He didn't wipe the tears, but instead allowed them to fall onto the bloody Ukrainian soil, each tear turning into a deadly fireball, scorching the forest floor. He could do nothing for Sergei now that he was cursed to wander for all eternity, looking for salvation. Azrael opened his wings and flew off in disgust, yearning to finish his interminable job and get back home.

PART ONE

AMUSE-BOUCHE

Bella

"JUST A BREATH of black sturgeon caviar with daily handpicked Sonoma county microgreens, wrapped in a taco shell of Japanese seaweed and dressed in Amabito No Moshio sea salt," pompously broadcasted the bearded, predictably tattooed server without cracking even the illusion of a smile. He continued the gastronomic lecture. "The chef displays it on black lava rock. Naturally, we spray our hand polished rock with locally sourced, 4-dithiapentane free white truffle oil. We infuse our oil with wild sorrel extract. The wine pairing for the first course is the 2013 Sonstige Winzer Krug Cuvee Brut. And how much did you love the chefs amuse-bouche?"

Before either Yuri or I could say a word, the server sang out loudly: "Wasn't the combo of black radish and pink scallop divine? And how about our signature sage-scented foam?"

"Divine," I echoed quietly, feeling overwhelmed; kind of the way I used to feel before an important exam.

"Wasn't the sage foam on point?" demanded the server more forcefully.

I didn't really get the point of the foam or the bitterness of the radish, but the raw scallop was easy enough to swallow. "On point," I mumbled again, smiling tensely, as we say in Russian, through my teeth.

"Enjoy!" commanded the beard, finally letting us be.

"Ha-ha, breath of caviar indeed—where is the rest, though?" said my darling Yuri, chuckling and shaking his haphazardly shaved head from side to side. I can't say I loved this new look, but he looked rather sexy-menacing, very much Jason Statham circa The Mechanic. As a rule, not much of a peacock, Yuri had acquiesced to wear my latest gifts: a pair of well-fitting Burberry jeans, a colorful Robert Graham shirt, and the latest in Gucci sneakers. (He removed the gray and purple Versace sport coat as soon as they seated us.) Mostly Yuri preferred to wear plain, no-press dress slacks and a simple polo shirt—he called it "the uniform." Since most of his insurance clients were Middle America, "mom and pop" business owners, he wisely recognized it was not good for business to dress like a Euro model, but when he was on "our" time, he allowed me to dress him up for fun.

"*Vot i 3* Stars for you!" Yuri added, mixing English with our native Russian—not that the hipster kid presenting the 3 Star Michelin dining extravaganza would understand his sarcasm. Yuri was pushing my buttons, but I remained composed since I had prepared myself for just such behavior. Imagine that of all the thousands and thousands of restaurants and diners and cafes, there were only twenty-two 3-star establishments in the entire United States! Overall, Yuri humored my passion—you could say obsession—with sampling only the best of everything, but I suspected that this dining "event" would probably test his true commitment to supporting my idiosyncrasies. Sometimes I'd get the notion that my husband disapproved of my "fixation" with food. I suspect feasting on this ridiculously expensive fare left him, shall we say, less than satisfied, as if he ever went hungry! While on this occasion I disagreed with him about the waste of money, I had to admit that after the tip and service charge, this evening would set me back close to a grand.

To make Yuri more at ease with the astronomical cost of our dinner, I had arranged a stay at an Airbnb near the University of San Francisco. I had taken walks on its most romantic, very European-looking campus when I thought our daughter might attend, but when Yuri found out it was a private Jesuit institution, he threw a fit. I think it was the tuition costs, though, and not his Soviet-born and raised-an-atheist prejudice against all religion.

Willing to appease my mate, I even promised him I would avoid shopping at my favorite Fillmore Street boutiques. (Well, maybe I'd shop a little on Sunday. I needed some new holiday linens I could only find in Chinatown.)

I had arranged for an economy flight from LAX to Oakland instead of flying into San Francisco, but I refrained from throwing a fit when Yuri insisted that we take the Bart across the Bay. Hey, people spend money on things they find meaningful. I don't drink expensive coffee or get weekly massages, so I figured this was a cheap outing. It's March 8th, and my daddy always spoiled his girls on International Women's Day.

When we first arrived in the States, I found it odd that Americans didn't celebrate this beautiful holiday in full force. I've seen some political demonstrations and protests, but that's not the way to celebrate! Eastern

Europeans celebrate all women on March 8th with flowers, perfume, chocolates, and no house chores! Not every woman is a mother or in the middle of a new love affair.

Lucky for me, I married one of our own: a Russian man taught from a young age to celebrate the women in his life. His heart was large enough for us all. Before we left LA, he brought chocolates not only to me but also to Alla Markovna, his widowed mother, and Oksana, his baby sister. I sent flowers and a care package to UC Merced, where little Polina, our college sophomore is studying Community Research and Service. I wish Polina studied something more prestigious, even something useful, like wine making, but I shouldn't complain. She is a good girl, if high strung and not interested in higher education. I guess she takes after her aunt Oksana and not her parents. If I compare her to a horse, my Lina is more of an Arabian than a Quarter Horse.

Just naming my only child was quite an ordeal! Despite hating the names popular among my Soviet-raised parents' generation, I went along with Yuri's wishes, permitting him to name our daughter after his grandmother, big Polina. Since Yuri's last name, Novikov, is typically Russian, I wanted an American first name like Amber or Danielle or even Sarah. I should have known better. Alla Markovna got her way with the name Polina by making me feel guilty, since her mother didn't make it through the horrific Leningrad blockade.

Well, she couldn't stop me from calling my baby Lina.

Just as I finally had relaxed, hoping I could savor the aftertaste of the previous course in peace, the bearded server returned. "Are you having fun with the lineup?" he queried us yet again.

"Sure!" Yuri answered for the both of us, sounding suspiciously sarcastic. Annoyed, I hit him under the table. The young guy pursed his barely visible lips and went on to pester another table.

After winking at me, Yuri swallowed the diminutive taco in one bite, making a surprisingly approving noise. I continued to savor the heavenly bubbles of Krug, gazing at my caviar taco with the eager anticipation of a child told to wait an eternity for her favorite ice cream.

"For this money, if you aren't going to eat it, I will," joked Yuri, emptying his trendy stemless champagne flute in one inelegant gulp.

"Don't drink like that! This is not a shot of vodka," I said. Yuri just shrugged my comments off as he usually did, without responding.

Over the years of marriage to my uber male, I've learned his cues about my nagging. If he's not responding to my instructions, he's telling me to back off. And I do—well, mostly. Still feeling a tad tense, I changed the subject.

"Have I told you how much I loved the peony bouquet you sent to the office last week?"

"You did," he answered blandly.

"Well, the flowers were spectacular," I went on ignoring his tone. "Where in the world did you find peonies in March? I'd gladly have settled for tulips or hyacinths."

"I asked my sister, and she recommended an acquaintance's flower shop in LA."

"You asked Oksana for advice? Wow, that's wonderful, but out of character, don't you think?"

I continued to engage him in conversation, worrying that his attention was waning. I love my man, but he has a short attention span, some would even call it adult ADD. That's why, a few years ago, after a rough patch between us, I decided that we would start a new tradition of dining alone. No kids, no parents, no friends, no Russian restaurants with all that low-quality gluttony—just the two of us.

I'm a positive woman and have learned to put the past back where it belongs; still worries about the future of our relationship linger. Losing his mortgage refinancing company during the last real estate bust and the ensuing recession was a major blow to Yuri's ego—along with constantly being reminded by people how lucky he was to have married such a successful woman—yours truly—and questioned why his wife had a different last name.

The subject of Yuri's sister wasn't always a pleasant one either. As much as he loved Oksana, her lack of education and suitable profession openly embarrassed him, not to mention her unsavory marital connections.

"Do you remember the name of the florist?" I wondered, genuinely curious. (At my dental practice, my office manager, Holly, usually handles all the business details, but flowers I choose myself.)

"Not really," he responded, still not looking at me. "I think it was something in the Valley. It started with a woman's name, I think—an ordinary name, something like Olga's or Anastasia's. Wait, I remember now. The owner's name is Alexandra. Just text Oksana: she'll give you the info."

Changing the subject, he asked hopefully, "Say, can I fire off one email?" Disappointed but resigned, I said as a compromise, "Maybe before the desert." I added yet another attaboy for good measure.

"I appreciate the gesture even more knowing you've never been the type for throwing flowers my way, even when we were dating. You know, the buketi-konfeti ritual," I said, jokingly referring to the common Russian courting tradition of sending loads of flowers and chocolates at the start of any proper love affair. What can I say? We love flowers! In many Russian cities, especially Moscow or St. Petersburg, one can buy a fresh bouquet practically twenty-four hours a day. As my grandmother said, if a man shows no effort while he's chasing you into his bed, what can you expect after the kids come along? At least that's how we see it.

"That's why I do it, my beauty," Yuri said regarding the flowers, finally looking directly into my eyes. "I do it because I know how much you love them." Then he grinned in that special way that made my heart melt. I smiled back, and something in my expression made him get up from his chair and reach across the table. To my delight, he kissed my still wrinkle-free forehead, just the way I liked.

Well, I thought, *I don't have to worry about the state of our marriage, at least not for the moment.* Thank goodness, my husband still knew how to show me how much he cared about my needs for affection. I've always needed the comfort of touch from those I loved. To my delight, our conversation was finally moving in the right direction.

"I must admit, you look attractive tonight," my stoic Yuri continued, offering me a rare yet sincere compliment with a twinkle in his gorgeous blue eyes and a sexy wink I've known and loved so well for over twenty years. I found it rather humorous how well this over-the-top Alpha male wore a public mask of a *podkobluchnik.* As I've explained to my American lady friends, a *podkobluchnik* is literally "a man living under the heel of his wife's shoe." The meaning ranges from an ideal husband, to an unsuccessful man dominated by his wife, to a lazy man who lets his wife make all decisions. Some psychologists say this type of man is looking for approval and perhaps associates his wife with his mother or grandmother. Eventually the man becomes weak and dependent, which sometimes erupts in marital problems, including break-ups.

Most men see being controlled or dominated by a mere woman as an insult, even if she's the more successful one. Personally, I think there's nothing wrong with pleasing your wife or being an agreeable partner.

If only others knew the private Yuri: a brilliant, erudite man; if only they could understand his emotionally subdued character. Since the day we made a life together, he's been my fortress—the one I trust most in the world and the one whose opinion is the only opinion that matters. So, I've learned to cherish every albeit small compliment coming my way.

Although I worked overtime to take an extra day off from my dental practice, I felt glam in my brand-new eggplant Escada pantsuit, hot pink silk tank, and midnight blue Barbara Bui booties. So what if my eyes were puffy? That's why you have lash extensions, and if you can't dress up for a Michelin dinner, when can you?

I will never get used to a prevailing disregard of basic dinner decorum, let alone wearing activewear even to the theater. The last time we went to LA's Disney Hall, the public was so shockingly coarse that it ruined my experience. Call me a snob—I don't care. What "they" call casual, I see as slothfulness.

And it doesn't take a lot of money to dress well either! When we were young and broke, I frequented resale boutiques, including Salvation Army stores, and still managed to look appropriate on a tight budget. Don't misunderstand me, I'm not like my ridiculously impractical sister-in-law who lives and breathes shopping, but even with my busy schedule, I try to look attractive for my husband. I never want to take what we have for granted. One can always change careers, get more education, or make more money, but a proper husband who is not an alcoholic or a cheater is rare, especially here in the West. How many silly mail-order brides think they've married George Clooney but find themselves married to a boring old scrooge? Some women are lucky to get out alive. Culture is culture. There are some decent men here, but personally I only know of one happy marriage between one of our own and an American. And it's a second marriage for both with no kids.

As on cue, our server approached, accompanied by a colleague, another young man with looks almost identical to the first one but a tad taller.

"Here is your second course, guys!" the taller of the servers said casually, introducing the tiny bites of something pink and shiny. "This is flash-fried Venetian soft shell crab with lychee jelly. We pair this course with Akita Homare sake. The Komachi yeast gives sake its distinctly floral aroma complimenting the delicate scent of the lychee fruit." I liked his attitude much better; it was enthusiastic yet reassuring.

All I could do was to marvel at the presentation, anticipating the pleasure. All Yuri could do was to hold back an obnoxious snort. I ignored him and wholly enjoyed the slightly flowery, beyond tasty morsels of crab. Just a mention of the dreamy Venetian Lagoon brought on a wistful smile. As I grow older, I understand what my darling father used to tell me about what made up a well-lived life: adventures and memories, not things.

While enjoying my crab, I passed on the sake—never my favorite. Yuri reached out across the table and drank my sake after quickly finishing his own. He didn't complain about the food. Yay!

"So far, I think this course is my favorite." I made my judgment clear, regaining my natural confidence.

"You think?"

"You know how much I love crab."

"I prefer lobster."

"Foo," I disagreed, using our favorite childhood word for "yuck." "When I was a child, they sold lobsters on the corner along with boiled corn and sunflower seeds. But for your sake, since we have a few more courses to go, maybe the chef will serve lobster."

"I hope so. Listen, how did you manage to snatch up a reservation for dinner only a week ahead of our trip?" Yuri inquired. "I tried to make reservations in December, and the earliest they could book us was April, on a Tuesday at 5:30. Remember when I tried to get us into Vegas Robuchon for your birthday? What a disaster that was," he added, still embarrassed.

I changed the subject without a snarky comment about him dropping the ball.

"I have my ways," I said, smiling mysteriously. "Impressed?"

"I'm always impressed with you, Dr. Bella." The statement alone is why I have hope that my marriage will go the distance, even in the face of ever-decreasing odds.

"Actually, it was Oksana's sister-in-law who got us in," I answered while playing with my chubby, stemless glass.

"Slava's sister? Fat Maya? You're joking."

"Why are you surprised? Maya knows everyone everywhere, and she thinks she owes me a favor. I referred her to Dr. Blumenfeld, the American dentist—you know, the older one with a "teenaged" wife? We met him at the dental convention in Scottsdale."

"Oh yeah, the nude dress and the lips. I remember. She was hot." I let it slide, but not before rolling my eyes.

"Anyway, Maya needed a root canal, and with her diabetes and other health problems, I thought she'd do well with a real specialist."

"That was good of you considering her husband is a giant creep, along with Slava, my bully of a brother-in- law. I think they both need a court-ordered anger management program, or better yet, twenty years in a Mexican prison!" Yuri spat out some of his food along with his disgust. "Mother still can't get over how I allowed my little sister to marry into that family—typical Odessa low-life criminals. We left Brighton Beach and moved to LA to get away from that element. Unfortunately, it was too late. You know Oksana when she gets something into that vapid head of hers. There is no reasoning with that girl. 'I want him, only him, and that's that.' The only silver lining to this entire mess is that Father is dead and buried. At least he can't see what's happened to his baby girl." Yuri finished his bitter diatribe, looking into the direction of the bar.

No matter how much I wanted to ignore his words, I couldn't keep my opinions to myself. "Oh, please. Stop being so dramatic; you're exaggerating. They're not criminals and not as bad as you seem to paint them. They're just trying to make it in America, like all of us immigrants," I shot back. "And hey, better be careful with your criticisms. I'm from Odessa too." Yet again I felt the need to defend my beloved city as if I were defending my family's honor. "For your information, Fat Maya and her brother came from Moscow. Only Vlad is a rooted Odessit and not a peasant interloper from the outskirts. Let's be honest—Odessa-born people can be snobbish about who was born where and how far back they can trace their lineage. You'd think they were born in Rome or Athens!

"Not to be mean, dear," I continued, "but your sister is a big girl and knew what she was getting herself into with Slava. She had heard of his reputation with both business and women. She knew life with him wouldn't be easy. Perhaps if she'd spend more time pursuing a proper profession instead of chasing the latest shoe sale, she could look after herself and the kids without depending on him. Who knows? Maybe he'd have more respect for her if she made money instead of spending it." I suspected I was being catty. Actually, I felt sorry for Oksana, but she and I were cut from a different cloth. I choose to believe only the best about myself. The world would tear me up on its own. Why should I cooperate?

"Oksana has tried to be independent, but she can't look after herself," said Yuri, continuing to vent and surprising me with the depth of his feelings. "She hasn't got the brains for education. Never did. That explains her attraction to that animal with his Odessa underworld connections. You'd think she'd be embarrassed, considering her own grandparents held advanced degrees. Our paternal great-grandmother graduated from the Stankevich Women's Medical Institute! Gaining educational degrees is our family legacy. There is no authentic class without education!"

As Yuri went on with no end in sight, I became irritated with his St. Petersburg snobbism. Thank goodness he redeemed himself by adding, "Don't be mad. You know I know that you're different. You have more class in your little toe than the lot of them, even with all their 'dirty' money. Look, if not for my sister and the kids, I wouldn't even spit their way, let alone have any personal or business dealings with them." Yuri raised his voice and added, "They're nothing but vicious loan sharks."

Although I was tiring of the entire conversation, I wouldn't back down; not yet anyway. "Again, you're exaggerating," I replied. "It's just private banking. OK, it's true that Maya lends our community money at high interest, but how else would many immigrants get the funds to start their business? Who'd give them loans with a decent rate? Personally, I admire Maya. I think she's fierce."

For some unfathomable reason, I felt the need to defend the woman. Not that Maya was a friend of mine or could ever become one. Still, I admired guts and success in whatever form it came in. "The only difference between your sister and me is that while your mother told Oksana she can do nothing right, my mother told me I couldn't do anything wrong," I concluded.

"Isabella," Yuri said gravely, addressing me formally, and as usual ignoring my comment about his mother. "I must insist that you never deal with Maya, her husband, or anyone associated with them again." This sounded suspiciously like a command. I don't like it when he pulls the Lord and Master card. No one orders me around, but now, in this place, I made a choice to keep my "tongue behind my teeth," as we say, and keep quiet.

Providentially, the third course arrived to interrupt our exchange, which was about to take a disagreeable turn. I did not intend to spend a thousand dollars on dinner fighting with my husband about his hairbrained sister and the cultural differences between our native cities.

Thank goodness, the food was flawless—a perfectly presented center cut of charred barramundi, the delicately fleshed Asian Sea Bass. Unlike

Chilean Sea Bass, I'm told, they source barramundi responsibly, and it's low in Mercury.

The chef nestled the fish on a bed of saffron-scented lentils dressed in lemon curd. It was a symphony of pink, dark brown, and yellow. Yum! I was beyond heaven. Although I already knew it, I didn't let on when our original server explained that their wild barramundi was flown in from Australia and traceable, meaning ecologically clean. Sometimes I find the educational aspect of fine dining is as important as the food itself, and that goes double for my seafood. Call me an OCD food freak!

Yuri and I ate in blissful silence, savoring the crisp, sweet, and salty interpretation of barramundi and sipping on a perfectly chilled JJ Prüm German Riesling. I know lots of oenophiles who turn up their noses up at the mention of German wines. However, in this case, I felt both delighted and justified by the chef's selection. You either hate or love this white varietal. I adored it, undoubtedly falling into the second camp.

A few months ago, while having a moment to myself to enjoy a glass of wine at the spa, I read a story about a late seventies vintage that sold for over six hundred US dollars! As far as I'm concerned, the chef's fish course, along with the wine choice, was a huge success.

"Now I understand what all the fuss is about. I'm so happy we flew in for this special occasion," Yuri admitted with a broad smile. Funny, I thought, how he fought me about getting his front teeth capped—just like so many of our folks who refuse to take care of their teeth, except in the case of a dental emergency. I mean, we've come a long way from needing full dentures at forty years young! After lots of nagging and pushing, my husband finally relented. Now, just look at him: he smiles all the time, even outside of our home. In fact, I'll take credit for both this newfound confidence and the improvement in his brand-new independent financial advisor business.

"Vkusniashki—you were right," Yuri said, repeating in English, "it was delicious," finally acknowledging all my hard work!

"You know, dear," I went on without my standard "I told you so," "I found a master sommelier course I can take online. It's only eleven weeks. I think I'll sign up."

"If you want to, go for it; but don't complain that you're overscheduled. I think you're spreading yourself too thin. What happened to taking those UCLA Extension writing courses? You have the talent, and you go around telling everyone how much you'd like to retire from your practice and write full-time, but I don't see you being serious. You know, Bella, creative ambition without focus is a recipe for frustration and failure."

That stung, and my eyes filled with tears. I didn't need yet another lecture—and from a spoiled-rotten man to boot. I was about to take it to the next level and tell him how I really felt: that it was all his fault I couldn't focus on my art, because I was the main breadwinner in the family, and the kids needed help, and the house, and his mother, and all the usual grievances, blah-blah-blah, but I kept it all to myself.

"The class schedule wasn't right. Da, you're probably right, but gosh, I'd love to take the time to learn about wine in depth: all that history, geography, all the fun cultural tidbits. Plus, when I was a kid and complained about being tired, my father always told me to 'switch it up' and do something different, not sit down and rest."

"Maybe your father was correct in his own way, but I think he would have lived much longer if he wasn't such a workaholic. You already know more than some wine store sales managers."

"I appreciate your confidence, but truly I do not have the proper knowledge of wine. I have a good nose, and I care about what I put in my body. You know, it must be all the foul-tasting food I had to eat as a kid. I still have nightmares about being forced to swallow that slop. Sometimes I held the food in my mouth for so long, I would throw it up! And look who's talking about being a workaholic! I'm positive you're about to excuse yourself and sneak into the toilet so you can answer emails."

"You know me too well." Yuri chuckled. "My apologies, but I do have to make a pit stop."

Alas, my sneaky husband didn't have time to leave the table. "Ah, here comes course number four," I said loudly in my deep, still accented voice in anticipation of yet another masterpiece. I hoped the meal would only get better!

The simple white plate framed the complexity of the food presentation instead of taking away from it. It was a savory root vegetable Napoleon with a roasted heirloom tomato gastrique. I recalled with dread my first experience with this technique of caramelizing sugar and deglazing it with vinegar. It was a god-awful New Year Eve Moet Chandon tasting, where each course tasted progressively worse. The kitchen used an altogether wrong type of vinegar, so the sauce smelled rancid. To make things worse, the service staff poured the gastrique over several medallions of pork loin. I know times have changed, but a rare slice of pork? I don't think so. Yuri was fuming because I refused to take a bite. I don't care what they say: raw pork is disgusting. We had a giant fight. He stormed off after telling me this was the last so-called gourmet dinner he'd ever pay for.

Well, that was then. Tonight's sauce was divine. I felt we were all talked out for a moment, and so we sat together in comforting silence, enjoying the over-the-top flavors accompanied by the soothing white noise of the establishment.

Despite its unexpected simplicity, the interior of the restaurant was an interesting choice of space allocation. I counted only a dozen tables, set against low-key neutral walls, accented with interesting if somewhat disturbing art lit by the latest in European fixtures. The star of the interior was an impressive open kitchen with enormous wood fire ovens. The bustling kitchen filled with more staff than customers fascinated me.

At first, I was almost disappointed by the open concept, the bare tables decorated with yellow dogwood branches arranged in distressed metal containers. However, after spending time in the space, I had to admit that, despite not being completely my taste, the room worked. It complemented the food beautifully. Both the chef's version of minimalism and excessiveness appealed to my senses. I even loved the crazy soundtrack, though Yuri found it jarring. Heck, he was never into my kind of music; he was a lifelong fan of Pink Floyd and the Stones.

Just then, one of my favorite Berlin tracks, "No More Words," cut through the humming of dozens of conversations. I couldn't help myself and sang alone, bringing another smile to my husband's handsome face. All the tension finally vanished as we enjoyed the feast.

For the fifth course, the chef spoiled us with a duck trio. Our servers presented us with perfectly pink Muscovy breast, a delectable duck leg confit, and a licorice-scented house-made sausage seasoned with an Asian influence; although I couldn't place the exact spice mix. A mind-blowing Shiraz from South Africa accompanied the course. The Shiraz so impressed my nonchalant man that he asked if he could take a picture of the label. I wanted more information, so our server called in the restaurant's manager, who was also in charge of the wine-buying decisions.

She was a surprisingly young Asian woman with severely razor-cut short hair, reminiscent of Debra Harry during her years as a front for my beloved

Blondie. The manager's hair was tinted a raspberry pink, and she had glossed her visibly augmented lips in the same pink, matching the hair color to a tee. Just like the rest of the staff, our heavily tattooed wine guide sported a large diamond piercing near her highly arched eyebrow. From my vast experience with consignment boutiques, I believed the girl was wearing a vintage Yamamoto, black and severely cut. I loved her entire look.

The young woman introduced herself casually as Aubrey and shook hands with us firmly. After inquiring about our wine pairings experience so far and getting a satisfactory answer, she explained the short history of the Saxenburg Shiraz Select with a genuine passion for wine culture. That I loved even more.

"So, let me understand," asked Yuri with a wink. "South Africa is in the top ten of the world's wine producers?"

"Yes," confirmed the young woman. "Actually, the South African winemakers have been producing wine for over three hundred years. The natural soil conditions are superb. This Shiraz, which I drink at home, comes from a farm dating back to 1700. That's older than most cities here in the US."

The lively back-and-forth went on for several minutes. I emptied the rest of my glass, seriously considering whether I should order another glass. Several more bite-sized courses followed in what I considered a rush; I guess it was getting late. I lost count after the sliver of wild-range beef filet, accompanied by a tiny hand-painted bowl of bone broth. The filet and broth came garnished with something the server called "their" version of Texas toast. And the outrageous wine pairing, to quote Eliza Doolittle, "done me in." It was a 2014 Joseph Phelps Insignia, so outrageous on my pallet that I regretted every glass I drank before it.

As we waited for the final series of presentations—Yuri's favorite, the dessert courses—my mind turned to our previous conversation about the family. "Did I tell you that I knew Oksana's Slava, Maya, and her Vlad when I was a kid?"

"You're joking! No, you've never said a word. Well, you'd better explain yourself now, before the dessert, so it doesn't spoil my appetite."

"Please, Bella, explain," I snapped at his rudeness, weary of him telling me what to do.

"Whatever. Please, Bella, explain," He said with just a touch of sarcasm in his voice.

"I'm not up to gossiping behind your sister's back—or Maya's either," I replied, feeling my face get hot.

"Since when?" Yuri raised his voice, switching to Russian.

"Since now!" I barked back in English, feeling the familiar burn of adrenalin rush turning my neck and face an embarrassing red. I've had trouble controlling my temper since I was in grade school, and it hasn't gotten better with age.

"Hey, hey, I give. Calm the fuck down." Yuri lifted his hands in a defensive position as he surrendered without firing a shot. "I thought you'd entertain me with one of your comical Odessa stories while we wait for dessert. You know, Bella, hearing your stories while I eat are one of the greatest joys of our marriage, since you can't make a proper meal to save your life. It's so relaxing, like listening to the evening news while having supper. You talk just like the TV presenters back in the USSR." Although he sounded sincere, I detected another hint of sarcasm. Was he now mocking my storytelling skills?

"Yeah, so go marry Fat Maya. I hear she's an incredible cook!"

"Ha. I'm putting on my running shoes right now." He laughed out loud. "I love you, silly. I can get plenty of borsch at my mom's. Her caregiver makes great borsch with lots of meat, and unlike Maya, she's young, good-looking, and thin!" He winked to show he was kidding.

When I didn't bite, he changed his tactic. "I'm sorry, kitty cat, if I wounded your ego," he said, offering a genuine apology.

"Well, since you regret your criticisms, I guess I can go on," I responded, not exactly feeling warm and fuzzy concerning his comments about my pitiable cooking skills. I realized I was a failure at what most husbands would expect of me. However, my papa raised me to concentrate on my creative and intellectual talents and not the stove. He told me to leave the kitchen to the babushkas or the other more housewife types. That man of mine sure knows when to challenge me and when to back down, I thought to myself, but then let it go to move on with my story.

"Are you ready to listen?"

"Like a pioneer, always ready!" Yuri reassured me, using our old schooldays motto. "OK, *nu, poehali.*" (I know the expression means "let's drive," but my father used it often when egging us on.)

I took a deep breath and began as though I were retelling a fairy tale: "A long, long time ago, in a place far, far away we—I mean, Maya and Slava and

Vlad—weren't friends or classmates. All three were older than I was. For a while, before we moved from the communal flat to the new neighborhood, Maya and Slava would visit their grandmother, who was our flat neighbor, during the summer holidays. Vlad lived with his mother in the next room. We all shared one dingy kitchen. I was born in that communal flat, close to the old historic center of Odessa, near Holy Assumption Cathedral. You know, it's a stunning place to worship. The commissars destroyed the original building in the thirties, but I've seen recent pics of the new church on Facebook. You'd love it—so bright and charming, so different from the usual doom and gloom. They built in the middle of a green space."

"Wow! I didn't know you were still interested. Would you like to visit?" Yuri said.

"I don't know if I'm interested in going back, considering there are still so many places we haven't seen. I guess curious enough I've kept up with Odessa groups through Facebook and live webcams." I stopped talking for a minute taking a sip of the now-room temperature Voss.

"Ah, I remember that church," said Yuri. "We didn't spend many summers in Odessa, but I was there twice with my folks, visiting friends. What a coincidence! So, you lived nearby?"

"What do you mean, a coincidence? I've told you we lived near that church. Sometimes I wonder if you hear anything I say."

"Sorry." This time it was Yuri who didn't want to get into it with me again.

"Later, Papa arranged for us to move to a brand-new flat outside the old city center where we didn't have to share the kitchen or the bath with neighbors."

"When did you move?" asked my husband.

"Luckily, before I started first grade, we were living like kings in our own twenty-five square meters! Can you imagine an entire family in the States living in some 270 square feet and thinking how fortunate they are? Papa always said, 'At least we're not living below street level, without a ray of sunshine.'"

"Hmm. He always saw the world in rosy colors, your papa: an innate American," Yuri interrupted, but I didn't mind since even thinking of not having my papa among the living still hurt. I took a deep breath and a sip of water.

"When I think of those years, for some inexplicable reason I have pretty good recollections of our old communal place, including Maya;

not so much Slava and Vlad. I don't know, but that girl left an impression. As a girl, she was so skinny—pathetically so. Maya never played with me because I played with paper dolls and clay. She hung out with her brother and the other boys in the courtyard."

"Fat Maya was skinny? I would've loved to see that!"

"She was tough, a true tomboy, and Slava was her second-in-command. Both kids were out-of-control hooligans—always dirty, spending all their time outside and getting into trouble with the neighbors. Their grandmother was worried sick about them when they returned to Moscow, since their parents were more into their careers—especially their mother, the minor theater actress. They shipped the kids off to Odessa every summer to stay with their paternal grandmother. On the other hand, Maya's husband Vlad was a whiny, sickly kid; all I remember of him is that his mother would wrap him up in some schmata, and his nose snot was always green."

"Ha, he's still a green snot!" Yuri snorted. "Those people are both crude and common."

"I agree, but you better stop interrupting me, or I won't tell you the most remarkable part of the story," I admonished Yuri with a sly smile, that special smile I use to appeal to his curiosity. "Let me tell you about Maya and Slava's grandmother, Zina. She was no ordinary babushka, that one, but a . . ."

"Here comes your final course: deep-fried mini beignets accompanied by fig panna cotta infused with lemongrass balm and combined with vanilla crema," our bearded server announced triumphantly as he brought out two matching square plates of delightful morsels of heaven along with two three-ounce glasses with the final wine selection. It was one of my favorites—a Renwood Cali Ice Zinfandel. The Zinfandel was a delicious blend of Viognier and Muscat frozen fruit, so delicate and exotically scented that my mouth watered with anticipation. I was so full, though, that I passed on the fried doughnut dessert and doubled up on the wine.

"Any coffee or tea to finish up?" our culinary guide asked with a satisfied smile.

"Not for me," answered Yuri.

"I'd love to try your organic green tea, "I asked with a nervous smile, hoping not to offend the staff or the chef.

"You got it!" the server responded in a neutral tone that I found mercifully reassuring. Sometimes I can't take all the condescension associated with fine dining. I mean, I am a doctor, and they are just food servers; you'd think they'd know their place. No wonder I find the American notion of class so confusing to us foreigners.

"So, what about Zina?" asked Yuri before I finished my iced heaven of a wine.

"You really want me to tell you now?"

"Why not—with how much this dinner is costing us, I'm sure we have the table for the rest of the night. Do you think we have the energy to go anywhere else?"

"No, I guess not," I agreed, deciding to indulge my husband with my curious story about Maya and Slava's moneylending grandmother Zina, as he indulged my dining choice.

The fermented green tea arrived, presented properly Japanese-style, and it was lovely: a perfect ending to a perfect dining experience.

Just then, we heard a commotion coming from a few tables away. I had already noticed the couple the staff seated after us because they were not only oddly dressed, but visibly uncomfortable with the dining experience. Both in their late thirties, the man wore wrinkled chinos and an ill-fitting navy blazer that clearly had been borrowed from the restaurant. The woman was not much to look at either; she wore a heavy wool work dress, scuffed black pumps, and dark-colored pantyhose.

It sounded as if the man was irate about the price of the wine. He saw the same bottle in a fine wine shop for a great deal less than they charged here. The poor woman looked like she was about to cry from embarrassment. The server called the sommelier over to explain, while the rest of us tried to ignore the conflict. I felt bad for the woman but went on with my story.

"As I already mentioned, I was too small to know what was going on, but I remember my family discouraging me from playing with Maya and Slava. Later on, I heard stories about their family history that would curl your toes!"

"OK, you've got my ears," interrupted Yuri impatiently.

"Well, settle down and listen to this." I promised, beginning my usual process of going back to the old homeland. "I'm sure you've heard of our most famous mob boss, Mishka the Jap (our version of Al Capone) or the infamous girl thief, Sonya the Golden Hands."

"Sure, who hasn't?" said Yuri, nodding in agreement. "I read Babel's short stories collection in school. I think someone named the area after the migrants from Moldova, right? How did he put it: two thousand bandits and thieves?"

And this is the reason I'm willing to put up with my man's personality quirks, I thought to myself. He's just brilliant, gifted with a photographic memory—the most intelligent man I've ever met. "Wow, I'm impressed you knew that. Well, celebrity gangsters were not the only ones who lived and operated in old Odessa's Moldavanka ghetto. The neighborhood was then, as it probably is now, a place with narrow alleys and decrepit buildings surrounded by noisy courtyards where life and death took turns. The place also reeked of hundreds of hungry stray cats, pigeon droppings, and piles and piles of hanging laundry. I called it the original no-go zone for the genteel set or even the authorities."

"What does that have to do with Maya and Slava's grandmother?"

"Ha! As much as the history of the Moldavanka gangs, their crimes, and even the invention of their own language became almost legendary, the true story of Zina, a ruthless moneylender, stayed hidden."

"Why is that?" Yuri asked, "Because it never happened?"

"No, wise guy. It was because no one would dare to go against her or her minions. Everyone needs money: the gangsters, regular folk, heck, even the cops! Zina, no one knew for sure if that was her real name, came to Odessa as a young wife from Vinnitsa. Vinnitsa was and still is a small town. I think the Americans refer to that area as 'the borscht belt.'"

"Where is it again?"

"Since you don't know Ukraine, the town is in the West-Central region, around two hundred kilometers from Kiev."

"Wow, let's see just over 120 miles: less than two hours driving."

"Probably an hour the way you drive! Moving on, I gather Maya's grandmother arrived in Odessa on the eve of the Stalin crackdowns, several years before World War II. Vinnitsa is a little place: lots of sunflower fields along the banks of the Southern Bug River. They have their own Gorky Park, not like in Moscow, but nice. Papa used to travel all around Ukraine for work, so once he took Mama and me along. He even took us on a river tour up the Dnieper River! I'll write about our adventures one day."

"Never thought of going to tour a *derevnia* in Ukraine," Yuri said with a sneer. I didn't expect anything different from my husband. I've heard the same from my mother-in-law, a typical snob, born in Leningrad, now

St. Petersburg. No one in Yuri's family would ever want to spend time in villages or provincial towns, let alone in Ukraine.

Yuri rubbed his eyes. I was losing him to that mind-dulling stupor that overtakes us after a full meal along with several glasses of wine. I knew I had to speed up my story by telling him something he didn't know.

"Vinnitsa is not a village! Sometimes you can be so condescending. It's not St. Petersburg. Hang on—the story gets better. Young Zina and her fellow had to escape a horrid massacre, a mass murder, really. It happened sometimes in the mid-to-late 1930s. You probably don't know Ukrainian history because you come from the north, but between 1937 and 1938, the secret police executed somewhere around ten thousand Ukrainians, both men and women. You know, with all those conflicts going on, I think the Ukrainian folks have never forgotten the atrocities. When the authorities excavated the remains, ironically they also found that a few Poles had been butchered along with the Ukrainians."

"Wow, I didn't know that—how awful." Yuri whistled softly. "I mean, I'm not surprised, but still to know that our own did that to civilians, not always the Nazis. It's upsetting. Say, why do you find Polish remains ironic?"

"Well, considering how much the Cossacks hated the Poles. Don't tell me you've never heard of Taras Bulba?"

"Ah, the bald guy with the weird skinny braid. Yeah, I remember the movie. That's where the Poles betray the Ukrainian Cossacks who supposedly saved them from the Turks. Right?"

"That's the one. Well, as usual it was a Hollywood version, but the old man kills his son. Tony Curtis was a hottie—and those blue eyes!"

"I like Hollywood versions of our history," Yuri said with a smirk. "Who played the old Cossack?" Wait, wait: it was Telly Savalas. Remember, I was obsessed with *Kojak*? As usual, we got to see it years later, after the show was already canceled here.

"*Net*. Not *Kojak*: Yul Brynner played the father, silly. He had Russian roots," I corrected him.

"Did I tell you I found *Kojak* reruns on YouTube? Sure brought back lots of memories." Yuri perked up, once again engaging with me.

"Should I go on with Maya's grandmother's story?" I asked, hoping he would give me the green light. (I use these moments to flush out ideas for my writing without him knowing it.)

"Go on," Yuri said, polishing off what remained in the breadbasket, apparently not satisfied with the elaborate meal.

"You can't imagine the worst," I continued, ignoring the bread. "The executions were mostly done by using small bullets to the back of the poor victims' heads, and because of that, a lot of them had to be shot twice or even three times! They found all the young women nude."

"Three times? Like with a 22 caliber? Fucking murdering NKVD," said my husband, referring to the precursor to the dreaded KGB.

"Isn't that the truth? I didn't know about the Vinnitsa massacre back at home either; I learned about it at UCLA when we were studying the origins of the resurgence of Ukrainian nationalism. I can see why the Nazis used it for their own propaganda." I ended my history lesson with a flourish. I know Yuri doesn't exactly love that pedantic, "know it all" side of me, but this is who I am, a frustrated teacher.

"Anyhow," I decided I'd better change the subject or lose him once again. "Our antiheroine, young Zina, was introduced to the Odessa criminal world by her husband's cousin, a small-time Jewish mob enforcer and part-time watch repairman. Everyone agreed she was quite a dish: curvy, petite, with long, thick black braids, blue eyes, and pink cheeks—a typical Ukrainian beauty, just like the gorgeous girls you see on the matchmaking sites. I guess she was hot to trot too, so her husband's cousin fell madly in love with her and kept her for himself. Being an honorable crook, he gave her husband an ultimatum: either leave Odessa without Zina or face a knife battle."

"Baba Zina, the original 'gangsta,' the OG of Odessa," Yuri said, whistling—impressed with my story, at least so far.

"What? You think love and crime is only for the Italians?" I joked.

"Go on," commanded my husband with another smirk. He had been obsessed with the American organized crime classic *Goodfellas* for years.

"I will if you stop interrupting!" I responded, thrilled with myself. "At first, practical and used to sexcapades, the cousins agreed to share one woman, but that's not what Zina wanted. She figured out that her prospects were much better with the cousin, whose day job involved pre-revolution jewelry liquidation and repairing clocks and pocket watches. What do you think she did?" I asked conspiratorially.

"I don't know," answered Yuri.

"Just guess!" I tried again.

"Killed her shmuck of a husband?"

"Nope—our clever girl orchestrated a confrontation. One night, she showed up at his doorstep with a broken nose and lots of nasty bruises. The lover went nuts and confronted the husband. Both were drunk, and the knife fight resulted in a murder.

"Unfortunately for our heroine, the husband came out on top. The Odessa cops arrested him, and he died in prison. His demise left Zina without either a husband or a lover, alone and pregnant. She tried to get an abortion, but that was 1938, the year Stalin cracked down on abortions, so she had her kid never knowing his true paternity, only proving the old saying, you can't sit with one ass on two chairs."

"That's funny," Yuri laughed obnoxiously. "So, you're telling me that somehow this uneducated, lone county girl not only survived the perils of the Odessa criminal world, but became a private moneylender, organizing her own gang, enforcers and all?" he speculated before I could finish the story with my usual flair. "That's quite a yarn you're spinning, not that I believe a word."

"*Sha!* We're still in public," I admonished him half-heartedly, as the restaurant was empty by now. "And every word is true, that and more, much more. Apparently, even my grandfather had dealings with her since he was a jeweler. He got a loan all right, but it cost him a pretty penny and a half an ear!"

"Wow! You know what? I really want to hear the entire story of how a small-time Vinnitsa gangster moll became a famous Odessa moneylender, but I'm getting a fish eye from the manager. Why don't we settle up and grab an Uber back to the Airbnb?" That was the most my husband had said to me in days! Then he surprised me further by adding: "Hopefully, you picked a nice flat. I brought a cigar and a small bottle of proper French cognac. We'll sit, relax, and I will listen to you until my eyes close."

"You can't smoke there," I told him gently, trying not to ruin the mood; so far, I was happy with his plan.

"Yes, I can, on the terrace, and I'll clean up after myself. I promise," he offered as a compromise.

By the time we got back, I never finished my story. Yuri was both tipsy and mischievous. He fell asleep quickly, but not before making love to me with sensitivity. I guess a thousand dollars' worth of spectacular food, outstanding wine, along with a good story win every time.

The next morning, we slept in. I had made a good choice of accommodations, considering the reasonable price. The high-ceilinged, elegantly wallpapered room was softly lit, the unexpectedly upscale bedding soft, and the scent of the vanilla and jasmine infuser soothing to my nerves. It was a Sunday. For once, there was no rush, and our plane wasn't leaving until 5:00 p.m.

We lounged around until ten, cuddling and leafing through travel brochures left on the nightstand. Neither of us felt like talking. Eventually we made it to the kitchenette. The gracious owners had set up a good-sized coffee pot and a tea tray for their visitors. While Yuri is a tea drinker, I can't get along without my morning coffee fix. The lovely thing about getting away is that, instead of getting our blood pressure up by watching the morning news, we sat and relaxed on the terrace overlooking the park across the street.

The mixed-use neighborhood was still sleepy but showing signs of life. The habitual morning fog was nowhere in sight. San Francisco smelled of freshly pressed French roasted coffee beans and fried dough. There's something about this town that not only appealed to my senses but made me feel at home; although lately I've seen many changes even here, not at all to my liking.

I remembered our first visit to the Bay area, as I sat blissfully sipping my favorite cup of morning java, the first one. We drove the coastal route all the way from LA in an ancient junker of a car, too afraid to take it on the freeway. It was a faded brown Buick Electra with a cracked side window, moldy seats, and a radio with only AM stations working. Yuri bought it from an eighty-year-old Hungarian immigrant, a WWII survivor who lived above my parents' first flat in West LA. I think the man took pity on us and sold it for a few hundred dollars. (He even took payments; God rest his soul for such kindness.) After driving for hours on end, we stopped in Monterey in a skanky motel near the main drag. Although, I wasn't hungry, Yuri wanted to try cheap seafood at the pier. Within an hour, I was vomiting so violently that we almost got back into the car and drove back to LA. In the morning, I felt a little better and gave my brand-new husband permission to continue driving up the coast. I've done the Pacific Coast drive many times since, always appreciating its wild glory, but that first trip I spent in the back seat thinking I would die from nausea. We skipped the planned visit to Hearst Castle because I couldn't even lift my head. Things hadn't improved much by the time we got to another crappy motel near Fisherman's Wharf. Yuri went out for Chinese soup, which didn't agree with me either. The next morning, I still didn't feel well, but I told Yuri to at least try to find some Russian food since we knew of San Francisco's Russian community. Miraculously, he found a Polish deli and bought pirogues with mushrooms and cabbage. The tasty dumplings finally settled my stomach, the fog lifted, and we had a great day. The funny thing was that when we returned to LA, it turned out that my nasty stomach bug was our oldest daughter!

Those were the days. . . . I reminded Yuri of that trip, and we had a good laugh. After a while, we ended up in bed yet again. Not that I complained about a little extra attention. Eventually we got hungry, and Yuri decided that we should walk to a Russian deli for some yeast dough piroshky stuffed with cabbage, chased by a porter-style Baltica beer.

Predictably, my low-key man preferred heavy root vegetables and meat, ordinary Russian food, and our own libations. To my chagrin, he forgot all about the previous night's extravaganza. Oh, well.

Instead of the BART, we took an Uber across the bridge to the Oakland airport, but first I needed a kiss of culture. Thank goodness I didn't have to talk Yuri, practically raised at the Hermitage Museum, into spending a few hours admiring high art. The museum displayed various collections with tact and decorum. We both adored the building, a gorgeous replica of the Palais de la Légion d'Honneur in Paris. Here was yet another bonus being married to a fellow coming from a city with the best museum in the world! We held hands and discussed the art we had seen before grabbing a bite in the museum cafe. My heart was at peace; we were in such a good place. I passed on shopping for linens. Even though Yuri promised that he'd accompany me to Chinatown, I decided not to push it, aware of his pathological dislike of shopping as a recreational activity.

Everything was going our way. We got to Oakland on time. After an annoying hassle getting through security, we settled in the first row and waited for the takeoff back to LAX. I had decided to upgrade—thinking that we needed a break from the hellish experience that had become the norm when we flew economy.

They served us drinks and snacks. I appreciated the most congenial staff that addressed us by our proper names; that alone was worth the cost of upgrading. I closed my eyes, feeling the familiar "going home" jitters.

"Bella, I have an idea," Yuri said out of the blue. Normally, his nose is in his phone the moment the weekend is over.

"An idea . . . and what would that cost me?" I said without opening my eyes.

"Don't know yet, but listen up. Why don't you stop spreading yourself so thin with all your usual nonsense, your poetry diaries, your little projects, your horse-riding lessons, and write a proper novel?"

"What nonsense are you referring to?" I snapped back, taking immediate offense. "I'll have you know I'll be riding with my equestrian group in the next Rose Parade! Do you know how many little parades I had to ride in to qualify for Pasadena? I'm not giving up riding—not for anything or anyone. I've waited too long!"

"Oh, stop being so thin-skinned," said Yuri, dismissing my feelings. "You know I only want what you want for yourself. For instance, that gangster story about Maya and Slava's grandmother—I bet that'd make a hell of a real novel. You always have so much to say about history and our culture, and you have an amazing sense of humor. Enough with the poetry: no one here reads poetry."

"Don't be a blockhead. Who would read my novel? Do you think the average American reader would understand what's really going on if the government or the so-called Russian studies "experts" can't get our basic national traits right? I can't even mention our point of view to Americans for fear of losing business or seeing their heads explode. My patients say the American president works for the Russians. They hate us. Plus, what sells here isn't literature. It's all soccer mom porn and vampires!"

"You're not Russian; you're 100 percent Ukrainian Jew. They like Ukrainians. It's me they hate. I think you're making excuses and being condescending. Just because they don't read and reread "dead poets," it doesn't mean they're not looking for quality. I don't read literature either, but anytime a great biography comes out or a new Patterson novel, you know I'll make time for it."

I pretended not to listen as I reached into my purse to look for a mirror and a lip gloss. If I thought my lack of response would shut him up, though, I was sorely disappointed.

"If you truly believe they don't understand, then make them understand! You're always freaking out about WWIII coming because

Americans don't understand our history and our culture. Here's your chance to make a difference." Yuri refused to let up.

"Look, I love that you believe in me, but I wrote a funny little story about me as a kid a while back and got up the nerve to show it to one of my patients who is a publishing consultant," I said, trying to defend myself.

"You did? Great! What did she say?"

"She liked my characters but told me to forget it in no uncertain terms. She said no one can afford to publish short story collections or take a chance on a new author without something she called 'a platform,' meaning thousands of followers on social media." I teared up, remembering how I had forced myself to ask the woman for advice and then felt both stupid and humiliated.

"You must've misunderstood her," argued Yuri.

"I did not! I saved her email; here, you read it." Since we were trapped in the air for another hour, I turned on my iPhone and showed him the email. I hadn't deleted it so as to remind myself not to be such a dope again.

Yuri read the email carefully, turned off the phone, and reached over to give me a hug. Without meaning to, I promptly burst into tears.

The email pointed out the realities of the current publishing scene. Specifically, the woman told me that unless one is writing a breakthrough pop novel of at least eighty thousand words or is a celebrity, a short story— albeit a fresh and poignant one—had little chance of getting published. She explained that the days of Jack London and O'Henry were over. She even showed me submission sites where the publishers and agents' guidelines stressed "absolutely no short stories or poetry!"

Still sniffling, I went on confessing, still feeling the sting of embarrassment. "On top of that, your stupid idiot of a wife showed the woman her beautiful "Thaw" poem. She didn't even know what the "Thaw" was—one of the most important political and cultural turnarounds in the history of the Cold War, an explosion of freedom in art and music and cinema. If they want to understand why the Soviet Union fell and not swallow the bullshit about Reagan spending us out of existence, they'd better learn. I mean, in so many ways these times were a bridge to Gorbachev's reforms, and she'd never even heard about it. I asked her about our poets, and she knew none of them; not even Joseph Brodsky! He won the Nobel Prize, for pity's sake. The Americans, they don't care about understanding anything except themselves! So, I told her that one day her cultural imperialism would bite her in the ass!"

"Oh no, you didn't!" Yuri shrugged his shoulders and chuckled.

"Oh yeah, I did!"

"And then what did she say?"

"She said before I consider publishing, I'd better hire someone called a "sensitivity" reader to make sure I write nothing to offend anyone!"

"WTF? How can you write about characters who say nothing?"

"Exactly my point! Can you imagine the pillars of world literature that would never reach the reader? Would they publish Mark Twain or Balzac or Tolstoy if someone forced them to check and recheck every word for sensitivity?"

"I agree, and I think it's sad."

"I think it's tragic when there is more freedom of expression in former communist countries than in the place where freedom of speech is a constitutional right!" I said passionately.

"I'm so sorry, baby." Yuri finally understood my frustration. It felt good to tell him. I took a deep breath and continued my diatribe.

"I guess book publishing has become just like all old-school print—you know, like magazines or newspapers. The day-to-day business has become something she called 'fused.' For the life of me, I don't know what she meant. It's all about the reality of competition from the internet and social media and platforms and guaranteed sales. Capitalists don't care about poetry, that's for sure. She said everything is in flux and that means there are fewer book publishers, their lists are smaller, and they are far less likely to take chances on projects they don't think will have a large payoff. To sum it all up, she said that publishing my poetry collections, if not impossible, at least is a very long shot. It reminded me what your mother told me when I made a stupid mistake and mentioned how I'd love to sell the practice and just work with horses and write."

"What did she say?"

"She told me to stop being childish, work in my profession, and write just for myself since, and I quote her, 'What use are poems? You can't even wipe your ass with them.'"

Yuri shook his head and reached out for my hand, giving it a firm squeeze. "Mama has her way with words. But I wouldn't listen to her—she has always been critical. Plus, I dare you to prove all of them wrong! I double-dog dare you!" He joked, quoting a line from my favorite Christmas movie and then gave me one of his most glorious smiles, the smile I live for.

"Honey, this lady, who I'm sure knows a good deal about the business end, doesn't know the real you. I've met no one more self-confident or tenacious. You've never backed down from any challenge since you were five when you broke that neighbor boy's nose because he was torturing a cat. Just think what an adventure you'll have and what a great example for our kids. Put your memories and your thoughts on paper. Let's face it, my soul, our entire life has been a long shot. So, stop crying and go get 'em!"

My husband's genuine support flabbergasted me. Then he used his propensity for black humor and added in his best imitation of Marlon Brando's godfather, "In the worst case, we'll just hire Fat Maya to make them an offer they can't refuse or cut off their ears!"

SEARCHING FOR GARY

Lullaby, lullaby, lullaby!
Lower than the thickest grass blade
You must bend your head
If an orphan in the world
You would live without grief.
Power bends and breaks all things,
Bend before it, bow and bow. . .
NIKOLAY NEKRASOV

Sasha

"DURING THE WAR everybody drank. It was "their" fault—the Red Commissars—as if starving half of Ukraine to death wasn't enough. They'd give us a full glass of ice-chilled vodka to drink up before each sortie; none of your shitty fruity modern mixers. That's all I can remember anyhow of our Great Patriotic War. I refuse to call it WWII. The world did nothing! The Americans lost, what, less than half a million—and no civilians. We lost millions! We were the ones who stopped Hitler. Young and cold and scared, we were happy to oblige. What the hell did we know? Yacov Osipov, our CO, was a big bear of a Siberian; he looked just like that fool Yeltsin. Remember him?"

Papa continues to reminisce about the War, sitting on a plastic-covered stool with wobbly legs at a mid-century oxidized gray Formica kitchenette. The set was his latest and greatest garage sale treasure, not that he could tell the difference between Eisenhower chic and Saturday garage sale junk. He pretends to be watching *Vremia*, the Russian evening news, on an ancient, kitchen-size TV, also bought secondhand. This one was a find from his upstairs neighbor Avi, the Israeli who never slept (at least not than anyone could tell).

"I was stone drunk the night I got shot down. See the burn mark on my wrist?" Yellowish gray hair covered his visibly deformed wrist. Something had taken a chunk out of both the skin and soft tissue, leaving the remaining skin puckered and shiny, even after more than a half of a century. A faded tattooed cross marked the inside of his wrist, along with the Cyrillic letters S and G for his first wife, Sofia, and his beloved natural son, Gary. An unknown artist had intertwined the letters together inside a rusty-tinged heart pierced by an arrow; the image vibrated dejection.

Papa reaches into his shirt pocket and pulls out a crisp linen handkerchief. Meticulously he unfolds it and takes out a piece of an old black-and-white photograph with burned-out edges; while most of the photo is missing, what remains is an image of two females. One is a stern, gray-haired woman with an exposed and very pronounced collarbone. She is wearing an ill-fitting frock with a small geometric pattern. A teenage girl with a sullen expression and unsmiling eyes is standing behind her. The young girl is wearing a French-style beret and a matching frock with a froth of white lace around her neck and wrists.

"Here's the photo I kept in my flight suit during the mission when the Luftwaffe shot me down. Look: the fire burned off half of their faces; the photo was of Granny and Mama and my sisters, but only the image of Granny and my youngest sister, Annechka, remain. All gone in '43, but I didn't know it until I returned home to Ukraine—or what the war left of my homeland. Can you believe it? By nowadays standards I was just a kid. Still, I was already flying my own Yak 1 with wooden wings and no radio. I thought I was a hotshot until I found out they gave my Yak to the women of the 586th.

"Did I tell you about Katya and Lidya, our great Soviet flying aces? Lidya had no luck. She went down in '43. Good thing I removed the sliding canopy—otherwise I'd have been trapped and burned alive. Six kills are not bad, is it? Mind you, I was no Misha Baranov, the real hero of the Soviet Union. He brought down five German planes in a single day! He took down twenty-one planes in the battle for Stalingrad, but his luck also ran out in '43—not in a battle, mind you, but just testing another Yak. Well, Eternal Memory to them all. Unlike the Westerners, we will never forget! Still, I survived, didn't I?"

"Yes, Papa, you did. Thank God," I tell him, gently looking at the burned photograph for the hundredth time as if I've never seen it before.

"I need some liquid nourishment, don't you see, Sashen'ka? I asked Avi to go to the store, and he said no. Can you believe he said no to a lonely old man who saved his people from the Nazis? I think he's ticked with me because I saw him with a swanky-looking blue boy, and I busted his balloon when I told him that the dandy was probably looking for a sugar daddy. Not that Avi has funds, despite all his Jew pretenses. And here I thought he was banging my neighbor's daughter. Did I tell you that one, Oksana, the light skirt, has married into the Bratva, our most powerful criminal society?"

"Oh no, Papa. Why even say their name out loud? I know Oksana— she's a good girl, married to a businessman. You've always taught me to see the good in people. I'm sure it's only gossip, and how could you be so rude to Avi? Please don't ask strangers to get you alcohol. It's not like back home: here neighbors aren't your best friends. Look, I'm here now. You know the doctor told you to avoid getting yourself agitated. Just wait; I'll get you some. I have a small bottle—just for emergencies. Here it is, and I measured it carefully. Drink up, na *zdorovie* (to your health), Papa."

"Thanks, thanks; you're my true soul friend. You're a real daughter to me, even if you're not of my blood; you, not Gary." Papa takes a gulp of the warm vodka, smells his fist, and chases it with a deep breath. "Why spend money on this expensive shit, when Smirnoff is what I wanted? And you'd better keep a tight rein on your son. That young guy I saw with the Israeli upstairs looked suspiciously like Jason. You don't want that filthy Zionist Avi to turn your boy blue, do you?" Papa says, using the common Russian slang expression for homosexuals.

Rendered speechless by his hatred, all I can do is shake my head.

"Tell me again why you won't buy good alcohol?" He continues to pester me.

"Because you like cheap vodka too much, and you know you shouldn't be drinking because of your blood thinners," I tell him. "It's Grey Goose—I thought you liked it."

"To be clear, I prefer samogon—the Americans call it moonshine. But it's all good. A soothing balm to my wounded soul," Papa waxes poetic as he throws the rest of the shot back elegantly, making a loud sound as though he just achieved a long-overdue orgasm.

"*Dobre, Dobre,*" he mumbles to himself in native Ukrainian, then switches to his usual Russian. "It went down good . . . now I can think much better. How about one more shot? Pour me another hundred fifty grams. No? Maybe just fifty grams?"

"Papa, you've had enough," I reply patiently.

"How about you have one shot with me, just for company? No? Your mama will be home soon, you are correct. Better no more shots. What was I saying, Sashen'ka?"

"You were telling me about the War, Papa . . . always about the War . . ."

"As I was saying, only we can understand and remember. Can you believe these Washington blockheads? No wonder a couple of greasy camel hoarders can blow a hole inside of the Pentagon. Two hundred guys die in the whole campaign, and the President of the United States of America, the most powerful man in the world, must go on TV and apologize. We lost 20 million, and I never heard Stalin apologize to us! The Americans, they started this last mess in Iraq. I tell you it's those CIA operatives and not Putin. I wouldn't be surprised if they're the ones who hired the Saudis to blow up those New York buildings, so they'd have an excuse to grab more territory while the New Russians thought the West was their friend."

"What are you saying? Stalin was a monster! Please don't be so cruel. Those are just boys and girls fighting over there. It's a tragedy for their families. How would you feel if it was our boy in Iraq or Afghanistan? And why do you always bring up Stalin? What does he have to do with the here and now?"

"Because you have to know the past to see what will happen in the future. Ah, you never understand me—all you care about is your flower shop! For your information, Stalin was harsh, but he was a just leader. Your boy is not stupid. Why would he fight someone else's battles? It's not like someone has invaded his own homeland. Plus, it's a job Americans get paid for doing. No one makes them." Running out of breath, he stops to use his inhaler.

"Are you all right?" I ask, hoping he's finished with all this crazy conspiracy talk.

"I'm fine—stop interrupting me, or I'll forget my train of thoughts."

"I apologize."

"Now, where was I? Ah, the Americans: we went to war because we had to defend our motherland. They fight to grow their profits. Ever heard of the Industrial-Military complex? Read Eisenhower. The Iraqis were fine with Saddam. What did he do to them? He sure kept the mullahs in check, and what about Mubarak, their friend? And that peacock Gaddafi? They promised him and his family protection—what a joke they played on him! I don't even want to talk about Syria—all the provinces are gone too. Look at the pictures: Aleppo is a bloody bathhouse. Before the CIA created the Taliban, Afghanistan was a paradise. Did I tell you about the woman doctor I befriended last time I was in Kabul, before we had to get our noses bloody defending our Allies?"

"Yes, you did, and she was lovely. Oh, Papa, please stop watching the news. Your blood pressure is already uncontrollable." I was so tired of his ramblings and politics and crazy conspiracies. I had bills to pay and family obligations to fulfill without losing my mind worrying about politics.

"Stop telling me what to do! I'm not your child! And where do you think ISIS came from? You know who. . . why don't they bomb the Saudis? I tell you, it's all about oil. They wanted to take the oil so Putin wouldn't get it! And how about that Wiki Mickey guy Juliette? Just listen to the young Tolstoy's political TV show. Nice kid and a descendant of the great Leo Tolstoy. Mark my words, he'll be the next president of Russia! I know politics. I know war." He goes on and on.

"Do you mean Julian Assange from WikiLeaks? We are lucky to live here, blessed—this is our forever home, and your grandson was born in Los Angeles." I try to reason with him, even though I know he won't listen.

"Ah, don't look at me that way. It's a free country, isn't it? I can have my opinion. God Bless America and all. Look at that fool in the White House: they will get rid of him for sure."

Oh no, now he will get up and give me a wet vodka kiss, I think to myself. I dare not refuse, though, for fear of hurting his feelings. It breaks my heart to admit it: my invincible Papa has the look of a withered rag doll. I remember the last time we danced together—an old-fashioned Boston waltz—his body was so fragile; I cried for hours on the way home.

It brought back memories of him dancing with Mama to the same song just before she took a turn for the worse. I held my breath as I watched their well-practiced moves on the parquet floor, proud and in control; her still-stunning Slavic features lit up from the inside with pleasure. I remember turning to my husband and asking him if he also saw the ghosts of their past love coming through. He shook his head, bringing my hand to his lips and telling me that only I could see them as they were and not as they are.

Mama ordered me to play that song at her memorial: Alexander Rosenbaum's poetry, both sad and comforting. His words stay with me: "How often do I see this dream, my wonderful dream, in which the autumn is dancing waltz Boston for us . . ."

No one here even knows what waltz Boston is. Papa told me they knew it as the One-Step Waltz, the Long Boston, and The Drop Step (on account of all the steps being dropped or eliminated except one). In London they also called it the Berceuse or Cradle Boston. I gathered it was popular with returning soldiers.

Papa apologized for not dancing it well, explaining that though the steps were deceptively simple, dancing it correctly was easier said than done. I don't know; to my eyes, Papa always looked perfect, gliding with Mama on the dance floor. But isn't it always this way? Simplicity is the most difficult to achieve. I use this philosophy when I arrange flowers. "Don't get mad, Sasha. I'm just an old fool. Not bored with my stories yet?" he asks me after the boozy embrace.

"Never! I want to hear everything about you."

"Sasha, I'm sleepy now. I'm going to lie down in the bedroom. Will you sit by me and watch my breathing? And if I die, wake me. Sasha, your mother isn't coming home, is she?"

"No, Papa."

"I got old, didn't I?"

"No, Papa."

"Still love me?"

"Always, I will love you, Papa. Rest, and I'll sit by your side while you sleep. You're safe."

———— ∞ ————

I was adopted in 1958—a great year in America, a year of Elvis and the fantabulous '58 Corvette. In England, chubby-faced Billy Hardy ripped the Manchester Theatre, filled to capacity by the sweaty neo-dandies called the Teddy Boys. One of my favorite French singers, Maurice Chevalier, made a triumphant return to Hollywood at sixty-nine years old and won an honorary Oscar for the musical *Gigi*. The West awarded Boris Pasternak the Nobel Prize for literature for his poetry, but most of us Soviets knew nothing of his international fame, let alone his masterpiece, *Doctor Zhivago*. He was dead in only two years, Western acclaim and all. The story of how *Doctor Zhivago* became an international sensation is a most curious one; something straight out of one of Ian Fleming's spy thrillers. An MI6 agent photographed the manuscript and then passed it on to the Italians, who published it, some say to spite the Soviets. I read an article in a Russian language paper about the entire *Doctor Zhivago* affair. Apparently, Pasternak trusted a few fellow academicians from Oxford to read his work because he was sure his poetic view of how his hero, a poet doctor, came to stand against the unstoppable tide of the Revolution would never see the light of day. The long-suffering years of battling the system took their final toll on his delicate artist's body. I imagine that being forced to turn down the Nobel Prize by petty Communist Party bureaucrats was a heartbreak. I saw his grave at the village cemetery of Peredelkino, where he lived—a lovely settlement near Moscow.

My real birthday is unknown. Papa chose one for me: May 30th. It means that I fall under Gemini, the sign of the twins. Funny, that's one sun sign I could never have been born under. I'm not at all witty or chatty. But I am adaptable; I don't fool around either. Papa's blood son, Gary, was born May 30th, the same day Pasternak died—coincidence? I think not. I wonder if Gary fools around. Why did Mama go along with that date? I think it's cruel to give one child the birthday belonging to another. Maybe Papa thought sharing a birthday would make me Gary's real sister—a star sister, anyhow.

Papa signed away his parental rights to Gary while he was in a drunken stupor. He never saw his only son again. His first wife, Dr. Sonya, remarried immediately and changed Gary's last name. Last we heard; the family had immigrated to Canada in the eighties.

Papa blamed his in-laws for his "tragedy." He blamed his new wife, his friends, even the law, but never "his Sonya." She was always good and kind, a true Tolstoyesque heroine—as if he ever read Tolstoy. Papa was strictly Hemingway and Erich Maria Remarque.

"A good doctor is always kind, and Sonya is the best," he'd tell anyone who would listen to his vodka-dampened stories. "She saved my hand during the Great Patriotic War. Do you know how few of my flying buddies came back with all their limbs intact? If only I could have stopped drinking . . ."

My adoptive mother, Klavdia Petrovna, is buried now, high on a hill overlooking the Ventura Freeway (or is it the Hollywood Freeway? I can never get the freeway exit right). My son tells me it's because I don't really want to go there. Mama waits for me beneath an evergreen, a Japanese pine. I get lost each time I go to visit her there. Her small, unremarkable headstone reads: "We Grieve Your Premature Departure." She said Papa would bury her, and he did—his bottle did.

I wanted her to live a little, enjoy the bone-warming California sun, but they moved here too late. Cancer. What else could it have been? All that pain and suffering can't be good for your health, that's for sure. She spent decades living with a drunk who brought God only knew what type of venereal disease to their bed, considering he used to disappear for weeks during one of his alcoholic benders. She'd never had regular pap smears in Kiev, and by the time I dragged her in to see my own doctor, they diagnosed her with the dreaded stage 4 cervical cancer.

"The disease is too advanced. We could try chemo and try to make her pain more bearable. But it's up to her. Otherwise just take her home and call a hospice. You'll need all the help you can get, especially toward the end."

We heard the same response everywhere we turned: from the best American oncologists at Cedar-Sinai to the most famous Russian émigré professors. Even the Chinese and the Tibetans told me to keep her comfortable and pray she didn't hang on too long. Papa heard of an Armenian faith healer from Lebanon who practiced in Glendale, but after consulting with her, even he gave up all hope. On a lark, I drove her to cancer specialists in Mexico, down south, past Rosarito Beach. No help there either. She wouldn't go for their approach: fasting, macrobiotics, and coffee enemas. "I'd rather die than eat that shit, "Mama told another Russian-speaking woman. Alla Markovna was a retired Russian physician, originally from St. Petersburg. The woman brought her own terminally ill husband to the clinic, apparently as a last resort as well.

Alla Markovna bonded with me over our collective sorrow, and we still keep in touch. She introduced me to her daughter Oksana. After we laid Mama to rest, I recommended my older friend to the management of the building where Papa Victor still lives. Fortunately, Oksana likes my flower arrangements and was kind enough to return the favor by putting in a good word for my flower shop with the other members of her family. Oksana's sister-in-law, Dr. Bella Ginzburg, a successful dentist with her own practice, has become a good client.

I can't help but wish Oksana's mother hadn't told me about her conversation with my adoptive mama. I know her intentions were good; still, it hurt. "My daughter's been in America too long. Who the hell does she think she is telling me what I must do? I need some good food and a little rest. Have you tasted their milk products and butter? Foo. No taste at all. Back home, in Kiev, cardboard tastes better."

Mama wouldn't stop complaining about all the wrong I've done to her, even as I drove her back North. By the end of the drive, I thought I'd killed her myself; at least that's what she told me. I don't know how I made it back without crashing into a freeway divider. We didn't tell Mama about the hopelessness of her prognosis. And what do the doctors know about "the" time? It's not for them to know—only God knows who will live and who will die.

When Mama slipped deeper into the quicksand of her disease, I pressed her to leave Papa and move in with me. She'd complain about him so bitterly. "He never helps; he drinks and sleeps or sits in front of his damn TV, yelling and cussing. He never talks to me, just listens to his Russian programs. I don't think he even knows how to bring me a glass of tea. He couldn't care less that I'm sick. I'm hungry. Why can't you bring me good food?"

"Mama, we want you to move in with us. I want to take care of you, but it's hard to drive to Hollywood from the other side of the Valley twice a day, and I started a new business. You'd like it. It's a flower shop. Maybe it's time you left Papa."

To my surprise, she got angry with me, furious. "Business, always business; what do I care about your American business? And a flower shop yet! You don't think your shop will last, do you? Why can't people grow flowers in their own yard? Everybody has a big house here, and you can buy silk flowers that stay fresh-looking forever!'

"Mama, please don't worry. I'll do the best I can." I tried to placate her, feeling overwhelmed with guilt and shame for not being a good daughter.

"Worry about you?" she went on mercilessly. "You are a selfish, ungrateful snake! After all I've done, everything I've endured with both of you—you want that I should be alone, alone at my age? You should have a man in your bed, but not me? My mother always warned me about you! She told me not to coddle an adopted viper next to my heart."

"But Mama," I protested gently, reaching out to touch her parchment-dry hand. "He's a hopeless drunk!"

I felt a sharp blow across my cheek.

"Who are you to criticize him? You're not even of his blood!"

"I'm sorry, Mama."

"He only began to drink after they took Gary from him."

"He signed the papers drunk!"

"Yes, but it wasn't his fault. We had a fight; I wanted him to give Gary up because I thought I was pregnant with our own child." She wiped her eyes with a shaking hand.

"Forgive me, Mama." Papa refused to let me take her home after the last hospitalization. He told me that if she died at home, he would never sleep.

Mama died alone early in the morning, just after I finally left her hospital room. It had been a long, sleepless night. I desperately needed to shower. As I left the Cedars parking lot, I decided to first check on my shop. I never made it home. When the nursing station called my cell, I dropped everything and rushed back. The kind nurse told me what happened. She asked if I wanted to kiss her goodbye. Mama was still warm, but no matter how I tried, I couldn't make myself touch her remains.

Forgive me, Mama, for not being your own child. I wish I could have been. I would've looked just like you: fragile, porcelain skin, strawberry hair and green eyes, eyes the color of a Fuerte avocado's skin. But that's not me. Papa wanted me for his daughter because I looked just like him: black hair and blue eyes, dark skin and heavy brows. Just like Papa . . . and Gary.

As soon as I came to America, let's see, over twenty years ago now, I bleached my hair blonde. I tweezed and shaved and waxed my brows. It's California, but I've never let myself tan, and I wear green-tinted contact lenses.

A full decade later, Mama and Papa received permission to leave Ukraine. When they arrived from Kiev, they walked right past me at the LAX arrival gate. Finally, Mama recognized my husband, Lee. It terrified me to hear Papa's criticism of my new look, but he hugged me tight and called me his American movie actress. Mama cried, holding on to Lee. She looked ancient and tiny. With loving care, Lee held her upright, giving me his wordless assurance, "See, they do love you!"

The last few months of Mama's illness were horrifyingly slow and painful until she finally gave in and allowed us to get her on a morphine drip. She lingered in the hospital for a full week despite her doctor's predictions of imminent death. After the first day, I was alone with her. Papa had drunk himself into a stupor while I sat beside her, hoping she wasn't in pain. I don't blame him for not being able to handle it. She struggled with every breath, but she never looked at me. I'm glad I was there until the end; I suffer no guilt, only relief. She's buried now. I've let my hair go natural, but it's not black anymore. It's white, just like Papa's, and maybe like Gary's . . .

Papa Victor doesn't live with us. Lee offered to share our place with him. He has a golden heart, my husband, but our only son, Jason, asked me not to let Papa move in.

Jason is our own private miracle. First, I couldn't conceive; then I lost one baby after another. I thought I was cursed. We were all set to adopt, thanks to Lee's love for me, but Jason made it through a difficult pregnancy with flying colors. That's why I named him after the ancient Greek hero who, unlike his little brothers or sisters, survived the wrath of the gods. I knew he would be fine. I delivered Jason before the doctors administered anesthesia. He looked just as he looks now: tall and beautifully formed, a deep dimple on his left cheek, gorgeous brown eyes, and a full head of dark blond hair. When I came to, the first face I looked at was his.

Jason is against alcohol; he thinks my papa sets a bad example for him and his friends, and he says I enable his alcoholism. At first, Jason offered to pay for a private alcohol treatment program with his own savings, or attend AA with Papa. I told Jason it wouldn't work. Jason tried to talk with Papa. I think he used up his entire Russian vocabulary.

"Come on, Deda, I'll help you lick it. It's time you kicked that monkey off your back. I'll be there for you, every day and night. We could do it together. For me, please. Say *niet* to vodka!"

"First learn to speak proper Russian, and then we'll talk. OK, Mister America? And I'm not even a real drunk by our standards. You know how to tell the difference between an amateur and a real professional drunk? It's when you're lying in the gutter and a woodpecker's drilling a hole in your head, but you're too drunk to say shoo!" Papa laughs out loud at his own tired joke.

"Addiction is not funny. It's a disease. I love you, Deda, and I don't want to burry you, not just yet. How can you be so selfish?" My son doesn't give up. I didn't give up easily either, not for decades.

As usual, Papa doesn't argue. He cries his vodka-tears and hugs Jason, but he doesn't agree to any help. Jason won't visit Papa's apartment because Papa still tries to push drinks on him and his friends.

"Drink up, boys. Are you men or mice?"

"Thanks, but no thanks."

"Drink up, don't be shy. I'm hiding a bottle of cognac too! Three stars, from Armenia! Not that you'd know where Armenia is."

"I know, it's in the Middle East somewhere. No thanks, I hate the smell of this stuff. Why don't we all have some soda?" my son calmly responds.

"Why do you drink American soda? Don't you know its canned poison? It causes cancer. I don't believe it: my boy's a girl! What are you, blue? And for your information, you can find Armenia in the south Caucasus Mountains. That's West Asia for you, dumb asses! Bet they don't teach you proper geography at your American school." Papa loves to prove his point about the superiority of the Russian education system.

"No, Grandfather, I'm not a girl, but I still won't drink alcohol! And I don't give a shit where your booze comes from. A toxin is a toxin," Jason fights back, sounding increasingly bitter.

What can I do? I can't change my father or my son. My boy is as kindhearted as his father, but still . . . he's young and a harsh judge. I never had time to be categorical in my own judgments. One must learn to adjust to the world of gray to survive. Still, I'm glad I raised Jason to feel safe: to see right from wrong and stand up for himself.

Jason also hates when Papa brings up Gary's name and my adoption. He says I'm emotionally abused. He doesn't understand. How could he, my American-born son? While I make America my home, I struggle to let go of my past.

I must believe that Papa's right about me needing to be more grateful; I'm so fortunate to have been adopted at all. I could've rotted in that orphanage. People just didn't adopt strange children in my country. They say, some do in this new Russia, but I don't believe it. Why then do they sell our abandoned kids to foreigners? All my life I've heard old women say that it's bad luck to bring such a child into your family. You never know about their blood. Maybe they'd grow up to be criminals! It's only natural that Papa and Mama never loved me as if I was their blood, but I was clean and fed and never hit with a belt. Mama helped me with my homework and sewed my school uniforms with her own hands. I had the run of her well-stocked, classical library, and in the summer, she took me to the family's country dacha. Mama's life was hard. Living with an alcoholic, no matter how nice of a person, isn't a party, but Papa, he was always so kind, so soft with me . . . and still is.

I never thought about my life before they took me in until I saw the pictures of Romanian orphans on *60 Minutes*. I let myself remember a little . . . I saw a dirty little girl with stubby black hair, barely grown out from being shaved because of lice, holding a small patchwork pillow. Until then, I wasn't embarrassed by my hair because I'd never seen a child with long hair. I thought you had to be a grown-up to have hair. All I can recall is a feeling of overwhelming happiness and joy. As if by magic, I was going home with the most beautiful couple in the world—my own handsome uniform-wearing papa and angelic, golden-haired mama. I shall always be grateful to them for taking me out of that cesspool.

"If you feel so sorry for me, my son, you bring a strange child, a throwaway orphan, into your home," I tell Jason when he pushes my buttons about Papa. Jason and Lee both hug me and tell me I'm their blood; they reassure me that they love me more than life itself, and I believe them. After one particularly painful confrontation with his grandfather, Jason chose a new birthday for me. He picked February 14th, Valentine's Day: a sentimental choice, yes. But a little melodrama suits me fine. America is a melodrama-loving country. How else can you explain their fascination with reunion shows or *American Idol,* not to mention author Nora Roberts? Over a hundred books written, and she's still young! I wish I could write just one before I close my eyes. I love her. Why can't all stories end happily, just like Nora's?

The phone rings twice. It's Papa's signal, so I call him back. Papa refuses to pay for calls to another area code, just the basic service. We bought him a smartphone in case of an emergency, but he won't use it; he says it causes brain tumors. It's not that he's poor—he receives Social Security, and his apartment is government-subsidized, but he wants me to call.

He wakes up early, listens to the news on a Russian-language program, and eats breakfast—always the same kolbasa and bread with sweet Vologda butter. He drinks a glass of kvass for indigestion. He believes the traditional Russian fermented drink—similar to kombucha—cures everything; although, after Mama's death, he learned how to make a cup of instant coffee. After coffee, he downs a short shot glass of whatever vodka he can stumble upon and walks a few blocks to infamous Plummer Park, the center of Russian-speaking immigrant life in LA, or so Papa believes. Jason calls it the old dude's Kremlin. He's right. Papa and his drinking cronies sit around just like they did back home. Some play chess, rather well; others prefer checkers, and they all discuss world affairs with gusto, as if they need to make up for all those silent Stalin years.

Today, the phone call goes on and on, and Papa seems especially agitated. Someone at the park told him he should go on an American talk show where they find your long-lost relatives. All his buddies know about Gary and offered their opinions.

"Those show people, they will fly me in and put me up in a hotel and even pay me!" Papa says, convinced he'll reunite with Gary on TV and make a dollar at that.

"But, Papa, you've hated airplanes ever since the war. Remember when we wanted to take you with us to Hawaii to celebrate our twenty-fifth anniversary, but you insisted that you'd done enough flying in the war? Don't you remember how we had to cancel our trip because you had a heart attack scare?"

"That's different, Sasha. For Gary, I'll get on the space shuttle." I guess he's right; Gary is his only real child. I still feel sad about that trip, though. Lee planned everything perfectly for me—the stunning Kapalua Bay Hotel, including a white limo to the airport. He bought a fresh flower lei for me to wear on the plane. The purple lei matched my brand-new amethyst earrings, also a gift from him and my son. No one ever brings me flowers now since I work among them. But Papa fell ill, and we never went. I guess we'll just have to go some other time, maybe for our fiftieth. Lee understood; Jason didn't. He told Papa he was being manipulative and ungrateful and an alcoholic.

"Papa's going on a TV talk show to find Gary," I tell Lee and Jason over dinner that night. I still can't believe we were able to buy our new place, a three-bedroom 1960s ranch with a private yard; it's everything I've ever wanted. The house needs lots of work, but I don't care. After all the years renting, I scraped together a down payment. Lee wasn't sure it was such a great idea since the prices here in LA are beyond high. Still, he went along for my sake seeing how much I love gardening. It will take us decades to pay for the mortgage, but I know I'll have something to leave my son when I die. I decorated my dollhouse with vintage lace and whitewashed the furniture I bought at vintage shops. I insist that we eat at the dining table in the kitchen—it's bright and cheerful and promotes conversation. And what a conversation it is!

"You're shitting me," Jason says, roaring with laughter and almost choking on his food.

"Knock it off and watch your language!" At first, I admonish him. "Good. You're choking on your words. Oh, no! Can you breathe?" I fret. I love him beyond reason, plus he is one of the few people in my life who can make me laugh.

"I'm good. Chill, Mom." Jason puts me at ease after drinking water and clearing his throat. Not much rattles his young nerves.

"What's going on, you two?" Lee joins in on our conversation. Normally he sits quietly, reading a sports magazine or some mechanical manual, always working.

"Somebody at Plummer park told Deda he could find Gary on TV," explains Jason. He goes on: "Say, parents, let's put him on The View with those loud New York chicks, that neck action going on and the booing audience. Or maybe on Maury—old Russian drunks who sell their children and now want back child support. They can even do a DNA in case Gary won't believe him."

"Jason, shame on you," Lee feigns admonishment. "He needs Sally Jesse."

"They canceled her show years ago," I speak up. Since I've always worked in a small business, I've enjoyed the freedom to glance at a talk show or an American soap opera.

"Who is Sally Jesse?" asks Jason.

"OK, then put him on with Geraldo, that guy with devil worshipers."

"Geraldo had his own show? Where have you been, Dad? Geraldo's on Fox—haven't you seen him crawling around the caves? But they kicked him out of Iraq. He's on Fox with the right-winged fascists."

"What fascists?"

"Never mind, Dad. Say, I have an idea—let's put him on *Jerry Springer*; he can duke it out with his ex and the in-laws. Or let's call the *Enquirer*— "My Son Was Abducted by Aliens."

That's when soup spouts out from Lee's nose.

"What about Oprah? She's still there, right?" Lee is confident about that.

"Nope, she retired," Jason says smugly.

"I give up! Oprah's gone too. I can't keep up with this country. Is she or isn't she a lesbian?"

"I hope she is, and I hope she marries Wendy Williams! She'd have the most expensive wedding ever and maybe Mom's shop could do the flowers."

"Who is this Wendy, and why are you always talking nonsense? When are you going to come down to earth?" Lee shakes his head in wonder. He's a practical sort who believes only what he sees with his own eyes. He grew up so differently and doesn't get our son, though he loves him madly.

"Why are you looking at me that way, Dad?" Jason says in his own defense. "It could happen. Read *The Law of Attraction*. I can also become a 'huuuge' success, just like that orange gorilla. I don't have to work my ass off like you do.

"What orange gorilla? Why can't I understand you? Are you telling me that you're finally interested in a good profession, something like law?" says my husband, opening his eyes wide. Lee and Jason don't see eye to eye on most things. Jason lives on Twitter and follows the most liberal sites, while Lee only watches conservative news—if he has time for anything other than work, that is. I'm lucky: most of the time, Jason and I have our own language. He talks to me. We spend time together, especially when he helps with larger flower orders.

"Hell no!" Jason spits out in protest. "I don't need thousands of dollars of loans to sit in some rigged court and lie. I'm a hacker and proud of it! And you, Father, should work less and watch more TV. Then you wouldn't be such a blockhead," Jason says jokingly, copying his father's heavily accented voice perfectly.

I've had enough of their banter and step in; the food is getting cold. "Stop it, you idiots." But by now, they're over the edge, laughing. I don't think it's so funny, but how can I resist their joy? And so, I join in.

After dinner and some obligatory return phone calls, I turn in to watch a few classic American films on Netflix. I often can't sleep, and the old stars keep me company. Next to *Doctor Zhivago*, my favorite musical is *Sun Valley Serenade*.

Sonja Henie plays a Scandinavian war orphan adopted by an American swing band. I adore the Nicholas brothers' tap-dancing routines. The bandleader expects a little girl but gets a beautiful young woman instead. In the end, Sonja and the bandleader (for the life of me I can never remember his name) fall in love and marry. How lucky for golden-haired Sonja! Being adopted in American movies isn't bad.

Why is everyone so angry with Hollywood? As Jason says, bringing attention to what's right and wrong has always been part of Hollywood history. Just think about how many folks made it through the worst of times escaping into the safety and magic of a warm dark theater, watching Fred and Ginger musicals and screwball comedies during the Depression and the War.

When Hollywood saw social injustice and prejudice, it didn't turn away. Think of *To Kill a Mockingbird* or *Look Who's Coming to Dinner* or *Boys Don't Cry*. And *Philadelphia*, *The Pianist*, and *Schindler's List*—even *Star Wars*! I'm so proud of my son who has inherited from me the love for the movies; even Lenin called it true art.

My memories come more often as I have crossed my fifth decade. They drift over my heart, sometimes misty, sometimes photographically clear. I was nine when the neighborhood kids called me a dirty gypsy. Papa wasn't about to tell me I wasn't his, but the kids did. Mama was glad; she couldn't pretend anymore. I was sad. I'd always felt different from my cousins. My grandmother never kissed me, but I didn't mind—she smelled. I pretended it was my personality or my looks that she found offensive. But once I knew the truth, I tried even harder. I was good and clean. I studied hard and received excellent marks in high school and at the City Art School I loved so much. I even surprised Mama when I married a wonderful boy from a fine family.

I believe I fulfilled my quota of bad luck right up to the moment I married Lee. He is my prince, my knight, my king. When Lee and his parents left Kiev, I reluctantly went with him to America, fell in love with California, and discovered my gifts. I got a private loan from another émigré to buy the flower shop in West San Fernando Valley where I first worked as an assistant. Lee and Jason came up with a catchy name:

"Alexandra of the Valley." It's a drive, but to be fair, it's the only time I can read. I've become addicted to books on tape!

All my nice American clients call me by my full name, Alexandra—that's formal for Sasha. We specialize in exotics: Hawaiian ginger, Anthuriums, the wedding favorite, the Maile vine, and my personal favorites, the unusual orchids you can't buy in a regular grocery store for ten dollars. I sing and coo and nurture my Dendrobium and Cymbidium babies from little cuttings. We do loads of weddings, funerals, and other life events, but lately I also won a few corporate accounts. Now I'm working on our web presence and enlarging the store's refrigeration. Life is full of beauty. Truly, I'm living my dream.

Before I left Kiev, I asked Mama if I had been born a gypsy. That would explain my special dreams, my way with plants and animals, my sense of people.

"Please tell me the truth; I won't be offended. I've often wondered why the gypsies on the street smile at me. You know, Mama, just before I met Lee, a fortune-teller on the corner stopped me, grabbed my hand, and told me I'd meet a handsome boy, marry him, and live on a green hill across the ocean. She didn't want money, but I gave her a ruble anyway."

"Always a big shot with our money," Mama said, shaking her index finger at me and poking me in the arm. "Are you crazy? Naturally, you're not a gypsy. Your mother was a young Ukrainian University student from the countryside and your father, her professor, was much older and married. Papa would never have adopted a child without intelligent blood."

And so she shattered my dreams of a mysterious background with psychic genes. That put my mind at ease. I left those dreams back in Ukraine with a clear conscience.

Now, what to do about Papa? I know him. He'll keep up with the drinking and this foolishness about Gary. Jason says Papa's a bipolar obsessive-compulsive, and that's why he's an alcoholic, not because of any war or Gary. Maybe Jason's right; he's studying to become a therapist. Later that evening, when Lee and I are alone, I bring it up again.

"Lee, I don't think he'll give up on Gary, and I'm afraid this talk show business would be so public. People know us. I think we should find him ourselves, quietly. It shouldn't be too difficult. I know his last name, and I've heard he's a doctor like his mother. I'll place a small classified in the Russian newspaper in New York; everybody gets that one. Or maybe Jason can look on the internet. Oh, and I'll ask Maya. She'll ask Svetlana, the owner of the day spa where she works. Svetlana really knows everyone. If they can't help, there's always Maya's brother, Slava, and his New York connections. I'm also going to a tea leaf-reading party on Sunday. Maybe the psychic will have ideas. Do you support me?"

Lee kisses his favorite dimple on my cheek, rubs his nose on my face, and mumbles, "Tea leaves? Oh, just put the old goat on O'Reilly. Don't tell me he's gone too! Go to sleep, my little gypsy." His arm drapes over my waist as usual. I sigh, thanking the saints for my blessings, and I sniffle as tears of gratitude roll down my freshly scrubbed face.

Just when I think Lee has fallen asleep, he asks gently, "Why aren't you asleep, dear? Another payment's coming up?" No matter how tired he is, Lee never just drops off to sleep without asking me how I feel. He is right about my restlessness.

Earlier in the day, I had to walk next door to talk with Maya about my loan payment. She had a few minutes between clients and was waiting for me in the backroom after throwing in a load of towels. She was snacking on a large slice of shiny, flaky homemade pirogue with meat, washing it down with a large glass of kvas. She offered me a piece, but my stomach was in knots. It embarrassed me to ask if I could arrange for special payments; after all, I'm the one who agreed to them in the first place.

We chatted about this and that while she continued to swallow one slice after another. When I finally got the nerve to ask if I could delay my monthly loan payment for a month or two because of the new house payment, she stopped eating and got serious.

"Sasha," Maya said grimly, looking right through me and speaking in the voice she used only for business. "I sympathize with you not wanting to throw money away on rent, but you must think about your priorities. Not everyone has to be a homeowner. Don't tell me you bought into this American dream propaganda? While I like your character and think well of you as a woman, I have my own business to run."

She continued to lecture me as I stood in front of her like a guilty child anticipating a spanking, shaking like a leaf and not saying a word in either explanation or defense.

"I'm very sorry to ask, Maya." I finally spoke up when she finished. "If you could find it possible just this once to give me a little more time, I promise not to let you down again."

"All right," Maya spoke, after taking so long to answer that I was feeling panicky. "I don't believe my grandmother Zina would approve of the kindness I'm showing you. It's amazing how easily people borrow money and how hard they find to pay it back. That's exactly the reason she had taught me to be firm with people, but occasionally she said it was fine to listen to my heart and make an exception. I will, just this time, allow you to postpone the payment, but only for one week. I won't charge you the additional interest, but you will have to add another five hundred dollars as a late fee. Late fees are pretty standard in any loan arrangements, aren't they?"

"Absolutely!" I answered, relieved.

"Believe me, Sashenka, it's for your own good; you don't want to have to double up on your interest next month, right?"

"I understand, and I'm eternally grateful for your generosity," was all I could muster in response.

Well, Lee didn't need to know what went on earlier today, so I cupped his cheek and lied a little. Even though I hate lying to Lee, I decided not to tell him about what happened with Maya. "I am worried a little, but I've got it. Maya's so nice and understanding and told me not to panic if I postpone a payment," I answered, trying to sound confident. "I think my new Russian client Flora will hire us to do her stepson's wedding in Vegas. It could be a big job. She also prefers that I go there to supervise the installation, so that will be an additional charge. They are a prosperous family."

The last thing my husband needs is to work more to pay off the flower shop expansion loans. I know he would walk through fire to pay my bills, but I'm worried about his heart condition as it is. If I can expand and get more business, maybe he could take a little break.

"A Vegas wedding for our store? That's exciting. Which Flora are you talking about? Not the one with the American husband?"

"She's the one."

"Are you're sure you can survive her?" he asks, suddenly wide awake. He had some rather tense business dealings with her recently.

"Yes, my heart. I met her stepson and his future daughter-in-law. They came to see me a few days ago. The girl was sweet. The boy, I don't know— there was something about him that bothered me. I'm used to guys being a little detached, but he seemed more concerned with his phone messages. I'm sure he's fine; flowers are usually all about the bride. Besides, it's far too much money to turn down. I got the deposit when I promised to be there in person. Don't worry—I'll be gone just overnight, and Jason will drive the van. If I could manage my own mama, I can manage Flora. She's not that bad, just lonely and lost."

"Sure, I'd be lost too with all their money."

"But it's not always about the money. She can't fit into American culture, and that makes me sad. She's a very interesting woman. I'll tell you her story tomorrow morning over tea, if you're interested. Did you know she came here after a torrid love affair with an American student? Remember when the government forbade marriages with foreign citizens?"

"In the morning I want coffee and fried eggs. What happened to all of us was a lifetime ago. Wait, I thought her husband was an electrical contractor? On second thought, why don't you tell her story now; maybe it'll bore me to sleep," Lee said, chuckling. Then he got solemn once again. "That's why you're my heart and the best soul I know. You see the good in everyone, even in a spoiled, demanding bitch like Flora," he said, giving me a sweet kiss.

"Come on, be nice. She's just high-strung. You know, she went to art school too. Except it wasn't my silly city school, but Serov's in Leningrad. Serov's kids got permission to paint right in the Hermitage! Flora's English is perfect because she didn't learn it from *General Hospital* and other soaps like I did. Flora worked as a technical translator at the Language Institute, and Ken's her second husband."

"Wow, I'm impressed that she can translate technical manuals. Bet you she hasn't worked a day since she married the American, though."

"The poor thing can't seem to adjust. I wish she loved our new homeland as we do. Where else could a throwaway orphan like me work herself up from nothing to own her own successful business?"

"Well, you worked for it with your own two hands, and all she did was lie on her back."

"Stop with the sarcasm and go to sleep, or I won't make cheesecakes for breakfast," I say, kissing his shoulder and turning off the TV. Another sleepless night looms ahead, but I'm not unhappy—just a little concerned.

I think I finally just dozed off when I heard the phone pierce the silence. "Oh, no . . . it's showtime . . . it's Papa . . ." I grab the only landline we have, my heart beating out of my chest.

"Papa, what's wrong? Did you press your alarm button? Are you at the ER?"

"Yes, it is I, your father," he answers, unmistakably slurring his words. "I'm perfectly fine."

"It's after midnight. Have you been drinking?" *God, when will it stop?* I think to myself.

"When haven't I been drinking, Alexandra? Listen, I must tell you something important. My conscience won't let me alone."

"Can't it wait until the morning?" My patience is wearing thin, and I'm getting annoyed. "Lee is exhausted—his doctor changed his blood pressure meds, and he finally fell asleep. You know he hasn't been feeling well."

"He should work less and drink more. It's good for his blood vessels," says Papa, amused by his own cleverness.

"Papa, I'm about to hang up," I say, desperately trying not to raise my voice. I can feel a funny headache at the base of my skull. Blood pressure again.

"Don't you dare hang up on me! I am your father and you owe me your life. Without me, you'd still be you know where? Nowhere! Don't interrupt, or I will not share with you. As Jason says, chill; plus, you will like what I have to say."

"Yes, Papa," I respond almost inaudibly.

"Are you sitting down? Good. Here it goes. I found Gary. I mean, I know where he lives, his profession, and the name of his wife. I saw his kids too. I'm a great-grandfather to two boys! Boys, Sasha, boys with my blood running through their American veins! Say, I even know where he vacationed. Last week he had his gallbladder out! Isn't it something? It looks like my son is just like me!"

"What?"

"Yes. I'm not a war hero for nothing. So, Maxim Petrovich, you know my chess partner, who is . . ."

"I know who he is; please cut to the chase," I shock myself by barking at the phone loud enough to wake up Jason's cat, Kotik. Kotik likes to sleep sprawled over my feet. I must be losing my mind to talk to Papa like this. I expect him to yell back, but for some unknown reason, he ignores my tone and continues the conversation.

"Shush, Sashenka, have patience! I'm an old man, and a drunk at that. Anyway, Max is on Facebook, so the two of us had a few shots and found Gary. It was easy. We put his name into the search, clicked, and then these

Facebook CIA operatives came up with all the right names. The third guy was him! See, I am a genius."

"Wait, then why do you want to go on TV show?' At this point I'm so confused and exhausted I can't think. Lee finally wakes up and asks me what's wrong.

"The old nutcase has found Gary on Facebook."

"Then why does he want to go on TV?" asks Lee as he rubs the sleep from his deeply hooded eyes.

"Exactly!" I howl, finally losing my temper. "Father, are you still there?"

"Where else would I be?" he answers, sounding a touch more sober. "Well, I've been watching this reunion show on Russian TV, and it seemed like a tremendous idea. I could use a little attention and I could say hi to everyone at the Park. Wait, why aren't you proud of me? Don't you want to meet your brother? What's wrong with you, Alexandra? Have you forgotten the circumstances of your birth? Have you forgotten who I am and how much you owe me? I am the man who took you out of hell! When did you stop being grateful? Mama is rolling in her grave hearing you talk to me this way—we didn't raise you to be so selfish!"

"Yes, Papa," I answer, giving up all hope of normalcy. "Whatever makes you happy, Papa. I congratulate you on locating your only son and your grandchildren. Lee and Jason and I, we support you. Good night. I kiss you. I'll call you in the morning."

THE LIBERATION OF LUCIANO PADOVAN

The Luciano Padovan shoe collection is often described as "refined, sexy and feminine." It is dedicated to the contemporary woman that doesn't sacrifice guilty pleasures in her daily life—a woman who doesn't go unobserved. High heels. Decisive shapes. Sensual colors and glamour. Meetings at work, drinks afterward or on a business trip. Luciano Padovan shoes adapt to every moment of her day.

Oksana
"ALLO?"

"*Mamachka*? It's me, Oksana, your daughter."

"Oksana is my daughter. Who is it?"

"It's me, Oksana."

"Why didn't you say so then? What's wrong?"

"Nothing . . . I mean a lot . . . I mean nothing wrong with me. I'm calling to ask you a for a little favor . . ."

"Diarrhea? Coughing? Bad menses? God save me and have mercy, it's the kids!"

"No, they're perfect, still in school."

"Slava?"

"At work, where he's supposed to be."

"Oksana, you almost gave me another stroke, and I'm alone today. That Polish *kurva* Bozena who's supposed to look after me got a hangover again. I called the little witch and she's still in bed. Migraine, shmigrain . . . nothing I do for this girl is good enough. Did you know that even your own brother hates her? Two hundred dollars a week he pays her, and I'm left alone. You live too far, busy with your own family. With the dollar so high against the rubble . . . let's see, two hundred times sixty . . . Oh no, we're paying her twelve thousand a week, times fifty-two weeks. Oh God, I'm making a caregiver a rich millionaire."

"Mother, have you lost it? Stop counting in rubles—and Bozena's Polish!"

"I don't care if it's in rubles. She can always leave me and take the dollars there. And my darling Yuri, your only brother, is married. I'm glad he married a dentist: she's a good girl, that Bella, despite being from Ukraine. Still, I lost him, and since your father left me too, I'm always alone. Ah . . . who cares about me? I shouldn't have allowed Bozena to go over to Bella's to help her mother after she had a stroke; hers was mild, unlike mine. I think Bozena likes Bella's mother better. She's always telling me how nice the house is and how Bella and her mother get along and love each other so much! Isn't she lucky to have a devoted daughter?"

"You have a devoted daughter . . ."

"That's what you think!"

"You know what, Mother? Just settle down and take your Valerian drops, not that they work like a proper medication, like Xanax. And you shouldn't call women whores. I hope you don't call her that to her face, and you best take the drops with a full glass of alkaline water this time. Why did I bother to get you a delivery service if you won't drink the water!"

"Not now. You never call and when you finally do, you hang up whenever you don't like what I tell you. I have things to say, but no one listens."

"I won't hang up. I'll wait for you to take your meds. I'm listening to you now, aren't I? Incidentally, I live fifteen minutes away and see you three times a week! And my brother pays for your help. Do you want me to call the agency to find you a new girl?"

"What new girl? Since when are you telling me what to do? I am the mother here. Bozena is clean and does things the way I used to do them. I don't want another girl. I want Bozena."

"OK, OK. You'll keep your Bozena."

"Ah, I see, you're jealous of her! Did I tell you she's a chemical engineer? My girl is a graduate of the Polytechnic Institute, and you never even finished technical college. First education, then kids . . . ah, you're not at all like me."

"I'm not jealous of your caregiver, Mother."

"You should be jealous: she spends more time with me than you, my own blood."

"Enough, *k chertu*! To hell with your Bozena. Forget I called. Farewell!"

"Don't you dare hang up on me! What you need this time? Besides, she's getting married."

"Wait, what? Married? Bozena has a fiancé?"

"Bozena hasn't got it wrapped up just yet, but there are two potential candidates for her hand and heart. Unfortunately, the fellows she usually finds economically appropriate are already married. Still, one must be optimistic and have hope."

"Bozena's having affairs with two married men at the same time?"

"Naturally Bozena sees more than one man. She is a free agent. Incidentally, both candidates are successful, but they have their own wives who want sex, so they send messages and pictures. Yesterday, a third candidate appeared on Facebook. Some military guy, an officer from a state called South Carolina sent a picture of his big penis."

"What the fuck?"

"It was a part of his resume. He wrote her that if she chooses him, this is what she can look forward to. She likes the other guys better because his penis picture showed too much pubic hair.

"Oh my God! Now I've heard it all! Enough of your crazy stories and your idiotic caregivers: it's my turn to talk. It was a good day at work, but after lunch something happened to the security on our computer system, and they told us to take the afternoon off. I didn't have to pick up the kids just yet . . ."

"Let me take a shot in the dark, you went shoe shopping—again!"

"No, I wasn't shoe shopping. I mean I saw them, but no. I went to Marshalls to get some kitchen towels for this Sunday's supper. Can Bozena bake your pirogue? But with meat this time; the kids hate cabbage. I love it, but they won't touch it, and can you bake your sugar cookies? Without walnuts?"

"Don't know, I'll ask her. Why no walnuts?"

"What do you mean you'll ask? You're paying her. Just tell her. Slava can't have nuts; he has gastritis."

"Meat is expensive and if he stopped smoking like a Siberian chimney, he wouldn't bleed out of his popa. He shouldn't eat meat, anyway. Meat is bad and full of antibiotics and hormones. Makes American men cry on TV. What's with all this crying?"

"You're confusing the cost of meat here and back home, and I'll pay you back on Sunday. Can I go on? Anyway, I'm at the store, kind of bored—and then I see them. You will not believe this one: Luciano Padovan shoes—at Marshalls! The last time I held them in my hands was when they opened the boutique in Moscow, and Slava was too cheap to buy them for me. He can be such a *zhadina-goviadina*: cheap, cheap, and cheap. He should be married to Bella with her red-soled shoes. Talk about expensive: nine hundred USD a pair! But these beauties were only $199! I couldn't take my eyes off them."

"What do you mean, nine hundred dollars? Is this how she spends my son's money?"

"Mother, shush. It's Yuri who spends his wife's dollars. Bella makes more than your precious son. She's a successful dentist!"

"It's not his fault they wouldn't accept his Russian degree! Especially since his degree is higher than his wife's. He's a candidate of sciences from a real university."

"Really? Candidate of bullshit. When will you stop making excuses for your baby boy?"

"Never! You've always been jealous of Yuri and me! He loves me!"

"I love you too, Mama."

"Sure. You love all I do for you. Let me go on a limb: you bought the shoes, and now you want me to lie to Slava and tell him the shoes are a gift from me. And as far your fancy sister-in-law Bella, I have news for you: dentists aren't real doctors, not like I was. Cardiology is the most noble of all specialties. How I miss surgery! Your father had the touch too. . . . How could he leave me alone? He promised I would go first."

"Please don't cry. Can we get back to my Lucianos? I didn't buy the shoes. See? You're wrong again, but you'll never apologize."

"Why should I? I'm the mother here! Mothers give you life, not offer apologies!"

"Fine, but let me paint you a shoe picture: they are black peep-toe platforms in real lizard, but the heel is an animal print—so classic and sexy and Italian. With my D&G black suit, I'll look like Madonna—no better, like Angelina in *The Tourist*. It's such a unique brand. Luciano himself is from Venice. I read online about celebrities like Britney Spears and Jessica

Simpson who wear them even to red-carpet events like the Oscars. I bet all the Russian social lionesses wear them too!"

"Why would I care who wears the damn shoes? If you spent more time learning something useful, maybe you could make something of yourself yet, and why do those women look like lions?"

"Those women are independent, influential, and happy! I bet they find high fashion useful! They are my idols. Plus, these shoes are just perfect for a lunch with you, or going to the theater, or traveling—anywhere and anytime. They are practical, too: black and beige; they go with everything and are so comfortable. Not like those metallic Jimmy Choos I got last week when Slava took me to the outlet. Torture, they make my heart hurt. Maybe I'll change my hair a little for his birthday? What do you think?"

"I told you, Jimmy Choos are too high. You're not twenty-five anymore. Your husband spoils you like Papa did. And I hate that Angelina. What a cat! And what's with the sailor tattoos? How could that Pitt actor leave that *krasavitsa*, beautiful Jennifer, for that vampire? There are no loyal men left. Your father wouldn't look her way, and leave your hair alone!"

"Fine, I'll leave my hair long. Wait, how do you know all this celebrity gossip? You don't even watch American channels. Angelina is the most beautiful woman in the world and does a lot of good. Tattoos are popular and no big deal—and my Slava is perfectly loyal.

"Bozena reads me from the Polish magazines, and they always talk about Hollywood stars on my Russian morning show. Tattoos—God said not to mark his temple, and your Slava's inked like a member of the Bratva, a common criminal. You should have him followed."

"Maybe they're just decorating God's temple. Wait, what? My Slava is not a gangster. He's a normal, successful businessman. I'm not going to have him followed, and people are full of envy!"

"Slava is a Jew. That's one thing Jews do well, make money. They sure can't fight."

"Can't fight? What about the Israelis? You always complain about Avi hoarding weapons upstairs. How's your neighbor, Victor from Kiev? I ordered a nice arrangement of blue and white hydrangeas from his daughter's flower shop. I think he's got his eye on you—and you well know that my Slava's only half a Jew."

"That's different. Avi's not a normal Jew. The Israelis are *Vostochnie*, Easterners. You want to put me with that stinky old Victor? In his dreams!

That Cossack alkie is nothing but trouble. Last week his daughter Sasha, poor thing, woke me up at 10:00 p.m. to see if her father was dead. He wouldn't open the door. No such luck. I got Avi to pick the lock and then call me. I guess the old half-a-liter was out cold, smelling like dirty Pampers. He's lucky he has such a devoted daughter, even though she's not blood. Devoted and a businesswoman! Sasha's always in his life. She takes him to the doctors, brings him gifts, does his shopping, and even cooks for him, unlike someone else I know . . ."

"Mother! Stop your jabs right now, or else!"

"What did I say? Poor Sasha: I guess Victor's wife, Klavdia, didn't accept her—or so I've heard around the building. If I recall, I met Klavdia at the cancer clinic when I took Papa to Mexico. She was an unpleasant, coarse creature. Supposedly at one time she was a great beauty, but I didn't see it, not even the remnants of true class. Maybe my impression was wrong. Well, those days are a blur."

"Yes, Mama."

"Say, was the bouquet you mentioned from Sasha intended for me? Because I didn't get it. Papa always brought me fresh flowers on Sundays, but I'd rather you came over more often than waste your husband's money on flowers. Are you still there? And what are you doing talking with Avi, anyway? Old Victor told me he thinks you're having an affair. I told him to suck his own cock!"

"Thanks for standing up for my reputation, Mama! But seriously, I think Avi's gay."

"Don't bother thanking me yet. Gay-shmay; and for your information, he goes both ways. I've noticed lately you've been shopping less and smiling more. Is there something you need to share with me? You think he will marry you and raise your kids? He's got an older girlfriend, you know. She will get him the legal papers to stay here."

"You know what? There's no talking to you, and no, I'm not cheating with Avi. What girlfriend?"

"Aha! Not cheating doesn't mean not planning on cheating. You're just like your father. May the earth be as soft as a featherbed for his old bones."

"Amen. The flowers were for Maya's birthday. She's always running around helping me, feeding the kids, nagging Slava when he's mean to me—even though he is her own brother."

"Hmm. Well, if she's defending you, that's because she wants something."

"What are you talking about? Let me get back to the shoes. My story gets better. I tried the left shoe on and was just about to get the other, when this *sterva*, a pushy bitch tries to snatch them right out from under my nose. She grabs the right shoe and tries to squeeze her stubby, hairy cankle into it. She's sweating and groaning, but she still can't buckle it. I ask her politely, what's your size? She says this is my size. I can see she is a size thirty-nine at least, and my Luciano's are thirty-sevens. I tell her, look these shoes don't fit you, and I tried them first. To make a long story short, we get into it; she pushes me down, twists my hand, and you know me, I must defend myself. I hit her good, but not too hard, Mamachka. You'd be proud of my temper. She thought she was dealing with an American."

"Oi, *gospodi!* Oh, Lord! My baby! *Dochenka*, are you injured? Oksanochka?"

"*Net, ne volnuiasia*. Don't worry. Our Krav Maga classes are paying off; Slava was right. He says no sense of being caught with your pants down, and I had my little 9mm on me, so I wasn't afraid."

"What's with the guns suddenly? First your husband, then Yuri, now you and Bella . . . I have nothing else to worry about? So, did you or did you not get the shoes?"

"Nope, we both got busted. The store manager called the cops, and they took us down to the station. As far as my gun, we need protection. Remember the riots? What's the big deal? We're an army family and proud of it!"

"I miss your Papa."

"Don't cry, *Mamachka*. I'm sure Papa is in heaven with our *babushka* and *dedushka*."

"Heaven? Heaven is for kids and Catholics—and your grandparents didn't get along here on earth, so why would they want to spend eternity together? God help me, your grandmother was a harsh, critical woman; I never could do anything right by her. No. When we die, it's over; lights out."

"I disagree; Papa is with Jesus and the saints. I believe in the afterlife."

"When did you get religion?"

"I've always felt it, even when you told me that science proved there's no heaven or hell, only cosmonauts. American astronauts believe in God; why can't we?"

"As they say here, whatever. You want me to get the kids? I can't. I told you I'm alone."

"No need. I called Slava and asked him to call Maya. She's off work today and always ready to pitch in. You know, we're getting closer. She's not at all like that fancy Flora. That prima donna wouldn't lift a finger for anyone. I texted her an esemeska, but she was at her face doc again, getting more injections. I swear one more syringe, and she'll blow up like a lamb's bladder. Look, Maya works like a horse, but still she is always happy to help. She'll get the kids and drop them at Slava's job site."

"Then what do you want from me? Let your low-life manicurist sister-in-law do it. Flora is the only one among your acquaintances I approve of. She's a class act. And what do you possibly have in common with someone who cleans people's toes? Plus, Maya is fat. I'd be embarrassed if they saw me with her, and in public yet."

"Stop criticizing already. The reason I called is to tell you that I'm a hero—I caught a big criminal! Get this: we're sitting at the station, the cankle and me, and I hear the cop, a very nice, pretty Chinese lady, call the cow Mrs. Galina Feinshtein. And I'm thinking, this woman is not one of us, nor married to one. Just in case, I ask her in Russian where she comes from. She doesn't understand a word. I decide to message Maya who has over a thousand friends. She's connected with everyone!"

"Facebook friends aren't friends."

"Oh, please: I know how you think, but this is our life now. Did you know that 80 percent of Russians are now on Facebook?"

"Lazy blockheads: I bet the same 80 percent voted for that fascist Putin."

"Well, there's where I agree with you. Anyway, I asked Maya if she knows Galina Feinshtein. She said yes and sent me to her page. Galina is this pretty, young blonde lady from Moscow. She paints or sculpts or does something artistic. I called out to the nice lady cop and slowly, without excitement, I explained this and showed her the real Galina's Facebook page. Then all hell broke loose: it turns out the fake Galina is a freakin' criminal who steals identities, they have a warrant out for her arrest, they want her boyfriend for rape, and wow—everyone was so excited!"

"Slow down, you'll stop breathing . . . remember you had asthma when you were a girl. Were you carrying an inhaler? So, the police, they let you out?"

"Not yet; I'm waiting for them to get to me. They still need to interview the witnesses in the store who saw her attacking me first, but I should be home close to dinner. I've made soup, and Slava can figure out the microwave without me. Anyway, I need you to get my shoes for me."

"You still want them?"

"*Odnoznachno!* My Lucianos don't belong in Marshalls on someone's ugly feet! What are you thinking? Before I got into the cop car, I handed them over to a Russian saleslady who usually helps me, Anya, and told her to put them on hold. She can't buy them until they're on final sale because she works there, but you can. Please, please, Mamachka, go get them. Ask for Anya. Please remember her name. Just use cash, and I'll pay you back on Sunday. Oh, and I slipped her my gun too. It's in the shoebox."

"Finally, you use your brain! But I told you I can't drive without Bozena next to me! I can remember a name; I'm old, not stupid."

"I'll call Bozena right now and tell her to get up here and I'll text Anya to look for you."

"Oksana, you'll be the death of me yet!"

"Mamachka, for me, please—you know you love me. I need you to get them. We can't leave them there. We must save them."

"Not this time, Oksana."

"Please, just this once: it'll be my birthday and my saint's day present and even New Year's!"

"When does Marshalls close?"

"When does it close? The store is open late, until 9:00 p.m. You'll have time even after your evening show."

"*Nu, horosho, ugovorila.* You talked me into it again. But remember what I'm doing for you the next time you say no to me when I want you to go to the cemetery to see Papa."

"*Blin,* always conditions! I agree to your conditions. But don't tell Slava . . . he will take away my Mastercard too. It's the only one left. Don't forget, it's our secret—just like when I was little, and you hid your Czech porcelain vases from Papa. Please? I love you so much, more than anything, even Luciano. I kiss your hands and bow."

"You, stupid girl, you are my life! And European porcelain is forever; your shoes will go out of style tomorrow. Ah, why argue? I kiss you. I'll bring your gun on Sunday with my cookies and my cabbage pirogue. I'll bring my Bozena too. But we can't stay too long. Bella's mother invited me for a tea leaf-reading party with a famous psychic, and I have questions about your father. I think he wants me with him. Do you want me to ask her about you and Avi?"

"No, I mean, yes. I mean, I don't know. I'm going now. Mama? Did you forget that Papa is dead?"

"Exactly! He wants me dead, too, so we can be finally reunited."

"But you told me you don't believe in life after death! Have you lost your marbles? I can't talk to you anymore."

"Then go! I'm not keeping you. You don't know my life. You're not taking part in my life. Goodbye! Farewell!" Click.

———⦻———

Did she just hang up on me? Why is my heart racing? Every time we talk, I feel like she just dumped an entire bucket of shit on my head; no wonder I'm nauseous. Maybe it is colon cancer? Maybe she's right about my asthma meds killing me? My neck hurts; I need a proper massage. Slava has such strong hands, but I don't want to have sex, and he won't do it without sex. Fuck, I must have a good talk with Avi, or my head will explode. Unfortunately, they still won't let me out for an hour. I better be quiet and let them do their job.

Exactly an hour later, just as I'm about to lose it, the clerk signs the paperwork and I'm finally free to leave. What's the plan? First, I must text Yuri about no longer needing a ride home. By now, I'm sorry to say, I'm used to stretching the truth. I'm sure he won't mind since all I do is "annoy" him. I'll tell him I'm using "rideshare" again; it worked before. Yuri texts back his usual "K." I take a deep breath of relief and order a ride. By the time I reach inside my vintage Louis V shopper and grab my lip gloss, the app says my car will arrive in four minutes, plenty of time to dial the familiar number.

Contrary to what my family thinks of my intelligence or lack of it, I'm pretty clever when it comes to covering my tracks. For instance, Avi's phone ID shows up as the name of one of my old coworkers—just in case my snooping husband gets ahold of my phone. It's not that Avi and I are an item, anyway—just BFFs, maybe we are more like something the Americans would say having an "emotional" affair.

"*Ma Nishma?* What's up?" Avi answers his phone in Hebrew. Although I don't speak my friend's native language, I've picked up a few words here and there.

"Nothing terrible. I mean, something has come up. Hey Avi, I just got off the phone with Mama, and she yelled at me at the top of her lungs and dropped the call—can you believe her?"

"Oi, that explains it. Do you need to vent?"

"Well, maybe, yeah. Do you have time to meet for a quick coffee and a ciggy? I'm dying for a smoke. Bring a few for me, will you? Slava won't let me have even one."

"He won't let you because you're a mother. He's right: you can't smoke in front of the kids. Say, will FaceTime work? Don't you have to get the kids?"

"No. Long story. I have some time to myself and could really use a hug. Can you meet me at our Coffee Bean? And can I ask you please not to be on his side, even if you think he's right."

"Fine. Then you better get yourself American friends. They'll lie to you to spare your feelings. If you still want me to meet you, it'll take me thirty minutes to get there."

"Of course, don't be sore. I'll wait. *Toda Rába*, thanks, Avi. You never let me down! Love you—see you soon."

My ride arrives right on time. It's a blue Chevy Volt driven by an older Middle Eastern guy who promptly looks me up and down with a disapproving look. Thanks to the Krav Maga training, I'm no longer afraid, so I ignore his rudeness. Not being afraid doesn't mean I'm stupid, so I climb in the back seat without saying a word. That's why I adore ride-sharing services; there is no need to talk or figure out the tip since the app is attached to Slava's credit card.

By the time we arrive at Avi's and my favorite hangout close to Santa Monica beach, I receive an apology text from my boy: running late. As if that's something new: I can't count how many times Avi has mentioned that being late was an Israeli national trait. He also explained that in his opinion, the Israelis did it to be utterly different from the Germans. Naturally, I responded by telling him he was full of crap. But to be fair, I don't mind if he was perpetually late or that some people think being late is disrespectful. I accept everyone as they are. I smile, grateful and excited to see him, texting back "np getting coffee nw." I get in line and enjoy the scent of freshly ground coffee mixed with caramel. That's something else we have in common, an appreciation for the roasting process. Once in awhile, Avi likes to pretend the coffee is too bitter, so he can get a free cup.

Just being here makes the rest of my day feel like a bad dream. I love hanging out at "our" place because of the vibe; everyone is chilled and comforting, the music choice, super indie. The staff is nicer than in other more commercial places too. I asked how long this place had been around and was surprised to hear the answer: since the sixties; that fact alone made me happy. Not that I'm a sentimentalist like my sister-in-law, but I can value the continuity, pretty unusual in LA.

When it was my turn, I order a blended mocha with almond milk from a twenty-something mixed-race beauty with shoulder-length dreads and amazing green eyes. He smiles warmly, remembering exactly how I like my coffee. That's more than anyone else around me has ever done—care about how I like things. Everyone here is nice and young and beautiful; just waiting for the next audition and stardom, I'm sure. I'm looking forward to the guessing game I play with Avi whenever we're out together.

Guiltily, I add a scrumptious-looking chocolate muffin to my drink order. It's been a bitch of a day. I think I'll skip dinner since fucking Slava will not be around anyway. All day long, I've had a powerful urge to smoke, but maybe good chocolate and caffeine will do the trick. I pick up my order and happily find a comfy chair, waiting for Avi, thinking back on how we met.

Life can be both weird and at the same time amazing. It's been about a year since Slava dragged me to the Krav Mag center where Avi worked as one of the instructors. I didn't even know what Krav Mag was, but Slava insisted we sign up for self-defense classes as a couple. As usual, after a few weeks, my "know-it-all" husband stopped attending since according to him, he could now teach the class all by himself! Surprisingly, I continued to train, and was I ever glad! With all my soul, I truly believe that meeting Avi has saved my, if not life, then surely my sanity. Since then, I've become an avid Krav Mag Twitter follower, especially because of all the celebrity influencers Hey, even Jennifer Garner mentioned she was a fan!

In the beginning, I didn't notice Avi even looking at me. To be honest, I didn't think he was anything special—just another undersized, rough-looking, dark-skinned, dark-eyed Jew with an almost incomprehensible accent. Then one day, after Slava quit coming altogether, Avi approached me and said I was ready for more intense training, and for some reason I agreed. He worked me over and over, using elbows and ribs, expecting me to complain, but no matter how much I wanted to stop, something inside me snapped, and I kept on fighting back.

After the practice time was over, he shook my hand, praising my guts, and smiled. I still remember thinking that his smile was so unexpected and totally out of character. The smile revealed perfect white teeth and a dimple. That smile rocked my world. Then he asked if I wanted to share a smoke and grab a cup of coffee with him. For some reason I still can't fathom, I was dying to go with him; however, Slava had told me to come right home, and I wasn't prepared to rock the boat. I thanked Avi and asked for a rain check, thinking about him and that encounter for days, hoping for another chance. Miraculously, that chance materialized several weeks later when Slava went out of town and I sent the kids to visit their favorite Uncle Yuri and Aunt Bella. We've been hanging ever since.

Lately, though, most of our heart-to-hearts have been over texts since Avi quit his job as an instructor. He took the job in the first place to help an old buddy. I always knew he had bigger plans than teaching a bunch of menopausal women to defend themselves from rapists and murderers, but I was terrified to think about what I'd do if he moved away. I don't rightly now how or when Avi had become my lifeline.

———— ∞ ————

"Chara, chara," Avi cussed under his breath as he hurried into the Coffee House. Fucking LA traffic—you never knew how long it would take to get even a block or two, and the time didn't matter; it was always crazy. For no reason he felt a stab of guilt for making Oksana wait so long. He needn't have bothered about her safety, though. There she was, sitting on a faded recliner, legs thrown casually over the chair's peeling arm as she chatted up a storm with a couple of hip kids at a nearby table. The woman was in her element.

Avi stood back and marveled at her ease with strangers, something he was never good at. She was an unconventionally attractive little thing: short and compact with softly styled naturally curly red hair, big brown eyes, and a gorgeously generous mouth. From sleeping in one bed (just once), he knew her breasts were small and naturally high, her hips curved without being matronly. She was also unexpectedly sweet, childlike, and straightforward; a breath of fresh air compared to the entitled cunts he was used to. In fact, it was Oksana's non-neurotic nature that drew him to her in the first place, since she wasn't his type physically. Not that Avi only slept with women—the Palestinians blew up Yonatan, his true love, in front of his eyes years ago.

Pestered by his folks, Avi married once and promptly divorced. Oksana liked that he was a father because he understood her life's problems. She could talk about the kids without feeling awkward. He showed her pictures of his daughter as well. He was a proud, albeit absent, parent to a stunning-looking fifteen-year-old girl; his only offspring lived full time with his ex-wife back in Ashkelon, where Avi had been born. Since he grew up right on the Mediterranean, he found Southern California—and particularly coastal LA— familiarly comfortable. He was a little worried about his family, since Ashkelon was located way too close to the Gaza strip, just thirty miles or so south of Tel Aviv. Not that he gave it a lot of thought. If you're meant to die, you'll die in your own bathtub.

Avi enjoyed telling Oksana all about his hometown's biblical history. She was curiously religious considering her atheistic background and her Russian communist parents. The native Israeli, commonly referred to as being a Sabra, told her many stories about the Philistines, King David, and the fact that Ashkelon was the place where the traitorous whore Delilah cut Samson's magical hair. Oksana was also color- and ethnicity- blind. In Avi's experience, lots of folks from the former Soviet Union were rabidly anti-Semitic; she clearly was not.

Even though they formally met at the Krav center, Avi had noticed her earlier when she came to visit her mother, who lived in the same eight-flat residence. She came several times a week, always alone or with kids in tow, schlepping bags of groceries from the Russian market a few blocks away. She was all smiley-bubbly when she came in, but she looked pitiful when she left. Avi suspected her pain-in-the-ass of a mother had something to do with it since he had enjoyed several entertaining run-ins with the old commie over some trash and noise. She clearly didn't approve of his friendship with the old vodka-guzzling drunk, Victor, either. Avi felt sorry for Oksana, but when he got to know her better, he was mortified at the emotional (and he believed) physical abuse she took like a trooper from both her mother and her husband.

Oksana was also an unbelievably talented and natural designer. What that girl could do with bits and ends of leather fabric and a few inexpensive stones she bought in the downtown LA Garment District was epic. She also drew, painted and loved crafting. Once, while killing an afternoon,

Oksana talked Avi into driving to Beverly Hills to check out the newly arrived collection of Dior shoes at Neiman Marcus. Avi, bored out of his mind, went over to the men's department and stood admiring an obscenely expensive Missoni sweater. Although Avi's San Diego lady friend would have bought it for him without a blink of her fake-lashed eye, Avi knew that Oksana had but a few bucks on her, let alone a Neiman's credit card. Just a few weeks later, though, she handed him an exact duplicate.

With little fuss, she had hand-knit a perfect imitation, presenting it to him for the Jewish New Year. The sweater was also beautifully wrapped in an Origami-style paper wrapper she decorated herself. Both flabbergasted and touched, Avi gave her a spontaneous kiss that he had regretted ever since.

Something inside his gut told him that Oksana's feelings for him, improbable as it looked to others, shouldn't be taken for granted. It didn't matter if she didn't cook or held any college degrees: not everyone enjoyed spending their lives in the kitchen or reading endless dribble written by those who preferred to make up stories rather than live them. To listen to her family, she was a shoe-obsessed, frivolous spendthrift with limited intelligence and without a proper profession—in other words, one big loser! Her family pissed off Avi to no end, making him declare his unwavering loyalty and heartfelt support.

To be fair, lately Oksana's ever-growing dependence was putting a strain on their rather unexpected friendship. Avi tried to put physical distance between them, spending more and more time in San Diego. He was hoping she'd get the message; so far, she hadn't. Since Avi had been breastfed on guilt, he learned to deal with it by going to no-contact, something the kids call "ghosting," but hurting Oksana by disappearing was not an option—at least not yet.

"Hey, I'm here," Oksana said, waving Avi over to her table.

"Here we go," muttered Avi under his breath. "Showtime . . ." He smiled unenthusiastically and walked over to her chair. He kissed the top of her head and put his hands on her shoulders, squeezing gently.

"Hey, yourself—what's up?" he asked.

"Have you got your java yet?" Oksana deflected his question, always sensitive to his moods. "You smell good. Did you find a new cologne?"

"No coffee. I've had my fill for today," Avi said, a little more forcefully than he intended, ignoring Oksana's compliment. "Stop sabotaging me.

You know I'm trying to cut back on caffeine," he added, pulling an extra chair from the next table without asking the kids still sitting there.

"I'm sorry. No worries, I'll just get you some sparkling water," offered Oksana, smiling cheerfully, ignoring his snapping tone.

Avi felt bad for being mean to her. "It's fine. Sorry, motek. I have so little time today and the traffic back to San Diego is a bitch this time of day."

She loved how Avi called her *motek*, a sweetie. "So, you're moving for sure?" asked Oksana quietly, her smile fading.

"Looks that way," Avi answered, again sounding harsher than he intended.

"Thanks for making some time for me, but I didn't get you here to cry on your shoulder about my mom or my bro or even Slava," Oksana proclaimed rather mysteriously.

"Really? No whining about mama drama?" Avi raised his left eyebrow and whistled, scratching his badly shaved chin. He didn't mean to sound sarcastic, but what did she expect?

"Yep, really." Oksana stood up to stretch her legs, finding Avi's habitual chin scratching sexy-hot. She was still dressed in her retail clerk outfit: black Joe's Jeans from the outlet mall and a Wild Fox sweatshirt that read "If you can read this, you're close enough to buy me a drink." She was comfy wearing flat-healed flowery Gucci slides she purchased from an online store offering high interest monthly payments through a secure service. She had to use her mother's credit card and email ID, but the hassle was worth it!

"*Nu, yala*, spill," Avi said. He was mildly intrigued but kept looking down at his phone as though expecting an important message.

"I will, but first I need your undivided attention."

"All right." Avi took some time turning off his phone as he placed it on a small side table next to Oksana's coffee mug. She refused to drink her favorite drink from paper or plastic. Since Oksana never asked to be his sole focus, he was genuinely intrigued. What was she up to this time: one of her harebrained schemes to make bank?

"I have a business proposition." Oksana pronounced solemnly. "I finally think I've come up with a killer idea, and I need your help. It's an idea about how to launch my shoe business . . . I mean, our business."

"You're jerking my chain," Avi said, laughing.

"I'm serious, Avi. This time even you're wrong! I believe in it with all my heart, and if you'd only shut up and listen, you'll see for yourself."

"Go on." Avi had never seen this side of Oksana before. He liked it.

"So, you know I've been dying to do something with my shoe designs forever, but it requires so much money for starters, and Slava told me in his special way to pretty much screw myself. You know how categorical he can be."

"That's an understatement. That fucking *hon saker*," Avi spit out in Yiddish, a language he picked up while living in LA with the Ashkenazi (European) Jews.

"Yeah, whatever," Oksana shook her head from side to side, making her curls jump. She didn't exactly appreciate Avi calling her husband a "cocksucker." Slava was the father of her children. But Avi was her closest and dearest friend, her soul mate. She couldn't deal with losing either of them. "Maya told me I need to do it alone anyway, just in case the business takes off and there are tax issues. So, I've been wracking my mind about something simple and easy on my pocketbook, something so unique but needed by all women, and I think I've got it. We don't need a lot of money, just enough to find a small manufacturing company here in LA and then set up an exclusive online store.

"You know, I just read a story in a fashion magazine about some very famous shoe designers going straight online, avoiding traditional retail altogether. What do you think?" Oksana reached into her large vintage LV shopper and took out her drawing pad, which was filled with dozens of original shoe designs, removable embellishments, interchangeable insoles, along with color swatches and notes. She held her breath as she handed Avi her future for his approval. She had been working on the sketches for over a year. Several times she tried to bring it up to Slava, but to no avail. Several times she gave up and put the notebook away, also to no avail. The dream wouldn't let her be.

"Take a good look! I think we can sell this even to the Italians!" she said.

"Fuck the Italians: we'll take it to HSN. I used to work in the warehouse of a company who supplied them with shipping materials. I made a contact there and even pitched my own idea."

"See? That's why I need you next to me!" proclaimed Oksana, looking at him with such adoration that Avi cringed with guilt. She was positively glowing with possibilities.

Avi took out his readers and carefully examined the concept drawings, struggling to read Oksana's juvenile scribbles. When he realized what she had come up with, chills ran up and down his arms. He took his glasses off and shook his head. *"Baruch H'ashem—thank you, Lord!"* he prayed silently. This had to be it—that million-dollar idea, his version of the American dream. This silly, desperate Russian housewife shopaholic had just handed him an opportunity of a lifetime, and she did so without hesitation and with unqualified trust. The years of missing his family and the loving arms of his friends . . . all the times he had had to eat shit and sleep on some acquaintance's couch . . . all the gut-churning head he had to give both men and women just to make a monthly car payment—it was all going to pay off. His mind was spinning with thoughts and ideas. *We will make it and make it big. I'll help Oksana with the business end. I'll protect her from her family. Fuck, I'll even marry her myself, even if I must deal with that motherfucking Russian mafia husband. After we're rich, I can always leave Oksana successful and free to raise her kids without fearing for her safety and move to my dream place. Yea, I'll buy my own place in Spain. The Basque country agrees with me. Maybe I'll finally fall in love, this time with the right man.*

Memories of that vibrant La Concha beach in San Sebastian brought tears to his eyes. Mile-wide La Concha, shaped like a precious seashell; Avi could almost taste the fresh Atlantic seafood served alfresco. Hell, maybe I will buy my own pintxo bar and name it after Yonatan . . .

"I'm with you until the end on this one, *motek.*" Avi promised, sealing the deal with a passionate kiss.

VINEGRET

"We may live without poetry, music and art; we may live without conscience, and live without heart. We may live without friends; we may live without books; but civilized man cannot live without cooks."

EDWARD BULWER-LYTTON

Maya

MY UKRAINIAN-BORN grandmother, the ball-crushing Zina, used to say, "If you want to keep your husband satisfied, little girlfriend, you have to work hard on your recipes. When you train your man's taste buds to recognize the difference between suppers cooked with love and care by *khoziaika* and slop thrown together after work by a *zasranka*, he will not walk off with the first vagina that winks at him. Maybe he'll look or even have a little nibble, but he will always come back to your bed! And remember, Maya, you are the lucky one to have a husband, so treat him right. Men are a delicate and rare commodity. Lord Jesus only knows how many years I've been without one."

Then she would share details of her sex life steamy enough to make a merchant marine blush. She's the one who made me curious about men and what they can do for a woman—besides give her a venereal disease, a black eye, and heartache.

And so, I have worked hard on becoming a *khoziaika*. That's what we call a genuine homemaker with a sense of pride of ownership—a real Russian housewife, but without all that plastic surgery and drunken girlfriend trips. I can be a lazy slob, but only with myself.

Don't get me wrong, though, I'm no Ina Garten or that Italian tart, Giada. I only have an hour or so to watch the Food Network and only when I get a bit of DVR space to myself. I still love Emeril, even though he's no longer the star; but I don't like Bobby Flay. I feel compassion for his poor wife. Nothing good can come out of a man spending more time in the kitchen than his wife. Plus, I don't need to learn how to flip a burger. That's not cooking! Cooking brings me peace and solace. I get a second wind after a long day dealing with business. While others brought family jewels along to their new homeland, I brought my grandmother's rolling pin, scorched by the kitchen stove and marked by years of wear and tear. Every time I roll my pasta or pastry, I feel her hands on it.

I loved Paula and her boys with her Southern flair for real butter and pork fat, but she was fired. Guess they didn't like the accent. My own kids won't even use real cream in their tea. "You need to use coconut creamer, Mom," they say. "It's better for you." How do they know what's better for me? Why live? I'm not going to die leaving a perfectly unused body.

"OK, I will use coconut creamer with my coconut cake," I answer slyly and giggle as they shrug their shoulders and sigh. First, I love food, and I'll be damned if I'll deny my family and friends life's sweet pleasures, and second, I work hard enough without raising my blood pressure at the smelly gym and making my heart race. I only get a finite number of beats. Why waste it on exercise when there's sex?

Now back to my still-missed grandmother. I don't know about you, but being called a slob by your own, most venerated *babushka* is not my glass of vodka. That's why I think that my version of borsht and sour cherry pirogue are simply, as we say, super, not to mention my vinegret: hands down, it's the best-tasting salad among my friends and family alike. Even our local Russian restaurants can't compete. My sons and husband agree. My husband's American boss Ken, now his partner, agrees too, and most importantly, I agree. After all, who's harder on me than me? I'm not at all shy about my cooking talents. As my kids say, "Our mom has no problem with self-esteem around her cooking." They want me to quit working as a manicurist and open up my own café, breakfast and lunch only. I wish I could, but I'm too old. Who opens her own business after forty?

Only Ken's Russian-born wife, Flora, turns up her pinched intelligentsia nose at my cooking. She thinks we're living in the past and eat too much anyway. She's so skinny; a Great Dane could run between her thighs. Girls at work say she had them sucked out with a vacuum cleaner. Don't eat fat. Don't eat meat. Now she won't even eat bread!

She runs. "Where are you running to, girlfriend?" I ask her when I clean her feet. She kickboxes. "Have you lost your mind? No real woman beats up another just for exercise," I say, trying to reason with her when she shows up, complaining about yet another broken pink-and-white gel-covered tip. Now she's into Pilates. Pilates, shmilates—it's just the same old Russian calisthenics we used to do in Phys. Ed. And for that she pays ninety dollars an hour!

What I really think and can't tell her to her face is that she is a stuck-up bitch. I hated doing her nails at Svetlana's Nail Palace, so finally I told Svetlana to take her on herself, because even the Vietnamese girls don't want her. Who needs the aggravation and her lousy tips—by a credit card yet? Fancy not having a few fifties tucked into your bra!

Flora brings in her own nail polish because "yours has chemicals and I'm chemically sensitive" and wears a mask. Sensitive, my ass! Let her try to work six days a week, nine hours a day breathing in acrylic dust and acetone fumes, and then she'll know what sensitive means. I can't smell anything anymore. The ENT specialist told me I burned the heck out of my sinuses. What can I do? We're not poor people, but the expenses, they keep on coming. Both boys are in private colleges, and I need to remodel my kitchen. Just today, Vlad installed my new Thermador stove. That alone cost us an arm and both legs! Plus, I hoard cash like no one else, just in case we are forced to leave again. That's why everyone who knows me calls me the "bank of Maya."

That's how I got Ms. Pilates to help Vlad with a job. I figured she owed me for all the late payments. Not that she needs to worry about money, living safely behind her American husband's back, as we say—like living behind a wall. Although she hides her dirty little plastic surgery habit and all the other shit, she does to herself from him. Like that crap is all natural? She never cooks for her Ken. Fucking *sterva*: how the hell did she get him to build that million-dollar kitchen? I've seen it with my own two eyes: it's gorgeous, huge, clean, and empty.

And here I thought I understood men. I've asked my boss and girlfriend Svetlana many times, "How can this poor Ken stand her? He's such a fine man, very Harrison Ford. Vlad thinks he is an excellent electrician, clearly successful, and the owner of a construction company that makes a shitload of dough. Of course, if you listen to Flora, he's a fool without a single intellectual cell in his brain. "Can't recite poetry, doesn't know history, has no soul, and doesn't drink either!"

From the beginning, Flora makes you think that she's something special—deeply rooted, as she puts it, in Russia's cultural capital, St. Petersburg. Far from it! Her parents barely got their official settlement papers before she came along. She still won't say exactly where they all came from—most likely some dusty provincial settlement . . . clearly not St. Petersburg. Even now, her mother resides in Moscow. I met her once when the woman was visiting, and I wasn't impressed. All she did was shop and run around bad-mouthing America.

If you listen to Flora, you'd think she has the worst life. During our last appointment, before I refused to take care of her, she told everyone at the salon that she suffers from "Stendhal syndrome." As if the American ladies even knew of Stendhal.

"I have chills. My blood pressure is so low, I faint upon standing," she whined, wringing her hands with their oddly stubby peasant fingers, considering how skinny the rest of her is.

"If you eat some meat, maybe some bread with good salted butter, your blood pressure will go up," I suggested sarcastically.

"It's not the meat," she barked back at me. "It's post-traumatic stress disorder. You don't understand. How fortunate for you that you're built strong like a Ukrainian cow. On second thought, you're just like Ken. You know, Maya, how much I love my husband, but sometimes I think he'd be better off with a more ordinary woman, you know, more earthy, someone like you. I'm a delicate creative spirit, and tragically I don't belong here."

"So, who's holding you hostage? What, have the Americans closed the borders? The last I heard they want to build a wall to keep people out and not in. This is not the old USSR. Go back if you hate it here so much!" *She's just a fucking peasant,* I think. *I'm the one born and educated in Moscow!*

"You still don't get me! It was my unfortunate karma to be born in the wrong time in the right place. Of course, as my yogi told me, I'm working on my ancestral karma."

"Oy, again with the karma," I mutter to myself. "Go back to *Rushka* and take your American with you! Let's see how easily he will learn our language!"

"Don't be absurd, Maya. Can't you see? I'm split between two cultures," she said continuing her verbal diarrhea. "Pardon me for even comparing our exalted ancient culture with this swamp. I don't live . . . I suffer through it! Do you know, there's a Russian professor who has definitively predicted that the US will implode, the economy will collapse, the states will separate, and race wars will wipe the whites from the entire continent. Just look at what Hollywood and their Jews have done to family values!"

"You don't truly believe that America will collapse, do you?" Sasha asks Flora without being even a tad adversarial. "I'm so sorry you feel this way." She offers her gentle support as I'm about to puke. "Feeling this way must be awful. I can sympathize with your dilemma, Florachka. Of course, you can't leave your husband and move back home. But have you considered Canada?"

"Or maybe you should investigate moving to New Zealand. My son, Jason, is always talking about moving there," Sasha, the florist from next door, says, trying to be helpful. "He says it's beautiful and environmentally clean with lots of nice people and low crime."

I just chuckle: Sasha has no choice but be nice to the bitch. I hear her shop got the order to arrange Flora's stepson's wedding. Life is not fair. Here's Sasha, trying to get some business done while Flora's getting a spa pedicure. Not that I'm upset. Sasha needs more business; after all, she still owes me money. Since Flora is silent for the moment, Sasha tries again. "I've been reading a lot about life in Bulgaria."

"Bulgaria? What has Bulgaria done to her to deserve such a punishment?" Svetlana interjects loudly as she walks by my chair. Never the proud one, Svetlana is carrying a load of soiled towels on her way to the back room.

Flora wisely ignores the comments, knowing through experience not to piss off Svetlana. "Sashen'ka, you understand me better than most," she says, turning back to the florist. "Didn't you graduate from an art school as well? You can see that America is my drug: intoxicating and costly. We all are corrupted by the standard of living, and we sell our souls for comfort. It's an addiction. I don't even recognize it anymore! I've become a stranger among my own, while being our own among strangers . . ."

What the hell does that mean? I can't believe that at first, I used to find her ravings fascinating, and I even felt sorry for her being married to an American. I must admit I love listening to Sasha, though. Her calming, tender voice with just a whiff of Ukrainian accent reminds of my grandmother Zina and my childhood in the South. I'm transported back in time when I spent hours listening to the rustling breeze, daydreaming of boys, as I lay on a plaid blanket in a field of sunflower-scented late summer grass, right above the Black Sea.

Sasha is a curious bird. Here she is, the oldest among us, yet even without any plastic stuff, she looks at least a decade younger. Just look at her creamy skin—and those cheekbones! Who the hell can get away with wearing their hair naturally gray and look like a model? I wonder if she knows how stunning she truly is. Sasha never raises her voice or gossips or complains. I mean, she's the orphan, not us, but she seems at peace with herself. I suspect it must be working with flowers and being married to a guy who doesn't hump every skirt in sight.

"Don't you know, truth is a porcupine," once again opines Flora, trying to sound like a philosopher, once again rudely interrupting my own search for inner peace. "It's all sharpness and needles, but inside it's a delicate piece of flesh, tender and easily wounded. I can't, I won't, lie to my husband, no matter what! I hate it here. Remember, girls, how we were spoon-fed lies by our parents, our teachers, and our party leaders? At least now I've made myself a sacred promise to remain authentic to my needs."

"There she blows," I mumble to myself as I shove hundreds of dollars of genuine Chanel flip-flops between her toes.

"Pay attention, Maya! You'll ruin my color," Flora snaps at me, continuing her rant. "During Soviet times, we all drowned in lies and corruption. The communist system fucked us—pardon me for using such vulgarities. So, now all you foreigners fuck the American system. I bet your Vlad doesn't worry about money, while my husband plays by the rules or faces the wrath of the government! Do you even understand the expenses of running a business— the regulations, the taxes, the insurance? They take money from us, the working classes, and give it to the lawbreakers! I doubt you get my drift. All you immigrants know is cash. Ah, why do I bother to fit in? What do I have in common with all you 'huddled masses, the wretched refuse,'" Flora said, raising her voice to quote from Emma Lazarus's words etched on the Statue of Liberty; "the 'wretched refuse' is now setting world's cultural norms!" Flora proclaims with a dramatic flourish as if she were giving a speech.

"Are you calling our sweet Sasha a refuse?" I ask with a menacing hiss, hoping to give her a bit of a scare.

"Well, not exactly . . . just educating you both about this country's founding principles," she said, backing down.

"Oy, again with the principles. . . . My next lady is here. Can you pay today?" I say, winking at Sasha.

"Of course, I can," she says, bristling. "But can you cash the check next Friday? My husband is away, and the money hasn't been wired into my household account."

Sterva! What a bitch! I like it here in the States, and I'd take one Ken over a dozen no-good, lazy-boned, arty-farty PhDs. They can paper their walls and wipe their butts with all their diplomas, but true street smarts can't be learned at the university. Can you eat poetry? People have a right to live where they can better their kids' lives, and I hate politicians in any case. They're all the same.

I survived the communists, and I'll survive the capitalists. I'm not blind; I see the problems. I see the tent cities and the crime, but what's different is that the Americans don't sit around crying crocodile tears into their vodka; they have the balls to change things that don't work. A woman is harassed by her boss; she sues, and more often than not wins! Her husband rapes or beats her, and he goes to prison, unlike back home.

They change their presidents whether the guy is good for them or not, and they keep pushing forward. They don't need a tsar. The Americans don't care what city, what state they came from, only where their address is right now! I can do business in America.

I'd like to see Flora try and vomit all that philosophical bullshit on my Vlad instead of feeding him three square meals a day and picking up his dirty socks. High Russian culture won't take care of your basic needs. I see what goes on when I watch Russian talk shows: the same old drunken fights at weddings, murder, financial thievery, government corruption, rape. I see that the basic living conditions for normal working people are as dreadful as they always have been. The roads are still a mess, and folks live in falling down shacks as the rich buy up the land, build their "cottages," and send their kids to London.

All you have to do is to drive a couple hundred kilometers out of Moscow and see for yourself. I don't deny that a liberal arts education can offer some cultural perspective, if you don't deny that the proletariat is the backbone of any economy. Or so said my grandmother—and she knew everything!

But back to telling you about my vinegret: you probably think I'm referring to the classic French dressing, but you're wrong. Vinegret is a vegetable salad, if you can call this delectable ambrosia merely a salad. It's colorful and full of contradictory flavors, sweet and tart at the same time. I have worked on my recipe since the day after Vlad and I got married back in Moscow. It's taken me fifteen years to bring it to the height of gastronomical perfection.

You see, the potatoes must be gently simmered in lightly sea-salted, distilled water. Don't ever boil anything in that poison that comes straight out of the tap! The organic carrots must be julienned, but roasted baby beets should be cubed. The tender green scallions (preferably Italian cipollini) should be chopped into tiny bits. I only use Clausen's pickles, unless I pickle my own Kirby cucumbers in the summer, and the sauerkraut . . . ah, the art of making sauerkraut! Why even our German-born neighbor Hans agrees that my recipe comes very close to his mom's. That's a great compliment from a German to a Russian. Naturally, we're the ones who invented it in the first place. I add a touch of sunflower oil bought at a Russian store and voila!

Oh, I forgot—in the winter, I grate one large Granny Smith apple and add it right at the end (otherwise the apple loses its natural tartness). I guarantee you that this dish is a conversation starter at any potluck. When I think of the pleasure that overwhelms my senses, I sigh. In my mind, I take a first bite, my mouth waters, and my stomach growls. What is life without pleasure? I love food just because it pleases me. Why don't you sue me?

But what's that stupid idea—potluck? At first, I thought you're supposed to bring flowerpots for a hostess gift, and then I figured maybe it had to do with bringing a nice-looking new cooking pot to bring the hostess luck. Apparently, I was wrong. Ken explained patiently to my husband that a potluck is a type of an American dinner party where the guests bring their own food. Now, that beats all. "Please, we're inviting you to our house, but bring your own food. At first, I couldn't believe my own ears.

"Are you sure? Are you positively sure?" I double-check, my eyes wide open and my mouth open, right down to my cute triple chin.

"Da! Sure, I'm sure. That's what Ken said," insists Vlad, as he shrugs his still-wide shoulders while unsuccessfully trying to button the top of his jeans.

"Ha! I don't believe you. They do very well. I'm sure that they have money for food," I responded.

"Then don't listen to me. Why do I bother educating you about them? You never believe anything I say. Remember, you didn't believe that they have beds full of water to sleep on or that their dogs eat cooked meat from a can?"

"Well, that was ages ago. I thought you could only eat what was sold on TV commercials too. Remember? All I'd buy for a while was cereal and beer. Still, not serving your guests food at a dinner party—even you agree that their manners are odd. Are you sure Flora isn't trying to embarrass me in front of her American? She's been so rude lately."

"You started it when you pushed her on to another manicurist."

"I couldn't take her abuse anymore—calling me Fat Maya behind my back! I was afraid to stand up to her just in case she'd squeal to Ken and cause problems between you two. And how do you know what happened? Did she call you?" *Oh-oh,* I think to myself, not being born yesterday in a truck full of cabbage heads. *Is that spoiled bitch complaining about me to my own husband?*

"Ken says that here in America people are working hard—everyone's so busy, schlepping the kids around, working out, or taking dancing classes. Friends want to get together, but this way there's no stress on the hostess." He circumvents my question about Flora without blinking an eye. He's got nerves of steel, that one.

"Who's got the time for dancing classes? And what stress does Flora have? She never lifts a finger at home, and she doesn't work! If you can't receive your guests properly, why give a party at all?" I ask, crossing my arms under my ever-expanding boobs. I swear, when I look in the mirror, I see my own Baba Zina. But she was so old, and I don't feel old at all. Maybe I should cut back on cream with my cereal just a little . . .

"Ah, you stubborn woman, you just don't understand!" If you haven't guessed, it's his usual response when I've scored a point.

"You think maybe Flora's right? You know, she's behind on her payments to me again! And do you think I am getting a little, you know, bigger?" I ask my husband, dreading his response.

"You look great, kitty cat. Don't lose even a kilo. What am I, a dog? I don't like jumping bones. By the way, let it ride with the Flora's payments. I owe Ken a favor. If you're short of cash, I'll front you."

"Let it go? Not on your life."

"I'm asking you. Do it for me."

Oh no, something is up. "Well, if you owe Ken, I'll call her and tell her." I agree, but my gut is telling me something isn't kosher between my husband and Flora.

"Ken is too good for her! Stop tickling me, you old horny goat. The kids are home, and it's only nine."

"So, we're tired and need our beauty rest. It's a natural thing: Mama and Papa together."

"They think we never do it."

"We don't."

"Yes, we do!"

"I'm going to give you a delicious piece of prime!" Vlad refuses to take no for an answer, which is unusual.

"OK, OK, you win. No use wasting all that energy in the kitchen. We've got plenty of leftovers; but turn the light off, all the way off. I mean it."

As he works on the lights, I watch him carefully and think to myself, *What a fool I've been.* Normally when I talk about losing weight, he gets nasty about my failures or offers to help. Then there's Flora's loan. Suddenly he wants me to forgive her debt too. There's no way he owes Ken a favor. Vlad is the one dishing out favors. And then I see it as clear as I see the past: that backstabbing whore Flora is banging my man. The thought crowds my head, and I can't let go, even during sex.

After a few minutes of grunting and moaning, the traitor drifts off and begins snoring. I go into my gorgeously marbled en suite bath, close the door, and call Oksana. Despite at first disapproving of my brother's marriage, I have come to see that I lucked out with Oksanochka. Not only my sister-in law, she has worked hard on becoming my best girl—no disrespect to Svetlana, who's in her own category, if you know what I mean.

If I can't share my grief with a trusted family member, I will explode. First, she listens without interrupting. Then, when I'm all cried out, Oksana says firmly, sounding so unlike her usual spineless self that I pay attention. "Stop all this wailing. He is not dead. Maya, you can't just give him to her! Let's come up with a plan."

"I don't blame Vlad. It's her that I hate. He's just a normal man with normal sexual appetites. Can you believe her disrespecting me, especially when she owes me a shitload of money? All I have to do is say a word to my brother, and she'll be left without her fake teeth or her American."

"I know; I feel for you, dear. Slava would take care of her, but you know how women are. She'll cry to Vlad who will feel guilty. She'll make him believe you're the one to blame. We must be clever. This is a delicate situation."

"You're right, Oksana. What was I thinking? I must keep my cool. If you think of something, please tell me."

"You can count on me. You are my sister now. We women must stick together. Say, I have an idea to cheer you up until we give Flora what's coming to her. I'll pick you up tomorrow, and we'll go to Santa Monica to my favorite coffee place. They make the most amazing Apple Charlotte cake with French cream."

"You have time for me?" I ask gratefully.

"I'll make time for you!"

"See you tomorrow, Oksanochka."

"Try to rest now. Good night, Mayechka."

I hang up the phone and think that even a strong woman like me needs to be propped up occasionally.

———⊗⊗⊗———

Although I feel a slight relief after the frank and supportive talk with Oksana about my personal dilemma, I still can't sleep. The leg cramps have gotten almost unbearable. I place my usual Russian-made homeopathic pill under my tongue and wait for it to take effect.

I don't understand what I did that was wrong. I fantasize about killing my rival, but likely I will have to resort to ruining her life financially. I won't feel a gram of guilt either. This is one sin I'm willing to take upon my soul—plus Ken deserves better! Too bad I don't know any "black" psychics who can put a curse on that whore.

I get up to pee, get a bite of leftover dumplings, and text Oksana, hoping she's still up. "r you asleep?"

"Nah," she answers, also awake. "Call nw. I'll pck up."

I dial and feeling relieved when she picks up. My brother must be on the prowl tonight. We may need to talk. "I was thinking: do you have someone, anyone who can do some 'stuff' to Flora?"

"What stuff? You mean like a curse or some black magic?"

"Well, maybe. I was just thinking out loud."

"Personally, I don't know of anyone, but I'm sure my mother does. Wait, does a tea leaf reader count?"

"I don't know; I guess, if she uses the dark magic to read. Why?"

"Then I have a plan. Mother can get you invited to my brother's wife's house for a tea leaf party this Sunday."

"Dr. Bella? The fancy dentist? The one who will barely speak Russian to her kids?

"Da. That's her."

"Oy, *spasibo* Oksanochka, perhaps I should go to the party. There's nothing I will stop at to save my husband from that wicked woman. I'm sure the tea leaf reader knows of someone who can do something about blocking Flora. Maybe she used black magic in the first place to seduce him. She is not his usual type. Yes, that would make more sense."

"Of course, she did," agrees my sister-in-law. "After all, he's an ordinary man. They don't feel bad energy like we do, being women and all."

"Yes, I have a feeling inside my soul she did something to turn his head, the both of them, I gather." Once again, humor saves my heart. "Oksana, what would I do without you?"

"You won't have to find out. Finally, a good plan: now we both can get some rest! I'll call Mother."

"She doesn't approve of me."

"She doesn't approve of me either: nevertheless, you're going. Bring lots of cash,"

"Sure thing, but will you come with me?" I ask.

"Wouldn't miss it for the world! Justice will be served!" chuckles my sister-in-law. "I've had a crazy day. Can we talk about this tomorrow? Go rest!"

"I kiss you, dear."

"Kisses right back."

I hang up. The meds are starting to work and I feel the cramp relaxing its grip on my aching calf muscles. But my mind is still active. The worst of it is how I feel about my own culpability. How could I have been so busy working, remodeling the house, and cooking that I didn't protect my home? Stupid blockhead, and here I thought he appreciated our life, our open-door hospitality, all the parties I give, my unquestioning devotion. Babushka was right. How can my man—or any man—know the torture and joy of giving a proper party, Russian-style?

The comfort of memories is a balm for my suddenly tired heart. I swear, I can smell and taste the briny saltiness of the sea . . . now I will rest. I decide to stay on the couch so as not to disturb Vlad. I know my size is ruining the cushions, but I can breathe better in the big room, and Vlad snores. I can't admit to myself another reason I like to spend the night in the family room: the proximity to the fridge.

I still remember my widowed grandmother's birthdays, celebrated not in a restaurant as they celebrate nowadays, but at her old-fashioned, one-and-a-half-room communal flat with its high ceilings, sparkling oak floors, and handmade lace drapes. She lived in a historic building, very close to the main beach, near the famed Odessa Port and the Potemkin Stairs—made famous by that silent movie, not that I go for the arty-farty stuff. For years, Slava, my obnoxious little brother, and I would travel by train to stay with her for the entire summer. South, south we went all the way from Moscow, accompanied only by our saintly nanny, Vera Stepanovna. We looked forward to the train ride in our own compartment; we loved the sweet tea and smoked sausage sandwiches served by the uniformed train conductor. (I heard that the crazy Ukrainian nationalists have just stopped the train service linking Odessa with Moscow: that just blew me away! How quickly life can change when men run the show.)

Our nanny, Vera Stepanovna, would deposit us in Odessa and turn right around, hopping on another train, this time going east. She herself had to travel further into the vast Russian countryside because her own family resided in Rostov-on-Don, the entire trip taking several more days. Vera Stepanovna stayed in Rostov with her grandkids until we were ready to be escorted back to our parents and begin yet another school year. How odd that I never minded being gone for the entire summer. I guess I was used to parents who seemed too preoccupied with their own lives to spend vacations with us.

We were always so happy when summer finally arrived. Pasty and sickly, with runny noses and lingering coughs, we couldn't wait for the "holy trio" of Black Sea, sun, and the beach. In a few miraculous weeks spent blissfully on the sand and in the sweetest of seawaters, my brother and I would morph into little golden gods, healthy and energetic, if a bit wild.

I was a different girl in the South. It felt wonderful not to be nagged and judged and pushed to perform by my parents. I happened to look like ballerina material: skinny, long-limbed, and freakishly flexible. But I hated classical music, the constant bar, and the mean dance teachers. Moscow was a tough place—lots of competition and pressure. I liked and did well in math, but my parents didn't think that was good enough. I finally figured out how to get out of ballet school. I started to eat anything in sight, even if my stomach couldn't handle it. If I'm honest, I must admit, I preferred being called Fat Maya, even though looking back, I was a completely normal girl, not a bit chubby.

But when I stayed with our grandmother Zina, I was a star! Here, in the South, under the blooming chestnut trees, I knew I was loved. I feel so bad for my kids who will never know this feeling of making someone happy just by breathing. Such was the width of our grandmother's love for Slava and me.

Toward the end of summer, by Grandmother's birthday on August 7th, we'd even lose some of our Muscovite "a-a" accent and pick up a bit of Odessa-speak, which was very mod at the time. We learned funny jokes, listened to the bawdy ones, and practiced throwing pebbles into the smooth surf. We had it all: love, acceptance, and freedom!

Three days before Zina's birthday gathering, the entire production would begin with a boring but necessary process of waiting in long, lively queues to get the foods that could be purchased legally. In Odessa—as in every other Soviet-era city, even Moscow—the queues wrapped around the entire block, but unlike in Moscow, everyone would be laughing and talking so loudly that our ears would ring for an hour afterward. The folks here loved to tell off-color jokes accompanied by wild gesturing and backslapping.

Odessa was nothing like Moscow, where you felt that even the dingy walls listened to your every breath. Phone calls to friends and family brought us what you couldn't get in the stores. Mind you, our babushka didn't have her own phone line, but the neighbor across the stairs did. He, the widowed Comrade Schevchenko, was a party *apparatchik*, a bigwig at the Port of Odessa—in other words, a gov-stooge. No matter; he'd let us use his ink-black rotary phone, regularly listening in. But Zina didn't worry since she always invited him to eat. Not that sharing a meal together would guarantee our safety from the KGB or most likely the OBHS, the domestic arm of the Soviet Secret Police. Plenty of people disappeared after sharing an intimate table with family and friends. No one could predict when and where one of those dreaded black Volga automobiles would whisk you away, to your final destination. But these were the 1980s, not the bloody thirties. We were getting bolder.

Zina, our commander-in-chief, barked orders in her sharp, authoritative schoolteacher's voice. "Maya, run upstairs and tell your Uncle Alec he must get the pork chops, the good ones with some fat around the edges, but not like the last time—too much lard. Ask Aunt Polina to get fresh caviar and smoked sturgeon and don't forget a can of crab for the salad. Uncle Lev can bring Armenian cognac. He's a hairdresser and they can get everything. Remember to tell him a minimum of three stars. Got it?" (Uncles Alec and Lev, as I later found out, weren't "real" uncles. They worked for my grandmother, making sure no one took advantage of her generosity in loaning money.)

Slava would slap his knees and, with a proper salute, reply: "Yavol, mein general!" Unlike now, my brother was a sunny-natured boy, a real jokester. Instead of being annoyed, Grandmother loved the clever way he made fun of her bossiness.

Before becoming a pensioner, she worked as a Ukrainian language teacher. She told us that after the war, Odessa's schools were desperate for teachers since so many had perished. Never one to follow the rules, she had one of her guys make up some papers showing she had proper credentials. Once a teacher, always a teacher!

Of course, her official job didn't take care of the basics, if you know what I mean. Like so many of our citizens, Zina always did what she had to do on the side, not only to survive but to be able to provide additional comforts. She taught me well to never depend on anyone, let alone a man or a government, to provide for my kids.

I turn my cell phone off, placing it on the ottoman that serves as a family room coffee table. I'm getting a bit chilly and reach for the hand-knit cashmere throw, a gift from Oksana. Despite my staggering anger with Flora and the overwhelming fear of losing Vlad, I finally close my eyes and calm my heart by imagining the long birthday party table.

Here it is in its glorious detail, stuffed with little plates of *zakuski*: herring with sliced onions and dill drizzled with sunflower oil. I can almost taste the smoked fish, the black olives and the creamy, mildly salted Bulgarian feta cheese. My mouth starts to water as I remember the delicate, garlicky aroma of the much-anticipated fire-roasted eggplant caviar served alongside newly dug-up, dill-boiled potatoes. In the middle of the table, near the vase overflowing with compulsory red carnations, I see a lovely display made up of light green three-day-old pickled cucumbers, red tomatoes, and rosy apples on a large Finnish platter. The sour, salty tomatoes looked fat and shiny, like the burnt shoulders of the summer tourists the local kids liked to torture at the Arcadia beach. A Chinese porcelain peony plate was reserved for my personal favorite, Grandmother's house special: sour watermelon (a surprisingly effective cure for a nasty hangover).

Grandmother came to Odessa from a small Ukrainian town called Vinnitsya. She had told us a few stories about her childhood, her parents, and her brother. They were shot by the Commisars before the last World War. I guess she was so beautiful that one of the executioners decided to let her live, although she still had a large, now-faded scar on the side of her head, where the bullet hit her. She was left for dead, with the corpses of her family on top of her. Covered with their blood and running a high fever, she made it to a farmhouse, where the kind people there cleaned her up and nursed her back to health.

When I cry hysterically, horrified at the very thought of not having her in my life, she holds me to her heart and tells me to be strong. "We are women. We survive the best we can. You have a sacred duty to take care not only of yourself, but your little brother. You know I don't trust your parents to do what's necessary to protect you. While I'm still in this world, sit next to me, Maya. Fight. Learn how I control men, and don't trust anything except your own inner judgment."

Back, back I go, remembering. Zina's birthday party table, covered with a Polish embroidered cloth, was made of two bleached wooden boards and took up the length of the whole room. This one room served as both her living and dining room as well as the study, yet it seemed huge to my then-unspoiled eyes. Everyone sat together, even the kids, except for the hostess/birthday girl herself, of course. She floated about, looking serene and proud, like one of the giant balloons sold by the local gypsies around the main town square. Her laughing eyes brought us joy, and her water-chaffed hands were always full of platters of more and yet more food. She loved to shout orders and make dirty jokes, and to me she looked gorgeous, the most beautiful grandmother in the world, bouffant henna-tinted hairdo, blue eyeliner and all, and a huge bosom that wouldn't fit into a proper brassiere.

We'd squeeze together, elbow to elbow, knee to knee, shot glass to shot glass. Even now I can smell the crispy, brown fried pork chops. Later, after gorging on appetizers, Zina would bring out my favorite course: steaming plates of handmade dumplings. Where in the whole world can I find such pleasure? I see myself as a skinny little girl, assisting Zina as she formed *pelmeni* Ukrainian-style with sour cream and her *piroshki*, both baked and deep-fried. I use a silver teaspoon to measure and fill the tasty handmade pastry with delicate morsels of potatoes, cabbage, beef, or hard-boiled eggs.

For dessert she'd bake a flawlessly golden *pirogue* with home-canned sour cherries and Golden Delicious apples.

In her later years, she mostly filled her days and nights with two activities: listening to radio shows and reading in French. (Mind you, she taught herself that language.) Funny how she preferred to read the sappy novels of George Sand, the notorious French cross-dresser, who chose her own lovers!

When Zina's eyes would get tired, she baked sugar cookies. She still spent a good part of her day cooking on an ancient one-burner Primus in that tiny, overcrowded communal kitchen. The kitchen had no hot running water, but it was cheery and bright, with one good window overlooking the courtyard filled with Chestnut and Acacia trees. She had lost her interest in the day-to-day money lending activities, but occasionally, faced with a particularly egregious disrespect, I overheard her giving directions to my "uncles." Perhaps I should have been terrified by the gory details, but I wasn't. It made me feel special to know her power.

Although I probably should return to the bedroom, I can't force myself to sleep next to Vlad tonight. Even under normal circumstances, as I put my weary head down on our living room couch, my mind drifts to the magical place of babushka's courtyard. Here reside the stray mutts and hopeless drunks who urinate anywhere they happen to pass out. There stands the hideous bucket where they drown newborn kittens. When I first see the execution of the innocents, I get hysterical and promptly produce an asthma attack. Then and there, I swear my Young Pioneer oath that I shall liberate the next batch of kittens. I succeed in enlisting babushka's help. She could care less about my heroic mission, but we can't have asthma attacks while vacationing, can we? I win.

During the magical summer of my thirteenth year, when I discover both my menses and my first kiss, she finds homes for each one of the blue-eyed kittens. I get really steamed at her because she won't let me keep a kitten for myself—all thanks to stupid asthma.

No matter how I plead, reason, beg and threaten to run away, I can't get her to understand. "I didn't get into a fight with old Klava for me to spend two weeks in the Children's Hospital caring for you!" She wins. My brother and I fear Auntie Nina, the cleaning woman and caretaker who hasn't spoken a kind word to anyone since WWII. The old neighbors say she saw her daughter gang-raped by Nazi soldiers during the occupation.

In the center of the courtyard stands the old water well, rusty and dried up. It holds a whiff of danger and excitement for all of us visiting grandkids. One summer, a small boy fell into the well, and the adults gathered all the courtyard kids together and told us that he disappeared forever. I cried, but my clever suspicious brother never believed it, not even for a moment.

"It's just grown-up propaganda; they're brainwashing us to scare us away from the well, just like 'they' scare us away from the foreigners," Slava tells the kids condescendingly.

"Shush, blockhead, you want to get us arrested and sent to an orphanage in Siberia?" I smack my brother hard, hurting my hand on his puny shoulder.

"Cut it out, Maya, you *suchka*, I'm only twelve," he says, pulling my auburn braid hard enough to bring tears to my eyes.

"Don't you call me a bitch, you hooligan, you . . . American cowboy! I'll tell on you. I swear by Huck Finn I will. (At the moment, we're both obsessed with Mark Twain.)

"If you tell, she'll punish both of us, and we'll have to stop playing. She won't care who started it. She believes in building solidarity between us."

"It'll be worth it, you cowboy!" I hate the cowboys and love the Indians.

"I'm sorry, Mayachka, I'll never call you a little bitch again. Promise and pinky swear. *Harosho?* Forgive me?"

I shouldn't have believed him, the little monster. I still shouldn't. Even now he owes me money. A big shot New York entrepreneur, he started by managing a few whores, then added the limo service, and finally he ran a strip club for his so-called friends, who used him as a front for their own money-laundering. I don't even want to know what crap he got into back home in the wild 90s; although, his tattoos tell the story. Thank God, he let me bring him to LA. Now, he's trying to make his fortune trading in "air" money. But only on the side—or so he says. I know he's lying.

I promised myself I'd make sure he's safe by keeping his nose out of my loan business, but I suspect he resents me for being our grandmother's true heir, being a woman and all. Ha! She chose me for a reason. It took discipline and guts to expand her operations to America, starting with just a few thousand dollars.

My brother, on the other hand, thinks it's beneath him to work with his hands.

You'd think he'd learn his lesson after the last brush with the law, wouldn't you? Slava, the schemer—never peace and quiet with that one. Vlad has had to call on his colleagues in Brooklyn to keep an eye on him more than once. He's got angels on his side for sure. He made it out of the Twin Towers alive; too bad his second wife, the young Chinese broker, perished. Slava refused to have a proper wedding, so I never got a chance to meet her. I'm afraid, as so often happens, he's still comparing Oksana to her memory.

I'll never forget that day, not that I forget anything. I took the kids to school and went to work early. Once there, I turned my cell off. My Tuesday 8:00 a.m. standing appointment, Mrs. Fitzgerald, is old-school: no phone calls and only speak English. Vlad was in Vegas, trying to win some money so he could pay off some bills. We have a TV in the nail shop, but no one turns it on except for Svetlana. That morning she did turn on the TV . . . and my world went black. I didn't know where my brother was. He was in the middle of a nasty fight with his first ex-wife, the urologist. I knew he could have been in Manhattan to meet with his attorney, so I tried to call for hours on end. He didn't answer.

Vlad reached me by noon and told me to stay strong. Luckily, he drove, so he promised to come home. He just didn't know when. He asked me to call his then-partner's wife and calm her down. The poor girl was hysterical, so I told her to come to the salon and hang with us. We all stayed put, but no one worked. We just huddled together, the Americans and the Russians, the Vietnamese and the Iranians, shaking our heads and weeping. I ran over to the drugstore and bought us an American flag. No one could think of anything else to do. I was furious—my dearest wish of escaping the nightmare of war had been shattered in a New York minute.

The school called and asked for the kids to be picked up. I had to stop crying. It's not good for my American-born children to be traumatized by seeing their mother out of control. I stayed strong for them. It took us three days to find out that my brother had survived. Gambler's luck! A visiting Canadian doctor pushed him out of the way of falling glass. He walked to the safety of Staten Island across the bridge with thousands of other shell-shocked souls covered with funeral pyre ash. I ended up in the ER by evening, even though I hadn't had a panic attack for years. We thought we'd lost Slava this time. I am the oldest child; I am still responsible for him.

He's all I have left of my family, and until that day in September, I believed we were safe across the ocean. Wrong. That's when I decided to really focus on building the money-loaning business. That way we can leave America on a moment's notice if we had to. God knows we're no strangers to worrying about our kids' safety or death.

I need to get up to pee again. My back is sore from lying on the sofa, so I decide to use the toilet in my master bath and then go to bed. It's still before midnight when I crawl in as quietly as I can next to Vlad, my anger spent and my tears dried.

When I was fourteen, we held a funeral by the well at the old courtyard. A young man, merely a boy really, went rock climbing in the Caucuses. The mountains proved too much for him, and he fell. They brought him back in pieces. Luckily for me the coffin was closed. No disrespect intended, but I hated to see an open casket. No one looked human anyway (we don't waste makeup on a stiff like they do here). Our well became the core of the requisite orgy of grief—the buckets of tears and the fainting, the bloodcurdling screams and the tearing of one's clothes. Grief is contagious in Russia. The women—my brother likens them to noisy black crows—remembered the dead: those who left to go to war and those who were taken by our system. Some taken by motorbike or streetcar accidents, others by alcohol overdoses, still others by suicide or cancer. Many cried because they anticipated their own unequivocal demise. After the stirring procession spearheaded by a local brass band and a heart-wrenching burial, the whole courtyard was invited to an enormous wake, where everyone, including the kids, ate and drank themselves numb. (Vlad told me the only thing that came even close was a funeral he once saw in New Orleans.)

That same year my second cousin Sergey died of leukemia. He was only eighteen. His mother, the redheaded Aunt Vera, was considered the unluckiest member in our family. Redheads have a hard life, or so we say. Grandmother was much older than her sister and treated her more like a daughter than a sibling. Grandmother Zina wasn't around by the time her sister was born, but she did send for her after the war when there was nothing left of their family home in their small town.

Poor Aunt Vera buried two husbands and a son—two out of three in the war. She went to the cemetery every day to lie on their graves. She smelled of grass and decaying flowers. Grandmother used to yell at her to snap out of it. She believed her sister liked spending her life among the dead because only there she felt alive.

I loved my auntie, feeling an odd connection to her, considering she was a simple small-town woman who never asked for anything. Everyone knew Vera had a weak personality, but was she ever a great cook! Her vinegret recipe was the most beloved in our entire family. To tell the truth, she felt the same about my abilities; I'm sure this is the reason she passed her recipes to me and not to her lazy, no-good college professor of a daughter-in-law, the wife of her one remaining son.

Even now, decades later, I can still hear the voices of my friends, arguing and shouting while rehearsing lines from a play, a surprise for our parents. The summer ends, and they come to steal us away from our grandparents. Back to the North as the rusty summer sun sets over the city by the sea and the first stars sprinkle the maroon-washed, smogless indigo sky.

We see our widowed grandmothers' faces, worn-out, shadowy with premature wrinkles, but illuminated from the inside with the certitude that tomorrow they will be needed again. I pray that my own grandchildren will need me as much as I needed my own grandmother. Vlad points out that we'd be lucky if we have any grandchildren at all.

Nowadays no one is pressured to get married and have kids. It's America, after all. No one needs anyone. We're supposed to be independent. And do I want to raise my children's children? Too much stress—it's not easy to raise American children. You can't even buy them a birthday present. It seems to me these brats have everything.

Maybe I should stop cooking so much. Lose a little weight, maybe travel. I promised Sveta to copy Grandmother's recipes, which she wrote in pencil on now-disintegrating paper. Sveta says there are many cookbook-worthy recipes that could win a prize if I entered them in a contest. She says I should go on the Food Network—she says I would beat any amateur and most professional cooks. I may do just that, but first I must deal with Flora.

I must have finally dozed off, and I must still be dreaming when when I hear my sons' voices.

"Mother? Dad? Parents? Are you in bed already? Mama, we're hungry!"

I'm up in a second. "I'm coming downstairs," I shout back, sliding off the bed and twisting my already sore foot. I know the boys can get their own food, but I also know they like me to make some fresh cheese pancakes. I cook, and they talk and share their lives; this is how it works. Of course, Vlad doesn't move a finger and pretends to snore louder.

"Hey lover boy, your brats are starving again. But don't you worry, I'll take this shift." I elbow him in the ribs and give him a light smack on the head. He doesn't budge.

I don't give up easily. "I'm going to the kitchen. It'll take a few minutes to fry up some pancakes and warm up leftovers. Do you want us to save you some vinegret? I made doubles for the potluck."

"Da, but add some salt to it, will you?" Now the dead has risen! "It doesn't need salt. Everyone at Ken's last potluck loved it. My salad is perfect!"

"Perfect for them because they don't know any better—I'm telling you it needs salt. I think you forgot the pickles, or maybe used the wrong ones, way too sour. You can't fool me," Vlad retorts.

"If you don't like it, don't eat it," I yell back. How dare he criticize my cooking! I take enough crap for everything else I do wrong.

"I'm going on a strict juice fast first thing tomorrow morning," I threaten. "And knock off the salt. Your blood pressure's through the roof!"

"Fuck my blood pressure. I know how I feel, and I'm telling you, I'm fine." He says the same thing every time we argue. "What juice fast? Are you nuts? You want to look like Flora, a stick with fake tits? What's gotten into you? Don't be so sensitive. Who loves your fluffy tits best, baby?"

"You do, my soul," I answer him with a full mouth kiss, cupping his balls tight just as he likes it and think to myself, *A stick with fake tits? You think I'm buying it?* Then all becomes clear, and I make up my mind. I will not allow anyone to disrespect my home.

It's about time I went to war to save my marriage. Sleep tight, my love. I will protect you from that bitch—plus she'll starve you to death, and that would never do. I promised your mother I would feed you well, and I will.

PART TWO

FLORA AND THE COSMETIC ARTS

According to the Liquid Face-Lift Association: "A Liquid Face-Lift is a technique for injecting advanced dermal fillers, such as JUVEDERM®, Radiesse® and Restylane® to lift and contour facial features. A non-surgical Liquid Face-Lift can be undertaken to accomplish any of the following:
  - *Gentle lift of individual (or overall) facial features*
  - *Reduced wrinkles, creases, line or folds*
  - *Restoration of natural, curved facial contours*
  - *A more rested, energetic look*
  - *A friendlier smile*

THE MORNING OF Flora's latest "artistic" cosmetic procedure, advertised as the "Liquid Face-Lift," arrived without incident, except for a peculiar dream.

Around 11:30 p.m. the night before, Flora took an Ambien, just as the Moscow-based nightly news *Vremia* went on. She chewed up an entire 10 ml tablet, chased it with a large gulp of organic coconut water, and dozed off quickly. She slept a tad easier while listening to the soothing comfort of her native language mixed with the rolling thunder setting on the Amazon-purchased sound machine. Years of California drought were taking a toll on her nerves, and their second home in the dusty Nevada desert wasn't helping either. She longed for snow; hell, she'd even take some rain.

As Flora slept, she dreamed of four black cats fighting off a huge crow. The altercation took place in the right corner of her yard, near the far end of her newly retiled swimming pool. The natural stone with flecks of sapphire-blue sodalite glistened in the eerily red-tinted moonlight. The water in the pool was bumpy, as if an earthquake had disturbed its usual Cali tranquility.

Cats gathered around a three-tiered stone fountain, decorated with genuine copper fleurs-de-lis, reflecting her lifelong obsession with France. The cats meowed loudly as they tried to chase the crow away.

The crow, a scruffy-looking black bird, had one white feather sticking out of its coat. She stared at the malevolent felines, which sounded like Bonnie Rait whores in heat. The wise-looking crow looked at Flora with her own mother's eyes, glasses and all, as she shed diamond tears. As soon as Flora realized the bad omen, she willed herself to wake up despite the heavy effects of the sleep meds, but not before she chased the cats away with an old-fashioned straw broom. Chasing away the "bad" while still dreaming was a technique she learned from her Reiki healer and personal psychic, an elderly Lebanese woman who lived with her ancient mother in a tiny back house among the Glendale Armenians. *Maybe that psychic tea leaf-reading party at Oksana's mother's house did get me riled up,* she thought.

Flora awoke with a foul taste in her mouth. Her heart pounded as fast as if she had just attended a spin class; her chest felt tight, as if she had just donned her parrot yellow Versace corset dress trimmed with metal safety pins. She could feel the tension in her jaw constricting her throat as it moved down her left arm. What now?

Flora was about to rub her eyes, but she remembered her freshly done lash extensions in the nick of time. Gently, she blotted the wetness with the edge of the top sheet, just as the familiar Russian National Anthem blared from the flickering flat screen. She had been so happy when Putin's government made it possible to return to the old Soviet anthem, albeit with new words. A surge of patriotism swelled in her gut and flowed down her cheeks. The New Russian ethos of imperial nationalism was blending with that Soviet-era legacy of socialist pride. For a while after the USSR collapsed, the people lost their bearing, looking down on their own history and trying to imitate the West with its corrupt family values and unabashed materialism. Things were different now. Russia had strong leadership that restored its national pride.

Flora hated herself for buying into the American myth of "democracy" and "freedom." Freedom to do what: be unemployed, homeless, do drugs?

When it came to her loyalties, her heart was always on the correct side! Why can't the Americans offer respect and well-deserved appreciation to all her country had sacrificed to defeat Fascism and save their cowardly hides? Why didn't they see that disrespecting other cultures and traditions can only lead to conflict?

"Ah, *bliat*," she cried, jolted out of bed and almost falling over her pink-and-gray Australian sheepskin boots, made in China. She insisted on leaving her shoes right by her side of the bed in case of an earthquake. A glass of water and maybe a little Xanax would do the trick. But first she needed to strategize, despite thick brain fog thanks to the aftereffect of the Ambien.

Hmm . . . black cats, she thought. *That means I have four female enemies or rivals; for sure there are lies and an unfaithful man. Blin, what else is new? Black means illness, but I did chase them away. That's good. There's a surprise in store. An old white-feathered crow crying—that means mama is protecting me. I wonder what the diamond tears mean. Diamonds are related to marriage. Aha, it's a warning to pay more attention to Ken. I'd better go to Vegas with him more often. He's a good man, but Vegas? Who knows?*

Was there water in the fountain? I don't recall, but I think so. That means happiness and maybe some money. Maybe the fat manicurist bitch will let me postpone the payment. How does she get all that money anyway?

Flora hated to borrow money from Maya, but she had to pay for several costly cosmetic procedures out of her miserly household allowance. She also couldn't use her credit cards because she didn't want Ken to know how much she was spending.

The pool water had waves; that means problems. Not too rough—maybe some little problems? I'm just nervous about the procedure, that's all. He's a good doctor. Let's not panic yet. Maybe I'll call Moscow and talk to Mama. Maybe after . . . I wish I could call him, but the cow is in bed, next to him. Why can't he let her sleep in another room? Ken does.

Flora willed herself to ignore her pounding pulse and turned on the over-the-top Austrian crystal lamp on her nightstand. She barely glanced at the vintage Baccarat crystal clock while turning on her newly purchased iPhone. Being surrounded by beautiful objects always made her feel safe, even as a small girl. She practically grew up in Leningrad and Moscow museums; unlike some of the others who came up in the provinces. It had been several years since she had been back home—yes, Russia would always be her only true home. She felt guilty for missing her mother's jubilee birthday coming up in a few months, but the personal loan interest was piling up, and she still felt unable to share the enormity of her debt to Maya with her husband.

The smartphone display read 4:00 a.m. She crossed herself three times and whispered, "God save me and have mercy." Flora followed the prayer by spitting over her left shoulder as she counted out her lucky number five.

That should do it. Lord, save my sinful soul, it's morning. Might as well get up and get ready for the doctor. No, let's try to sleep a little longer. It's just my nerves. Vlad should be up too; maybe he'll answer my text? No, I must punish him. Lately, he's been mean to me—and cheap. Let him fuck his cow and see how he likes it! I hope I look fabulous by the time Ken comes home. I wonder if he'll notice this time that I had something done.

Often Flora ingested only half of a sleeping pill, just to take the edge off the ever-present insomnia. But once a while, she would awaken with a jolt of adrenalin, always at 4:00 a.m., the "widow's hour," and just lie in her snow-white Duxbed listening for strange noises. She was alone again. When her stepson finally had enough of the quarrels and moved out, Ken offered to get her a pet for company, but Flora balked at that idea.

"I'm done taking care of things. I want to be completely free. You just feel guilty for always leaving me alone," she told him without the slightest hesitation, while narrowing her eyes to the point that she felt her lash extensions poke her eyeballs. "I know what I want—travel and attention from you, not a dog!"

"Why should I feel guilty? That's not it at all, hon. I think you'll be happy with something living here in the house: a fluffy little pooch, nothing that needs too much training or walking, something to entertain you at night. Still taking your pills?"

"A dog is an animal, not a person. What's with you Americans and dogs? Spas for dogs, doctors for dogs, organic food for dogs: your dogs live better than kids in the rest of the real world. You're such an idiot. How did you ever run the business without me? I don't even want to imagine; you're nothing but an uneducated fool." Sometimes, she felt a bit guilty for being so honest about his humble background, but mostly she let him have it, and he took it straight up—although she wished he'd yell back or do something to show he still cared.

This morning, Ken wasn't home, yet again. Another Vegas project had kept him out of LA for nearly a month—a substantial landscaping job in Summerland, off the ever-morphing Strip. He told her it was a lucrative and high-profile project for his new but already burgeoning lighting company. Therefore, he had just gone through the huge expense of opening a separate Nevada office. Flora was no dummy; she understood the financial opportunity, but she still resented his time away. When he made noise about being in the wrong, Flora jumped on it and extracted a promise that he would take her on yet another cruise in between this project and the next.

In the meantime, she decided not to sulk; instead she would get some "things" done. She'd been undergoing a few minor procedures (mostly a touch of Botox to lift the brows, laser lipo on her thighs and knees, and a few chemical peels to lighten the spots). It was probably time to freshen up the implants Ken bought her a decade ago, but Flora simply couldn't recover by herself. She was thinking her breasts would have to be redone in Moscow so her mom could take care of her and the cost would be minimal.

Naturally, these "tune-ups" were done while hubby was out of town. He never seemed to notice, merely complimenting her on how well she looked.

"You're looking sexy—it must be your new diet or that exercise class. I bet you're sleeping better too, hon." Ken complimented his wife so sweetly, unlike Vlad. There's got to be something wrong when your own husband treats you better than your lover. *Stupid Russian men,* Flora thought. *I bet Vlad would treat me like a princess if I was younger.*

The preliminary "no-charge" consultation with her doctor, the "artistic dermatologist" as he sternly referred to himself, went relatively well. The derm guy was a slightly built Middle Easterner with shiny, baby-butt smooth skin and crow-black hair plugs pulled back into a thinning ponytail.

After looking at Flora through a magnifier, he forcefully recommended multiple injections with Botox, some amazing long-lasting European wrinkle fillers, and a cool touch laser to smooth and freshen up her face and neck. Total cost: four thousand dollars in US currency. He agreed that it was a little expensive, but said it was a worthwhile investment considering there was no downtime and instant results. She tried to get him to offer a discount, but he held fast. She agreed to make an appointment since his reputation was impeccable. As his brochure proclaimed, he was a "dermatologist for dermatologists."

After a forty-five-minute power walk with weights and a blueberry kale smoothie that helped shake off the med-induced brain fog, Flora arrived at the Medical Day Spa by 9:45 a.m.

She was fifteen minutes early, knowing there would be more release forms to sign. She never read the forms, judging them as "too scary." She believed in going with her gut and pushing forward no matter what. As she told her acquaintances on a few occasions, "When a woman is too lazy for 'maintenance,' she should expect to lose her man to another woman. Men love with their eyes, while women love with their ears."

Occasionally a young woman would tell her that such sexist talk was offensive bullshit, but mostly no one wanted to risk her verbal wrath.

Flora signed the release forms with a flourish, her handwriting well-practiced and slanting sharply to the right. One could always tell the level of education and class by one's handwriting, unless one was a physician.

After she finished signing the forms, Flora had some time to look at her surroundings. The reception room was designed with a great deal of aplomb, and being a true Taurus, Flora appreciated high style. In fact, it was hard to believe that this luxurious, beige-and-cream, flower-filled, softly lit environment had anything to do with the practice of medicine. It was all about spas and vacations and making you feel well taken care of. Of course, there were a myriad of brochures strategically placed on low marble-and-glass tables introducing the waiting patient to the other wondrous procedures that could change their lives in miraculous ways in the span of a lunchtime.

She recognized Alexandra of the Valley's signature white "Ice Cascade" cymbidium orchids, "Snow White" cattleyas, and lavish, buttercream-colored peonies. The flower arrangements looked very expensive, very chic, and totally unexpected, combining the over-the-top exoticism of the tropics with the sweet innocence of a beloved European classic. The flowers were presented artfully but simply, complemented by red-lacquered Japanese bowls. Flora had always wanted to learn two things: the ancient Japanese ikebana technique of flower arranging and calligraphy.

That Sasha's doing all right for herself, considering her background, she thought with just a touch of resentment. Well, that's America for you: from a stinking orphanage to owning your own business. Everyone knew "her big adoption secret," thanks to Sasha's papa and his big mouth. To be fair, Flora liked Sasha. The florist was naturally pretty, petite, and acted somewhat refined . . . for a Ukrainian. Not entirely acceptable, but passable enough to have an occasional chat and order a small arrangement, normally for a funeral. Sasha also had an uncanny psychic intuition, probably due to her gypsy blood, which intimidated Flora to a degree. Flora took a class after class, read all the books, and had readings, but it wasn't in her blood. As her father used to say, "The only thing in life for certain is your blood and your homeland."

A romantic heart, Ken had patronized Sasha's storefront on more than one occasion, often to order flowers to be delivered while Flora was getting her nails done next door at the Nail Spa. He knew how much his cranky, hothouse flower of a wife liked getting attention in a public place. The girls at the nail salon couldn't believe Flora's luck.

"Mrs. Flora, we're ready to take you back for your numbing," a stunning, twenty-something Asian assistant called out from behind the desk, her breasts squashed together to better advertise the double E-cup implants, her lips puffed up and lacquered a modern nude.

Flora prided herself on noting even the tiniest of details: *Good-looking implants, but not too big. I wonder if the "artist" did the job himself or farmed it out. Too bad her skin is pimply, and what the hell is she wearing? These American Asians, they simply have zero taste. They should take lessons from the girls in Shanghai or Tokyo.*

Flora followed the second assistant, also a young Asian with blown-up lips and tattooed brows. The girl opened the door into a brightly lit treatment room, which was not nearly as glamorous as the reception area. She told Flora to relax and sit on a worn leather dentist-style chair covered with rough-looking plain white paper. OK, two cats down.

A middle-aged woman dressed in scrubs was waiting for Flora in the coldness of the room. "The doctor will be with you in a couple of minutes. Let's numb you up," said cat number three with a mild sneer. The nurse was also obviously augmented, a dried-up Orange County-looking blonde with a huge diamond on a chain hanging around her ruddy, freckled neck and chest-long, stringy hair extensions. *Rich ex,* thought Flora instantly.

"Let me pop a Benadryl first," said Flora, rolling her Rs. She liked to show off her accent when she felt uncomfortable. It put folks on notice that she wouldn't take any crap.

"Why? Have you informed the doctor? Are you allergic to Novocain or Latex?" asked the blonde, sounding irritated.

"Yes, the doctor knows. No, not allergic, just a little sensitive to smells," snapped back Flora with equal disdain.

The numbing gel first tingled and then stung. Flora wished she'd added just a bite of a Xanax to calm her nerves. She couldn't fall back on alternate nostril breathing, but she was able to take several Ujjayi pranayama breaths to calm her nerves.

"Aren't you excited?" asked the nurse.

"Not yet," answered Flora. So far, she was not pleased with the service. "Don't worry—he's amazing with the needle. I just love his lips," the annoying woman chattered on. "He gave me a dental block and then shot me up from the inside. I had a date with the girls, and no one noticed," she continued. "You know, you can fool a guy, but a woman is another story."

"I know. He is very good. I wouldn't go just anywhere," agreed Flora sourly, as she started to feel her area go numb.

"Fabulous! Just relax, and he'll be right in. Oh, and make sure to like us on Facebook."

"I'm not on Facebook," answered Flora. She actually was, but she would never admit to anyone what she was doing in terms of maintenance.

"Well, if you join, then," said the pushy nurse, not giving up.

"I don't think so," Flora said, trying to raise her eyebrow without success. "Look, can you just go get him? I'm very busy today."

"Sure thing, ma'am," responded the blonde acidly.

Just then, Flora's iPhone chimed, a song from the late eighties band White Roses. It was one of her favorite songs sung by teenaged Yuri Shatunov, the dazzling leader of the boy band, Gentle May. The naive, romantic song still brought back memories of wonder and hope, longing and nostalgia—nostalgia for who she used to be. Based on the ringtone, she knew the call wasn't coming from her husband. It was also the first song she danced to with Vlad at a Russian New Year's Eve celebration. She was so happy that night, thinking she'd finally found her soul mate.

Now he replies. I better not miss it, she thought. She'd been texting Vlad for several days without a single response.

"Can you please reach into my Burberry and pull it out?" asked Flora as she felt her nerves tingle with familiar excitement, these days brought on only by Vlad. For the first time in her adult life, she knew she was in trouble.

Before the woman could do as Flora asked, the doctor burst in with his usual oily smile and strong smell of something spicy.

"All numbed up?" he asked his nurse.

"Yes, Doctor," she answered with a bright, flirty smile that made her look at least ten years younger.

"Okeydokey then, let's make you look amazing," he confidently proclaimed. "There, there, darling; trust me, I do these all day long," he added, addressing his visibly nervous patient.

"I know. I trust you completely. I just wish someone had come with me."

"Don't worry. We're not doing anything that requires a driver, but if you feel a little more comfortable not driving, the front office will call you an Uber and your husband can pick up your car later."

"He's gone."

"Oh, I'm so sorry, darling."

"No, I didn't mean like gone forever: just working out of town, like always."

"Ha," cackled the dermatologist. "Glad to hear it. Let's get started."

Almost an hour later, Flora sat in the front reception area with an ice pack, sipping on Voss mineral water as she waited for her Uber. The injections didn't go as planned, and she felt nauseated, her face already showing signs of bruising. The doctor started with her nasal folds and lips and then moved on to her forehead. Her lips hurt like never before because she asked for a little more volume. The injectable around her nose stung, too, and although her forehead didn't hurt at all, when the dermatologist stuck her neck with the paralyzing substance, something didn't go as planned.

Flora felt an electric shock as her mouth was overtaken by a flood of saliva. She cried out, and the doctor stopped. A few minutes later, she felt another even stronger wave of nausea and an immediate urgency to go to the bathroom. The doctor was calm and patient, telling her that they could take a little break and resume after she felt better. She waited for the nausea to pass, but it didn't, so they decided to stop and resume the following day since he had other patients waiting.

When Flora got home, she texted her stepson and asked him to get her car and hang around at the house until she felt better. Zack texted back, telling her he'd get the car by the evening but he wouldn't be able to stay because he had stuff to do. She responded by telling him that he was never there for her and she couldn't wait to tell his dad. He ignored her last text.

After taking a shower, Flora tried to eat something small and bland as she felt the usual post-injection headache coming on. She decided to lay down in the darkened bedroom with another ice pack and fell asleep having forgotten all about the text from Vlad.

She woke up with a terrible taste in her mouth and a sharp, stabbing pain in her lower abdomen. *Lord, what's wrong now?* she thought, still groggy from her nap. The clock read 6:00 p.m. Suddenly the urge to evacuate her bowels forced her to get up and rush into her en suite bathroom. She barely made it to the toilet. The cramps and the diarrhea made her break out into a cold sweat. She could barely get off the toilet before a strong dizzy spell brought her down on the Carrara marble floor. She vomited some yellowish liquid, and her heart rate took off so quickly that she almost blacked out.

When she finally was able to crawl into the bedroom and reach the phone, she dialed Vlad because he was the only one she could think of. The call went straight to his voicemail, which was full as usual. She then texted him, "Pls call smtg wrong"

He answered, "WTF? hme Maya here"

"Pls SOS dying"

"Call hubby In VS"

"F-ck Pls help"

"Call son"

"Busy"

"F-ck. K, calling 911"

"No, need you. Come"

"Calling now"

Within minutes, emergency sirens shuttered the neighborhood silence. Flora slowly went downstairs, hanging on to the ornate banister and opened the front door without turning off the alarm, clutching at her chest and gasping for air. The alarm went off just as the young, good-looking female paramedic rushed through the door.

"Can you turn the alarm off, ma'am? Can you hear me? What did you take? Any chest pains? Do you have asthma?"

"No. Nothing, I took nothing. I can't take a deep breath. Dizzy. The code is 2201. The pad is right there," she said, barely able to point to the wall panel as her head swam. She was having trouble swallowing. "I can't breathe, my chest hurts, and I think I fainted earlier. Cat number 4 . . ."

The young woman and her male partner went to work. They slapped a 12-lead on Flora, took her vitals, and performed an EKG. Everything looked stable, except that her heart rate was abnormally high, and her oxygen level was lower than normal. She was going for a ride to the hospital.

Flora felt both hot and cold as the back of her head and neck went into a spasm. Every nasty fearful thought she'd ever had rushed into her consciousness, and there was zero she could do stop the downward cycle. This was the end she so dreaded and so longed for in her darkest hours.

Just as she was loaded into the ambulance, Zack pulled into the newly refinished driveway. He remembered that Flora didn't want him to park in front of the garage to avoid the leaks that could stain the stamped concrete. *WTF?* he thought. *Mom's really sick.* He felt a sharp twinge of guilt as he dialed his father, his hand shaking.

Ken picked up, saying, "Hey, son!" Lately he sounded like his own dad, Kenneth Sr., also a Navy vet. Zack heard the fatigue, as well as comforting warmth coming at him through the phone.

"I don't know how to say this, so brace yourself, but Mom's really sick. They're taking her by ambulance somewhere. Hang on—I'll find out where and follow them."

"What? Oh no, please hurry."

"Hold on. I'll be right back."

A few minutes later, Zack relayed to a terrified Ken the information he'd received from the paramedics. The older paramedic explained that, while the patient was not critical, they needed to rule out a few potentially dangerous problems and were taking her straight to Valley Presbyterian.

Sounding both composed and concerned, Ken instructed Zack to stay near his stepmom until he could get there. Too many years in the service prepared him for pretty much anything, and besides, since 9/11, it was faster to drive than to hassle with all the extra security.

"I'll be there in four hours. Just tell her to be brave—and tell her I love her."

"I won't leave her sight," promised Zack, sounding more like his cocky self.

———✦———

Just after Vlad called 911, he received a detailed email from Ken asking him to call the job site in Vegas first thing in the morning—or even better, to get there in person because he was driving home due to a personal emergency. Of course, Vlad pretended not to know anything and asked if he could help. Ken thanked him but responded in the negative.

"What's going on with all these texts and calls?" hollered Maya, who was still in the kitchen finishing preparing one of her elaborate suppers. This one she had gotten off the Barefoot Contessa site. "You can't eat fried meat and dough every day; your cholesterol is over 300!" she had proclaimed just last weekend.

"Yes, I can. Stop nagging! I'm a man, not an American dishrag," Vlad had fought back. He was good and tired of getting shit from both his wife and his mistress. "My grandparents lived into their nineties, and they ate what they wanted!"

Now he told Maya reassuringly, "It's nothing serious, zaichik, it's only the American. He's coming home early from Vegas and needs me to look after the site; I may have to leave tomorrow." He tried to conceal how shaken up he was by the texts from Flora.

"If he's leaving work, it must be something to do with that crazy cunt," Maya said, loudly enough to be heard in the next room.

Vlad entered the kitchen and went over to give her a hug.

"What's that for?" asked his wife suspiciously. *He called me* zaichik, *as if I look like a little bunny. Something's up for sure.*

"Nothing, just thanking you for not being a crazy cunt," Vlad replied, nuzzling the little space between her short neck and round shoulder. She smelled like fried onions and sugar, so unlike his mistress, who poured something called essential oils right on the pillowcase to calm her fucking nerves. The smell of those oils made him nauseous and his cock soft.

"Hmm, feeling guilty for not looking after Her Majesty while Ken's away?"

"Hell no, why would I? You don't think I have anything to do with her, do you?"

"Ney, she's way too much trouble for you. You're used to me catering to you, and she's used to Ken kissing her ass. You two would be like oil and fire: my spoiled prince and the prima donna. Incidentally, that kid of theirs, Zack, and his loan are becoming an issue. You want me to handle him?"

"Nope. All's good. Glad we straightened this out. But seriously, if you are uncomfortable with me and Ken, I can always get another job. The economy is humming along."

"Don't be a putz. Business is business. But mark my word—this is all about our Queen Flora. I can feel it in my bones."

Vlad just shrugged and left the room. He turned on the TV and pretended to listen to Hannity. Usually he paid close attention to the ever-worsening political situation in his adoptive country, but this time his mind was on the situation with Flora; to be more precise, he wondered how to get rid of her once and for all. The affair, while exciting in the beginning, was taking its toll. Not that she was his first tango at the school dance. Still, tonight was a close call. *As soon as she gets well, we're going to have that talk*, he decided, and immediately felt better. Time for a nice large snifter of Martel's VSOP and a hot plate of borscht. Even though Maya was experimenting with some French stuff, there was always a plate of his favorite soup simmering on the Viking. His girl sure had style!

Back in the kitchen, Maya picked up her secondary cell phone, the one she used for personal affairs, and quickly dialed her confidant, Oksana.

"It's me. Shhh, don't talk, just listen. That fucking camp whore Flora is at it again. She's been contacting Vlad, and I overheard him calling 911 for her. Then his boss called with "an emergency." You don't think she did something to herself, do you?"

The conversation continued for a few more seconds, and then Maya hissed, "Da, da, da and blah, blah, blah. Whose side are you on, anyway? I've got to go. But I think the time is coming for us to have that special talk."

Four hours to the minute after he hung up with Zack, Ken walked into the hospital ER, which was beginning to fill up with the ever-increasing numbers of migrants who used the hospital as a walk-in clinic.

To be honest, he made the drive in three-and-a-half hours, but he first stopped by the house to pick up a silk robe and cashmere shawl, knowing Flora couldn't stand institutional wear. He also cleaned up the mess in the bathroom, shaking his head: his fastidiously clean freak Flora would never leave the vomit on the floor if she wasn't terribly ill. It looked like the fluid would leave a stain on the marble. *Oh well, one more thing I'll have to take care of before she gets home—if she gets home. No, stop! Zack said she was not in danger. Nothing better happen to her. I can't do without her.*

After parking in the designated emergency room lot, Ken entered the glass doors and saw his son sleeping in a chair. He walked over to the reception where he gave his name and relationship status, signed in, and was ushered in through the security door.

Flora lay on a narrow hospital bed in a back cubicle, her eyes closed. She looked strange dressed in a stained faded blue-and-white checkered hospital gown. Ken noted that her right arm was hooked to an IV and several monitoring machines were reading her vitals and oxygen levels. He knew how to read the numbers, thanks to several years caring for his folks. Everything looked normal, except for her oxygen levels. No wonder she looked pale. It was so unlike her to appear disheveled under any circumstances. Ken also noticed that she was seriously bruised; his heart did a flip as his hand tightened into a fist.

"Honey, baby girl, open your eyes. I'm here," he said gently, trying to wake her.

To his relief, she opened her eyes, licked her lips, and then saw his expression. As soon as her eyes focused, she began to cry softly.

"Oh no, my baby, don't cry. I told Zack to tell you that I'd be here in just a few hours." He held her tenderly so not to disturb the plastic tubes and cause her any more discomfort.

"Kenny, my dear, I'm so relieved you're here. I was so scared and alone. I haven't seen Zack. I asked him to come, but he said he was too busy. I was scared and so sick. I think I'm going to die. What's wrong with me?" went on Flora in her best baby-doll voice, the one she occasionally saved only for her husband. Her normal tone was quite edgy.

"No, my silly girl, you're fine, just very scared, dehydrated, and your heart rate was too high. Your breathing was a little off, too, so they wanted to keep an eye on you; it's probably just a touch of the flu or something you're allergic to. They don't know what caused it, but they told me all the tests were fine, and you're stable now." He reassured her in his best papa-bear timbre. "They say you're good to go home. They've given you good hydration and an antibiotic shot, something for nausea, and some Ativan to make you sleep.

"I'm not dying?"

"You'd better not be, my honey; I can't be without you." Ken picked up her hand and kissed it gently, controlling his anger. Flora was overwhelmed by emotion. Relief, gratitude, guilt, self-loathing, and gut-wrenching love for her husband made her head spin. Tears poured down her face as if the faucet had been left running.

"Dear, I'm sorry. I'm so sorry. It was entirely that damn dermatologist's fault. He told me that the anti-wrinkle stuff was safe and so easy, and I'm so stupid and I did it." Flora continued to ramble on. "And you're always gone and the girls in Vegas are so young and so beautiful, and I'm getting older, and I'm so scared."

"OK, stop now, just stop. You know I adore you. You are my life, and there will never be another woman in my bed. You make my life beautiful. Look at our home and our businesses. And what about Zack? I know he's a pain in the ass, but he adores you too. Who stayed up late doing his school projects with him? Not me. Who always pushes him to study and teaches him manners and art? Not me. Who looks after him as if he were your own child? Who has a PhD in Literature, for Christ's sake? Who speaks four languages? You do! You are all that and more, and we both adore you!"

"Oh, Kenny, I love you so much!" cried Flora, choking on her tears. "You're my hero, and you're the best of the best of men. You're the only one except my mother who sees me. I feel as if I'm behind a stone wall with you, always safe and protected from this cruel life. I just miss you so much. I don't need more stuff. I don't need anything else, but I must tell you something bad; I did something bad. I don't know if you can forgive me this time, but I must tell you . . ."

"Just wait a sec," interrupted Ken, as he took her face into his hands. Normally, his wife protested loudly complaining about the roughness or his musty smell, but not this time. She closed her eyes and nestled against his palm. "You can tell me. There's nothing I won't understand. It's OK. Just take a deep breath and spill," he continued calmly and patiently, although his heart dropped all the way down to his groin. *Oh no, she's leaving me.*

"OK. I will just have to trust our love. I did something so stupid; I can't even believe it myself. I owe Maya money."

"Is that all?" Ken took a deep breath and blew it out loudly as he looked up.

"You don't understand. I owe her a lot of money. I've been making payments, but I missed the last one, and now she's charging me daily interest."

"What? That fucking bitch! That's usury! OK, thank you for telling me. It's going to be fine. I'll cover your debt. Don't you give it another thought! I won't even ask why you needed her money: just promise me that we're good and you forgive me for making you feel so bad about our life."

"You will?" whispered Flora, as another jab of hot guilt squeezed her heart muscle until it ached, even with all the meds inside her system.

"Consider it done," her husband answered gravely.

"Thank you, thank you. You don't even know what this means to me. I want to tell you. I borrowed money for my stupid cosmetic procedures, so you wouldn't know that I was looking old," Flora said, feeling the entire weight of lies and deceptions lift from her body.

"It doesn't matter what you use the money for, hon. Just forget it. I'll move some money from the business to our joint account, and you'll just write her a check. Or does that criminal bitch want cash?"

"It's a lot of money."

"It's fine. You are my wife and you deserve my support."

"Kenchik, I love you."

"Christ, you haven't called me *Kenchik* for so long," the relieved man felt a familiar tug at his innards. "Look, I'm so sorry about the baby. I know I should listen to you more, and I will. I promise. It's just been so long since we lost our baby. And I just want you to forget, to move past it, but I know you won't. So I must accept it. I don't want you to hurt anymore, and I do understand why we couldn't keep him." Flora began to cry again.

Though her head was in the right place about the loss of their only child, her heart would never let go. The lingering guilt and anger and resentment and every ugly emotion a woman like her could experience came up to the surface. It's been a long time since they had spoken about the loss of their only pregnancy. Flora thought that those who say the loss of child brings a couple closer are idiots.

"I'm sorry, I'm so sorry, but he was damaged, and I couldn't handle giving birth to a sick child and watch him suffer and then die. Or even worse, what if something was to happen to us, and Zack was left to take care of him. Zack was so small, and he needed so much attention and care after Joy left. I know I sinned, and I know God will never forgive me, but I took that sin on my soul willingly for our baby and for Zack and for you," cried Flora, overcome by her long-buried guilt.

Now it was Ken's turn to shed the tears he had kept buried for over a decade. He felt as bad as his wife about the loss of his dreams for their baby, but he had Zack, while she had nothing to show for the marriage except for the things he would and did give her. Ken could only be miserable to a point; the years in the service and then on active duty during Desert Storm had changed him completely. One got on with it, like his father before him, or wasted years suffering from the dreaded PTSD.

"Let's just leave it for now, hon. Please rest; I need to get some coffee. Is that OK?"

"Of course, please go and get yourself something to eat too. If they're sending me home, it'll still take a while. Please go; I'll just close my eyes." Flora said reassuringly, sounding more and more like her usual in-control self.

Ken wiped his eyes with the back of his hand and walked out of the little cubicle. Feeling overwhelmed by what just took place, he needed a stiff drink and soon.

Flora closed her eyes as an intense calm came over her body. *Enough. I've suffered enough, Lord. If you want me dead, then just take me. I'm not afraid. I'll be with Papa and my son. But if you still have plans for me, then forgive my sin and set me free,* she prayed. *I will make it up to Ken. I make a solemn oath. It's time Vlad and I had that talk.*

LAST MEAL AT LOS PESCADORES

Bella

"WHY ARE THINGS always changing? Why are so many places not here anymore?" I pondered, addressing myself more than my husband and dinner companion. "Even the pier over the ocean where we used to kiss has been torn down." I played with my bottom lip in between taking measured ladylike sips of my favorite 2011 Two Brothers Pinot Noir. Alas, the restaurant served the wine in a Cabernet glass, a fact I found annoying.

"Pinot should always be served in a Burgundy-style glass," I continued, seemingly talking into thin air. "You'd think that for that much money, they'd present the wine in a proper container." I was dressed comfortably in a red cocoon-style cashmere sweater set and chic form-fitting slacks that probably cost more than the servers made in several weeks. Bulgari-inspired Caboshon ruby and diamond earrings along with a classic equestrian-style Hermes bracelet completed my date-night ensemble.

Always looking for something new to learn, lately I've been on a wine-tasting, wine-drinking, and serious-wine buying kick. I'd never really developed a taste for the "usual" vodka and cranberry, sickly sweet champagne, or harshly scented Armenian cognac. The entire wine culture and all the lovely bits associated with it felt both decadent and comforting—and by golly, I deserved to feel both, considering how hard I'd been working and all the usual family crapola.

Having recently returned from an extravagant gastronomic weekend in San Francisco, I was in the middle of planning our next getaway: a wine-tasting trip to California's Central Coast wineries. Maybe soon I'd plan an even more amazing visit to the wine regions of Portugal or Spain, but for now, Paso Robles would have to do.

"Uh huh," answered my husband absentmindedly, looking down at my latest gift to him, a brand-new iPhone, as if all life's answers were inscribed on its large screen. Being well-trained to be a supportive mate, he was also drinking wine, but I know he would have preferred an expensive Scotch.

Clearly distracted, Yuri hadn't said anything complimentary about my appearance yet. I knew, though, that he still found me attractive. He always told me I was one of the few impressive, elegant women left; however, he understood that no one would call me beautiful. I'm not a hot, California-style busty blonde with an upturned potato nose like the Polish caregiver Bozena or a petite, red-haired spitfire like his sister, Oksana. I'm tall and stately with naturally thick, curly brown hair without a slight tint of red. My best features are my dark, almost-Asian, almond-shaped eyes and full-lipped mouth, thanks to newly injected cosmetic filler.

Leo by birth sign or not, Yuri makes me feel that I was a winner by any standard. He appreciates that I am both a serious moneymaker and a devoted family woman. I ski, play tennis, and ride a mountain bike. I've had a lifelong love of horses, and I'm quite a skilled equestrian. And now, I've finally decided to write a book.

I continued my one-sided conversation with Yuri. "I mean, I can go anywhere in Europe or back home after years of not being there and still find my favorite bar and boutique, not to mention the same parks and museums. What's with this place? I'm exhausted just trying to find a place for a nice supper on a Friday night!"

"This place has a fun scene, and you like the farm-to-table menu, right?" Yuri responded, still looking down. "We can't be spending a grand each time you want to eat," he added, referring to our recent San Francisco dining experience. *Sometimes Bella's never-ending demands and expectations really piss me off,* he thought.

"Agreed," I said. "I suppose this place is nice enough. They just opened a few months ago. I mean, everybody's been here already, and the wine list is pretty good. Still, they don't have a sommelier; they probably won't last a year. I miss the old standbys."

"That's why I don't get you, my nostalgic sentimentalist. Funny, you're more Russian than I am. Even after all these years, you're longing for some dumpy joint we had to go to when the money was tight."

"I am what I am, and that's a Leo. We're known for our loyalty!" I lifted my now-empty glass in the air to let the passing server know I was ready for another glass. *Sometimes Yuri's condescension really pisses me off,* she thought to herself. *After all, I'm the one paying for our increasingly extravagant lifestyle.*

"Crap," sounded off Yuri, as he saw yet another SMS from Bozena, his mother's caregiver. "Oh-oh," he said, finally looking up at me. "Bozena says Mom's blood pressure is up, and she wants you to come over right now to look her over."

"Seriously? How many times have I told her that I'm a dentist, not her cardiologist! Tell her to call her doctor or Oksana."

"I know, *moya belochka.*" Yuri tried to soothe me by calling me his little squirrel, a nickname given to me by my father. "But you know Mama—probably another panic thing or something. Bozena wouldn't bug us if she could handle her or find my sister." Yuri tried to explain, feeling both exasperated and guilty—in other words, normal.

"*Nyet.* Not going this time. We must stop spoiling her. I'm not running off. I worked all day without a break for lunch. I have to eat," I said, putting my foot down. "Just text your sister and tell her to dial 911." I made up my mind then and there to draw the line despite having to deal with Yuri's guilt. "Wait. I have an idea. Why don't you text your mother and tell her to use the BP cuff? I left it in the kitchen. If she can't find it, tell her to ask Bozena."

"Ok," Yuri said, approving my plan. A minute or so later, after a slew of back and forth texts, he shook his head and said that the blood pressure measurement was insanely high, his mother was freaking out, no one could locate his sister, and Bozena was calling 911.

"I'm sorry, we have to go, dear. I promised her we'd meet them at the ER."

"Fine," I said firmly. "There's no rush, though. They won't let us in for at least an hour. Let's finish dinner and head over then."

"What if it's another stroke?" asked Yuri, now clearly nervous.

"What if it rains on Thursday and mushrooms will grow out of your nose?" I quipped back, quoting a popular Russian folk saying. "Well, if she's talking and bitching at the caregiver, it's probably nothing; in any case, she has plenty of time to get a TPA shot once the ambulance comes." Over the years, harshness has become a permanent part of my reactions to these sorts of "health" scares. I'm astute enough to understand that matter-of-factness and detachment are necessary forms of self-preservation. Maybe I'm "only" a dentist, but a doctor nevertheless is a doctor.

"Right—you're absolutely right. But still, let's hurry and go there. Finish your wine, but let me get the bill. Should I use your black card to get the extra points?"

"Sure, I guess we can always use more points," I agreed, not at all surprised by the fact that I would be paying for yet another spoiled evening.

"Bozena says that Mama is crying and carrying on in Russian about my father. I guess she found out on Facebook that someone she knows just dropped dead, apparently at a young age. Most likely, the unfortunate fellow died from a massive heart attack, like Papa. Guess it set her off."

"Ah, that makes sense. Well, then she might as well get some extra meds and hydration." I wondered who had passed away. "We better go now, before the usual night ER rush," I continued in my best medical professional voice. "She'll be fine; I can feel it. Negative emotions are a terrible thing for stroke patients; that's why I want to discuss the possibility of her not leaving the hospital without a script for antidepressants."

"Thank you, dear, but I don't think Mama will agree."

"*Odnoznachno*, we will make her agree. Look, I do feel a little guilty for not dropping everything and running to the ER, but I'm worn out from the lot of them; neither my maternal nor my paternal grandparents were like them. They were strong and capable, and they took care of us," I reminisced wistfully. "Your mother and my mother and everyone's mother and poor Sasha, having to deal with that horrible old man, Viktor, who she calls father. All of them are pains in the ass, except for my dad. He was an amazingly tough man. I never saw him cry, except once."

"Well, that was then; another time, another generation. They had to be resilient: revolution, war, hunger, gulags," said Yuri. "Your father was a jewel, though, real sunshine. I miss him too. You'll have to tell me his tears story next time over dinner. I so love your stories; too bad you think you have to be published and can't simply write them down for the kids."

"It's not that, babe; I need time and space," I said, knowing I was just making excuses. Yuri smiled, took my hand in his and gave it a lingering kiss. "Perhaps when you don't have to work at your practice anymore."

"Perhaps one day. I love you," I whispered, unexpected tears forming in my eyes. "Maybe one day I will write down our family stories—at least for the kids. I want them to know who they are and where they come from. But we both know I'm not retiring since neither of us is willing to struggle again."

"Da, but I want you to know how much I love you and the family you gave me. Aren't we lucky to be together?"

"We are lucky. Still, let's go. You know, I'm still wondering whose passing would upset your mom so much that it sent her to the hospital."

⸺ ❧ ⸺

It turned out that it was a good thing that Yuri's mom was admitted to Cedars. After a plethora of tests, the resident physician concluded that she was severely dehydrated, had forgotten to take her potassium pills, and was suffering from a nasty UTI. The doctor also suspected she may had have had yet another mini stroke, a TIA, but he couldn't prove it since TIAs didn't always show up on the MRI.

The ER staff pumped her full of antibiotics and got her hydrated. The doctor decided to be conservative and keep her overnight for observation. She was released to Yuri's care the very next day. I wished she had stayed for a few more days, but Medicare denied the request.

The doctor advised her to ask her regular physician to prescribe antidepressants and a mild tranquilizer. She refused both and told the nurse, not in a very nice way, to leave her alone to die in peace.

Since I was still at the office, Yuri was the one to bring his mother back home. He told me he wasn't coming home until the next morning. Bozena wasn't scheduled to stay the night, and Oksana was spending most of her free time with Maya.

Evidently, the fellow whose passing put Yuri's mother into the hospital was Vladimir, Fat Maya's husband and my old childhood neighbor. Since Vlad, as everyone called him, was Oksana's brother-in-law, Yuri's mother considered him a member of the family.

After much carrying on, she explained to Yuri that once Vlad did her a big favor as well as offering numerous kindnesses after the death of her husband. When Yuri questioned what type of favor and kindnesses, she refused to tell him. It sounded like the manner of his passing reminded her of her husband's death, triggering a lot of painful memories. Since his mother never dealt with her grief like normal people, Yuri wasn't surprised that the trauma of hearing about his unexpected passing shook her up.

Furious and concerned, Yuri texted me their entire conversation blow by blow. I could tell he was pissed about just how deeply Maya and Vlad's claws had penetrated his family. I asked him to calm down, reminding him that his mother was under strict orders to avoid stress, but he wouldn't listen. The disagreement about the in-laws blew up into a huge argument, and Yuri asked me to come to the apartment ASAP so he wouldn't strangle the disloyal "witch."

Tired and hungry, I left the office earlier than I should have. I decided to leave my car there because of the horrific traffic and took an Uber to the West side. I was resentful, if resigned. Yuri never left me a choice. How could I say no?

When I got there, my mother-in-law was red in the face, fanning herself and lying on the sofa. My troublemaker husband was on his laptop, pretending to be busy. He greeted me with terse thanks for coming and asked if he could go get something out of his car.

I could tell Alla Markovna was relieved to see me. Never a demonstrative woman, she gave me a chapped-lipped kiss on the cheek and began to complain about Oksana. Funny, here she just had a tongue-lashing from her son, but it was still Oksana's fault.

How dare she wasn't available to take care of her own mother!

"Nu I vot-poevilas kralia," the old woman said under her breath, just loud enough to be heard. "You have arrived just in time, Isabella." She addressed me oddly in English. "I need a medical professional near me. I recognize that you're a simple dentist; still, a doctor is a doctor. Take my blood pressure. I think my heart is stopping." I think the tone of her voice alone could make me hate her, let alone her sarcasm: calling me, *kralia*, meaning a beauty. As if she ever offered one single compliment about my appearance!

"You're fine, *Mamasha*," I never could bring myself to call her Mama. "Now, take a deep breath. Good. Better? Now, take a sip of water," I said calmly, crossing my eyes, just like I did as a little girl. I placed the wrist cuff on her left hand and turned the monitor on. She made noises as if she were in pain. I ignored her. True, her numbers were a little low, considering she was lying down, but nothing to freak out about. Hell, I'm sure my own blood pressure was far worse just then.

"Poor Yurik! Poor boy!" she cried with a straight face. "I must confess, he's upset with me. Of course, he's irritated, but I don't blame him. He already spent too much time looking after me. He must work. Oksana, she's the woman and should take care of her mama. What else does she have to do while her American brats are in school? What? Play with clothes at Marshall's?"

When I didn't respond, she switched gears, saying how devastated she was not to be able to attend Vlad's funeral and that she hoped Maya would not hold it against her. After an hour or so of moaning and bitching, I took charge and commanded her to close her eyes and rest. At last she settled down.

Since I still hadn't had a bite to eat, I dug a piece of gum from the bottom of my Burberry bag and went onto the balcony, thinking, *Damn, I wish I didn't quit smoking just about now.* It was a quiet afternoon. Across the street, a young Russian-speaking woman in tight yoga pants was pushing a stroller, while talking on a smartphone. She was loud enough for me to overhear a few bits of conversation. She was bitching about the baby's parents never being around and not paying her enough.

Trying to ignore the stupid little *suchka* across the street, I looked down. Just to the left of my car, I noticed Yuri's car. The gorgeous dark gray BMW X3, yet another birthday present from me and the kids, was parked too far from the curb. When I put on my glasses, I saw my husband sitting alone. His head was slumped over the well-padded steering wheel. He wasn't talking on the phone or looking at his laptop—just sitting there so still; I became concerned that something was wrong. Then he raised his head and sat up, still not exiting the SUV. *Oh-oh,* I thought; *he's had it. I better do something.* Without much thinking, I dialed my mother's home number.

She picked up immediately, seeing that it was me.

"*Moya devochka!* Has something happened?" The very sound of her voice calling me her little girl was better than popping a Xanax. Having just spent a few hours with my impossible-to-please mother-in-law made me feel thankful to still have my own mama, despite all the health scares and caregiving needs.

"I need your assistance," I said gently so as not to jolt her own nerves.

"*Konechno, solneshko*; anything you need." I was still her sunshine! Mama never said no when I asked. She told me it made her feel good to be of any help since she hasn't been able to be an active grandmother to the kids after her stroke. She was doing well, considering the damage: working hard on moving around her apartment, keeping herself busy with little projects, and enjoying a rich social life with her old friends. I'm not saying that caregiving was easy, but she was so sweet, supportive, and appreciative that I wanted her to have the best of everything.

"Look, we just brought you know who from the hospital; she's fine, but kvetching as usual and Oksana can't stay over. Yuri promised he will sleep here on the sofa, but could you possibly send Bozena over for a few hours so Yuri and I can grab dinner?" I said, explaining the situation.

Not surprisingly, Mama not only agreed but insisted that after dinner we go home and rest.

"I'm having a good day," she reassured. "Auntie Rita and her friend are here for tea, and she will help me to get ready for bed. Bozena can go. She gave me a bath earlier, ahead of their visit." I felt guilty, but I decided to accept her offer, promising to check on her first thing in the morning.

I heard from Oksana a few days later. Not surprisingly, according to her, Vlad's funeral was the largest funeral anyone had seen for years. I wanted to tell her but didn't want to let her know what I thought of the entire mess. Why would anyone make such a fuss over a cheating, vile prick, without a decent bone in his body? Oksana said she guessed the flowers must've cost a hundred grand, and I didn't even want to know about the restaurant bill. You'd think it was Steve Job's funeral—or Elvis's! Not that I ever had any love for Maya—she was undoubtedly a predatory piranha— still, she must be grieving.

On the other hand, knowing how those people operated, I suspected Vlad's funeral didn't cost her a penny. Maya probably put the squeeze on the vendors and got everything comped.

I smile when they say "died suddenly." All death is sudden. Or when they say "it was unexpected." All death should be expected. In any case, I had to cancel an entire day of riding to pay our "respects" the following weekend.

Phew, such a stressful few weeks. Well, they were behind us. I was thrilled to have a nice, comfy dinner, a glass of good wine, and some conversation that didn't involve my in-laws.

Eating out has become not only our "entertainment," but also a time when we can just relax without interference from the kids and the remaining "parents," usually with the caregiver in tow. Even if I'll be the one stuck with the bill.

Usually Yuri and I sit across from each other at restaurants, but for some reason, tonight Yuri decided to sit next to me. "The chair looks rickety; move your cute behind," he joked.

"Really? You know I like to see your face across the table when we talk," I replied with a smile. "I'll tell you my Papa story after we've had some libations. It's been a day and a half."

We sat on cracked, stained, faded, fake brown leather, so popular back in the last century. How odd to say "last century"! We were dining at Los Pescadores, the last old-school seafood restaurant in town, left over from when we were still dating. I was attending junior college in between working in the school library, tutoring math and babysitting. Yuri was making a little cash, driving old wealthy Americans to their doctor appointments and painting houses whenever he got a gig.

Well, that was then. As I looked around, an odd feeling came over me. I had to face reality: the place was a dinosaur, and I recognized the inevitability of its demise. This was clearly our last time here, my silly penchant for nostalgia or not.

As it happened, I was correct, because the very next week, the place was shut down and eventually demolished to make room for the new Trader Joe's parking lot.

But for now, we sat next to each other, sipping on God knows what-brand of bourbon and fountain syrup coke. Yuri had to get our drinks from the musty-smelling bar, since the wine list was truly frightening. Needing to zone out, we sat without speaking, our heads down, checking our Facebook accounts for both news and entertainment.

We ordered another round of drinks from tonight's server, yet another dinosaur. Refreshingly, she was not one of these erudite foodies, or glammed-up boys, or "I'm putting myself through sommelier school," or "waiting for a big showbiz break" young professionals, but an authentic old-school waitress. She had finally made her appearance just as Yuri was about to blow and get up to leave.

The waitress looked both dead tired and annoyed, but I had a strong sense her mood had nothing to do with us. She wore the same old uniform I remembered from years back: a permanently soiled white shirt and a short, "used to be black" late 1980s skort. The dubious skirt-over-short number was propped up by red suspenders, decorated with tiny sailboats and faded gray sharks. Her flabby legs were encased in white fishnet stockings.

"You kids ready to order?" she asked blandly.

"No," Yuri answered firmly, waving his hand at the woman. "We are not ready to order. Come back. Oh, and I'm ready for another drink, but make it a double this time. If I wanted a soda, I would have ordered a soda," he continued, sounding irritated, not at all like his usual humorous self. Usually I'm the one who is the more verbal, or as he says, "discerning customer." He added sourly, "And I asked for extra lemon."

"Sorry, sir, but the kitchen will be closing early, so I have to put your food order through now," countered the waitress, looking down at her old-fashioned, wrinkled, and stained order pad. She shook her head as if trying to come back to reality.

Without being asked, she proceeded to recite the evening's specials, which she said included the best food in town.

The seafood sounded good to me, and I squeezed his hand to signal my wishes. "We'll have two T-bones, medium rare, a couple of scalloped potatoes and extra sour cream," ordered Yuri, still sounding unnecessarily gruff.

"Anything to start from our specials?" the waitress asked, trying to up-sell us.

"Manhattan chowder will do," he decided. "I doubt their produce is up to par," he said, talking to me but clearly addressing her. What had gotten into him? He wasn't a "foody." Something must be upsetting him. I wanted to ask, but I had a feeling it wouldn't be a great idea.

"Any sautéed mushrooms? It's our specialty. Or maybe our famous cheesy garlic toast?" the waitress got his not-so-subtle message and attempted to appease him.

"No, not tonight," Yuri snapped. Once again he dismissed her with a wave of his hand while looking down at his phone. Men can do that, you know; they can just wave our spirits away, especially as we get old. You spend an hour fixing your face as you try not to look past your chin; you put on strip lashes and a glob of moisturizer to smooth out the wrinkles, brush on some color, and say to yourself, "Not bad . . . not too scary." Then some guy just waves his hand, and you magically cease to exist. The expression on the waitress's face told her entire life story. There's no respect for older women, not in this culture. No wonder we are all filled with fear and anxiety, doing crazy stuff to our faces and our bodies. I was beginning to regret the entire evening. Yes, Oksana's increasing marital woes and his mother had been causing him stress, but that was not an excuse to be an asshole. Tonight's resurfacing of some of my husband's old personality traits were not making me happy. I decided the evening's mood was ruined, so I had nothing to lose in speaking my mind.

"That was unnecessary. You were extremely rude to the server; I don't like *hamstvo*." There are some words that defy simple translation. *Hamstvo* is what Russian-speakers refer to as that particularly noxious blend of vulgar insolence and insensitivity. I never could hold my tongue when faced with *hamstvo*. I've seen it translated into English as "arrogance" or "being brazen," but that's not accurate.

"Was I?" he responded without taking me seriously. "Sorry, dear. Who cares? You always say, 'No education, no respect.'"

Oh no, I wasn't about to let him off the hook with a sarcastic "sorry, dear."

"Who cares?" I shot back. "*We* do. Therefore, Russians feel disrespected by American businessmen and politicians. If you can't take the time to see what matters to another culture, you'll just keep making erroneous assumptions, and that will surely lead to distrust and conflict. That's what my papa used to say, always a frustrated politician."

"Whatever. Why you wanted to eat here is beside me," Yuri said, defending his actions. "We could have gone to Morton's or Ruth Chris. As you keep reminding me, we are not poor immigrants. Fuck, if you insist on a more modest place, Outback Steakhouse is just around the corner." He was on a roll now. "And all the new places in downtown LA are like wow. I think it's time to put this stinky place to bed, along with that skanky old woman. What a slob! Why can't she wear something age-appropriate? Fishnet stockings: give me a fucking break!"

"It's their uniform. I'm sure she doesn't like it either," I said, attempting to both explain and excuse the poor woman's appearance, knowing well it was an exercise in futility. Out of the blue, I felt a fog of exhaustion envelop my entire body. Another time, another place; I was simply too tired to fight.

"Anyway, do you want to hear about Papa or not?" I asked, changing the subject. I love my husband, but I can't continue to explain my attachment to the past, to all that gives me the illusion of stability.

People, places—they all tend to disappear on me. I've already left so much behind. Yuri's a man and not at all schmaltzy by nature; the Russian gene has been suppressed. That was one of the main characteristics that drew me to him in the first place—an inborn lack of melancholy and a penchant for moving forward without looking back. My Yuri doesn't cry vodka tears while listening to our childhood songs; in fact, he never liked them in the first place. Rock and roll forever!

The Manhattan chowder arrived before I could start my story. Yuri was right again. "This is not chowder, just some dishwater with tomato paste and raw potatoes." Yuri took a sip, made a face, and then proceeded to gulp it down, right to the bottom of the yellowish, cracked soup cup. I smelled the soup and decided to pass, but without making a fuss. I ate the little fish-shaped crackers and took a sip of my drink. Occasionally, I just want to connect and talk it out, rather than eat quickly and run to a movie.

"He only cried once."

"What? Who?"

"Papa—I only saw him cry once in my entire life. A long time ago, in Vienna."

"Why Vienna?" Yuri has this "endearing" habit of interrupting my Kerouac-like stream of consciousness, but he does pipe down eventually and follows my yarns with genuine curiosity. As we say, my tongue is well hung, meaning I'm a talker. Since our main course is delayed, I decided to tell him yet another family story.

"Do you remember the story about our trip from the border to Vienna?"

"I think so. That the one where you fought with the border guard and then were thrown off the train?"

"Well, not technically fought; just had words and was shoved a few times," I said, wanting to put things into perspective. "Anyway, we were left across the border without money or tickets or passports. We were like those poor Syrians, the true homeless and stateless. My heart breaks when I see the children. I know exactly what they're feeling. It took us days to get to the relief workers in Austria, but when we did, a kindhearted Austrian woman took us into her own flat because there were no more places at the pension."

Without saying a word, Yuri stopped chewing on a cracker, reached out, took my hand into his, and offered a reassuring squeeze.

I think my husband had a bit of immigration guilt. He had an entirely different, infinitely more civilized experience. After taking an overnight train from Leningrad, the four of them simply boarded a plane in Moscow and landed in New York, but then, they left home later than we did.

"Go on," he encourages me, just as our steaks arrive, well done of course. He cuts into his, looks up at the Hispanic food runner, and tells him to take it back and bring the check. The man apologizes and offers to make us another plate.

"Never mind," Yuri says, raising his voice. "Tell the manager we're done with this dump." He gets up and throws down a fifty, telling the poor man it should more than cover the drinks and the disgusting soup.

I follow him into the parking lot, and as he gets in without opening my door, I look back at the restaurant and my eyes tear up. This is not a fitting ending to all the years of good memories, but it is what it is. I get in and close my eyes.

The drive is short and wordless. At home, Yuri asks me to make him a smoked salmon omelet. I comply, but do not join him. A piece of cold chicken and a yogurt will do. I've lost my appetite.

After finishing his meal, Yuri promises that next week he'll make plans. I'm too tired to talk. I leave him in front of his computer, skip my skincare regimen, and go to bed early.

The ghosts of my emigration memories won't let me be, especially now that I'm getting older. It's funny how the impressions of some experiences become foggy at best, while others continue to come more into focus. I continue to remember . . .

After that first sleepless night of freedom, Papa took me for a walk along the river Wien, leaving Mother behind to recover from the travel ordeal. Silly me, I wanted to see the "blue" Danube, but Papa explained in his gently instructive way that it was the Wien, not the legendary Danube that runs through the city of the waltz. It was a damp early morning in June. Vienna smelled like rain and possibilities. We must have been in a haze, walking for hours until my stomach began to gurgle so loud that my father noticed.

"*Nu da*, Mama will kill me if I don't get you something to eat," he joked. "Hungry?"

"Not really," I answered, not wanting to complain.

"Right. Well, suddenly I'm famished. Let's see if we can find a little snack. When I was in the army, guys stationed in Germany talked about street vendors selling pretzels; the fellows said they were almost edible."

Just like that, we spotted a tiny butcher shop. Despite a nagging sense of fear and discomfort, we decided to try our luck, hoping there would be some food available for takeaway.

Since Papa spoke a good deal of German, I knew asking a question or two wouldn't be a problem. Taken aback by not seeing a long queue outside the front door, we went in.

The shop was oddly empty. For a second, I thought it was closed. Then it hit me, an overwhelming scent of smoked meat and cinnamon that has stayed with me ever since. My mouth watered. Then my stomach gave an embarrassingly thunderous gurgle. As we both stood at the doorway, not knowing what to expect, I noticed a man. He sat at a little table covered with a crisply ironed, immaculately clean blue-and-white-checkered cloth; the largest cup of steaming hot liquid, probably Viennese coffee, placed to his right side. A neatly folded newspaper lay on his left. He was puffing on a large carved wooden pipe. Next to him, a small furry creature wearing a knitted sweater snored away, its soft underbelly moving in and out, in and out. My heart melted, and I felt an irresistible urge to touch the sleeping puppy.

Papa gave me his usual "Let's go now; we don't belong here" look and, without a word, put his hands on my shoulders. Before we were about to exit, the man smiled and greeted us with a cheerful "Guten Morgen!"

"Guten Morgen, mein herr," responded Papa bravely, raising one of his bushy blond eyebrows and giving me a wink.

"Grub Gott," the owner said, turning to me. As I later found out, it was how Austrians say "hello."

"Bonjour, monsieur," I automatically answered in my second language, my face instantly turning vivid red, betraying my inner confusion.

While I didn't speak German, I was raised around plenty of old Jewish women who conversed in Yiddish, and I gathered that the owner of the shop asked my father if he could help us with anything. The two men spoke for a minute. As for me, I was fascinated with the creature, now up and about. I suspected that the little dog liked me as it wagged its fluffy, perfectly styled tail and rubbed against my foot. I wasn't raised around dogs because we lived in small flats, but this little guy stole my heart with his outgoing personality and adorable mug. When the pooch realized I was paying him attention, he rolled over and offered me his sweet belly for patting. That's when I realized that he was a *she* and fell in love. From that moment on, I made sure that I had a dog sharing both my life and my bed. It's one thing I will always fight for, even with Yuri.

After a few minutes of cooing and petting, something made me look up at my father. By now, emboldened by the warm reception, Papa moved closer to the counter accompanied by the butcher. I noticed he was standing with his mouth open, tears running down his ruddy, unlined cheeks. There he stood, balling his blue eyes out—Papa, my hero, who never complained about the horror of starvation, the war, or the military service. Papa, who never shed a tear at funerals. Papa, who always laughed at adversity and only saw the good in everyone. He washed the bodies of our dead loved ones and never cried.

He had left his entire family behind back home, knowing he would never see them again, and never cried. I was beyond shocked as I heard him saying something over and over.

"Papa, what's wrong? What are you saying?" I asked, feeling alarmed. He didn't answer. "Papa, should we go now?" I touched him gently on the shoulder. And then I heard it. "Sausages, blood sausages, wieners, pork, schnitzel, kielbasa, pastrami, ham, salami, sausages, sausages . . . sausages."

"Papa! Are you ill? Please don't cry!" I tried to get him to stop, but he was beyond reach. I stood there, not knowing what to do or what to say. The old butcher left us in peace, returning to whatever he was doing before we came in.

I stood by and let him feel whatever he was feeling. "They lied. They lied. No one was hungry, just us," he stopped crying and wiped his eyes angrily, so unlike his normally cheery, even-tempered self.

"Who lied?" I tried to engage him as calmly as I could. Although I knew only too well what he meant, I needed him to return to his normal self. He shook his head and asked me to go outside. I complied, willing to wait patiently, my appetite gone. We returned to the flat without a word, stopping by a corner store to pick up some yogurt, a box of pastries, and three bottles of Orangina soda.

Papa never said a word about his butcher shop meltdown. I kept my mouth shut as well. It was simply too much to bear. The hunger, the fear, the lies, the control, and more hunger. As I look back, I remember that it took a few days before his natural personality returned. Only those who were truly hungry could understand the trauma he felt; even I, brought up during the lean times, couldn't quite grasp it.

———— ∞ ————

The next day, after work, I decided I needed to visit with my mother. When

I arrived, I was greeted with a sunny smile and sweet kiss, although I noticed that her color was off. Bozena was on her way out, so I told her I would help my mom to get ready for bed. I made tea and served a few slices of Polish chocolate wafer cake. We chatted about this and that, and then I talked her into looking through the faded photo albums. As I explained to her, I was trying to keep memories of Papa close. The albums were kept on top of the bedroom closet, out of the way, but easily accessible.

In the few black-and-white photos that had survived the years, Papa resembles Harvey Lavan "Van" Cliburn. No one had to tell me the amazing, true story about the young American pianist. In 1958, the gifted, charming Texan shocked the Soviet musical establishment when, at the height of the Cold War, he won our most prestigious Tchaikovsky piano competition. He also won the hearts of our people, despite the Communist Party's displeasure. I've seen that performance a thousand times. The sheer romance of his fingers is overwhelming to my senses. Van Cliburn sadly is gone, as is my darling papa.

Here's another photo of Papa, the one that still breaks my heart. The picture, crumbled and faded from black-and-white to gray and yellow shows off his perfectly etched profile, a shock of luxurious hair blowing in the wind. Papa is sitting at the edge of a pier, looking out at the stormy Black Sea. There's another one that also brings a smile to my face. It's black-and-white too, but in much better shape. A little heavier and a tad older, Papa is sitting at the head of a birthday table, shoving a huge pork chop in his always hungry mouth, while family members toast across the table with vodka-filled cut crystal shot glasses. In yet another one, Papa is playing chess and enjoying more vodka shots with someone whose name I have now forgotten.

As Mama and I continue to leaf through the memories, I noticed that her eyes are filled with tears, so I make an excuse about having to make dinner (both of us knowing I don't cook). I help her get ready for bed and leave with a heavy heart.

Let the past stay in the past, I'm told by my husband. Nostalgia is both seductive and dangerous. Look at Facebook romances with your high school sweethearts, for example. The impersonal contact makes rekindling affairs easier; I assume. He is correct, and so I promise myself that I will put the past to bed. Maybe I'll write a book for kids instead—something about horses?

A few busy weeks later, one late evening, my cell phone goes nuts with text messages. I glance at it with a good deal of resentment, expecting my office or a pesky patient looking for a pound of flesh, but this time I'm wrong. This is personal. Six group texts come through, one after another. I see the names: Bozena, Oksana, Bozena, Oksana, Yuri, and Bozena again. It's showtime one more time—a definite health crisis with my mother-in-law. She's had a major stroke and they're rushing her to the hospital by ambulance. Bozena found her unresponsive in front of the television, her face contorted and her tongue half-bitten. The hysterical caregiver called 911 and in just a few minutes, off they went to the ER.

No matter how hard I try to set up personal boundaries, life gives me the finger. I'm trapped by obligations and duties, and I've just about had it with them.

I get into the shower, scrub my face, and stand there for a nice, long time, feeling the hot water infusing me with energy. I'm sure it will be at least twenty-four hours until I leave the hospital. I'll call my office manager from the car, take some precooked Italian food out of the freezer, and get going, but first, I just want to stand in the dark and let the water beat on my neck, just for another minute.

HOLLYWOOD FOREVER

THE LARGEST INDIVIDUAL flower order in Alexandra of the Valley's business history arrived at the crack of dawn. If the shop had been open, the staff would have fainted from both glee and panic. The burial services for Maya's husband Vlad were set for the fabled Hollywood Forever Cemetery in the heart of old Tinsel Town, just a stone's throw from the old Paramount Studios. That was peculiar, since the flower shop usually serviced the bland, ever sprawling Forrest Lawn Cemetery in Glendale.

The cell phone rang at seven, just as Sasha was fixing some cranberry tea with organic orange blossom honey for herself and frying some *sirniki* (cheese fritters) for her boys. She was thinking of making her daily morning call to her father to see if his night went well. It was her sacred, if dreaded, obligation. Lately their conversations had grown increasingly hurtful and tense. She could always count on some sort of verbal conflict, but the increasing levels of anger coming from Victor was still unexpected.

Victor started his day early, listening to the Russian and Ukrainian news channels and getting increasingly irate and full of venom. By the time Sasha would call to ask about his health, he'd vomit out all that angst. Last week he became obsessed with the president of the United States being a Russian spy and a notorious secret gay who was being blackmailed by the devil himself, Putin. The Hollywood Jews and the blacks have ruined the culture and were now coming to kill all the Christians. The Muslims have already overrun Europe. And on and on . . . who knew what was next?

After the politics came Victor's complaints about not getting enough attention, his musings about his son Gary's business successes, and his bitching about Jason, who he started to call "the little blue boy," meaning homosexual. According to him, the homosexuals, not nuclear war, would bring down the entire Western civilization. He then would recite the entire passages from the Soviet-era translation of Edward Gibbon's *The Decline and the Fall of the Roman Empire*. At the end of his days, Victor decided he would become a history expert, plus one of his park cronies, a retired history professor, had died, and his kids threw out the man's much cherished, now useless books.

Sasha was past emotional exhaustion. She was also caught in the middle, since the rest of her family had long ago lost patience both with her father—and even more painfully, with her enabling of his behavior. How could they understand? They weren't adopted.

When she looked down at her ever-present cell, the screen read Vladimir Kanevsky, the honored dead himself, and that alone gave Sasha the willies. *Oi Gospodi*, she gasped as she crossed herself twice and then answered reluctantly. Obviously it wasn't Vlad, but still, just seeing the dead man's name made her shiver.

"Is this Alexandra of the Valley?" a man asked with a perceptible irritation in his voice, with no trace of an accent. This is Flora's husband, Kenneth. I buy flowers from you all the time."

"This is Alexandra, but the florist shop is still closed. You've called my personal cell, but yes, I do remember you, Mr. Bowman," answered Sasha as pleasantly as she could. It was not in her nature to show her own irritation about being called at the crack of dawn, and on her personal phone to boot.

"I see. Well, at any rate, I need to place an order for some sympathy flowers for tomorrow," the American continued without offering an apology. "It's for my late business partner, Vlad."

"Yes, of course; my condolences on your loss. May the earth be like a featherbed to him," replied Sasha.

"Featherbed? Hah, that's an interesting expression. If there is God's justice, more like a bed of nails." He heard a gasp on the other end and made a coughing sound. "Anyway, I want to send flowers directly to the cemetery and I want them big. I don't know what you people think is suitable, but whatever it is, just double it."

"We can do that. I'll be going to my store shortly. You can decide now if you want a standing wreath or an easel heart or just a large arrangement in a container?" Sasha said, trying to clarify. "Also, what type of flowers would you prefer? We received several large orders overnight, and I may have to drive to the downtown flower mart for more merchandise."

"I don't care; I'll leave it up to you," Flora's husband said, sounding annoyed.

"May I ask your budget?"

"Whatever you think; just make it impressive. I know how you Russians like showy funerals, and I don't want our arrangement to get lost."

"Are there some special colors you prefer? I know your wife is very particular," Sasha asked again, trying to narrow down the choices. She had a terrible premonition that this funeral would cause her some serious grief: all expense and no profit, at least when it came to Maya's order for sure. Maybe Alicia, her newly hired design assistant could hold down the fort while she drove to the mart before going to the shop. Of course, the traffic would be horrible this time of day. To be fair, the traffic was a nightmare every day, all day long, and she needed her SUV to transport the flower-filled buckets along with more floral supplies.

"My wife is not to be disturbed," warned Ken. "I'm calling from my car on the way down from Vegas. All hell's breaking loose. I'm trying to make it down, but I may not make it in time for the cemetery. Flora is not feeling well, so I'm leaving it up to you, as I said. There is no budget," he clarified again sharply.

"Very well, Mr. Bowman; We'll take care of your order, and to make sure you are completely satisfied, I'll even do the arrangement personally. Again, please accept our sympathy."

"I'll have my assistant call you with the credit card info."

"I understand. We mostly deal in cash, but I can send you a PayPal request if you wish."

"PayPal? Sure. Why not? That way, I'll know what I'm spending. I don't want Maya to think Flora and I are being cheap; no offense, but what a waste of good money. Flowers are just for the living. By the way, are you going?"

"Yes, we will be there to pay our respects," answered Sasha, ignoring his comments about Maya. "However," she continued, "the formal wake is a private event and since we're not providing flowers for the restaurant, I won't need to supervise."

"A formal wake? What? Is it black tie? Never mind. I guess we're done. I hope Flora will be satisfied with your work."

"I'll do my best, as usual. Have a nice day, and thank you for your order." As Sasha wrapped up the conversation, she felt another tension headache coming on with a vengeance.

———— ❧ ————

Oksana was having a meltdown about her shoe choices for Vlad's funeral and the following luncheon. She sat on the wholesale-priced carpet, right in the middle of her Home Depot-installed master closet with its revolving shoe rack, a glass of cut-rate Prosecco precariously perched next to her. She knew Maya wouldn't notice her shoes, since she didn't give a rat's ass about fashion—being fat all her life—but everyone else would. She needed something that complemented, not overpowered, her black Dolce pantsuit, an outlet find. The heels would have to be elegant and chic, but not too painful, for the send-off would surely last well into the evening hours. Oksana was beginning to think it was Mission Impossible; she couldn't very well ask for a second opinion. Mother had just been released from the hospital; poor Maya had just lost the love of her life.

Just recently, Oksana had found out that Maya and Vlad had known each other since childhood. How sad, and what a shocking exit!

She still couldn't believe that she and Slava were at Maya's home when the unthinkable happened. It had been a regular Sunday. Vlad had come back from another job in Vegas. He was in great spirits and overflowing with extra cash. On the way home, he texted Maya his preference for dinner and asked her to invite a few couples to celebrate the completion of a big project, something so big that he also promised he would take a break. He even told her to finally book a cruise of her choice.

Tears filled Oksana's already puffy eyes when she remembered Maya's joy and anticipation when she texted the invite. Little by little, Maya had begun to confide in her sister-in-law about the increasing problems in her marriage. Maya also missed her brother. Slava had been out of town looking after Maya's business interests.

When everyone had arrived, Vlad was still in the shower, so Maya gave them a little tour of her newest addition: a brand-new Tesla SUV. *You'd think it was a house,* Maya thought, *not a fucking electric car that cost as much as a house in any normal place other than LA.*

Choking on envy, Oksana gulped her wine like water. As usual, everything was perfect: the fabulous home-cooked meal, the expensive tequila, and of course, Maya's signature Kiev Tort, served with generous pours of Louise XIII cognac and Italian espresso. Oksana had tasted Louise XIII once in Las Vegas, at the gaudy Chandelier Bar in the Cosmopolitan Hotel. When she found out the cost of a one-ounce pour, she gasped and told Slava for that much money she'd rather buy a pair of designer shoes! He told her she was just a classless *dura*. She ran into the smoke-filled lady's room in tears and Facebook-messaged Avi. Knowing he had recently moved to La Jolla to live in a big mansion with his much-older American lady friend, she was happy he responded.

She never told anyone about their special friendship. Mama was wrong. It wasn't an affair; yeah, they messed around once or twice, but it was so much more than that. Hell, her husband was great in bed. So what? Avi saw her potential; he nurtured her love for design. He admired her work. He saw her. He promised he would be her business partner and stand up to her husband. He was the only one who wasn't afraid of Slava.

She could message him night and day, vent about Mama, the kids, her demeaning retail job, her frustrations with Slava, and he never called her stupid or a superficial shoe-obsessed bimbo. They had plans. As soon as his immigration papers were final and she got the seed money, they would form a made-in-LA couture shoe manufacturing business together! She knew of Avi's other sexual preferences, and she was jealous, but she'd never allow her personal feelings to stand between her and her destiny. Avi was omni-sexual or whatever he believed. Oksana never thought that sex defined a relationship anyway. Look at Maya: she had regular sex with Vlad, but did their good sex life stop him from acting up?

For all she knew, Slava was screwing around just like Vlad or planning to dump her for a younger woman. Da, he'd take care of their kids, but she'd get *duli*, zip, nada. He'd always been a generous father to his now-grown son from his first marriage. Oksana didn't know about Chinese wife number two who died in the Twin Towers. Slava told her there was a woman after his divorce, but he wouldn't share any details. Maya's money was her answer, and Avi was her future.

After that fateful dinner, the guys went into the bonus room to play pool. Slava told her that Vlad had begun to feel very hot and sweaty, so he went back in the kitchen where Maya was just finishing up the dishes and opened the refrigerator to get some iced tea. That's when tragedy struck. None of the guests saw him fall. Since the playroom was near the kitchen, the men heard what they later told the paramedics and the police was a terrible thump. When Maya turned around, she saw her husband hit the floor—so hard that he split the side of his head, blood gushing out on the stone floor.

Maya screamed for help, thinking it was an accident. God knows he'd fallen when he was drunk before. Thinking about it now, Oksana felt more tears filling her eyes. *Must be the hormones*, she thought.

Vlad hadn't exactly been nice to her ever since she married his wife's brother. At first he compared her to Slava's first wife, the Saint. Then he tried to get fresh with her, which repulsed her. Since she wouldn't go for it, he paid her back by making sure she knew her place, having Slava control all the money, and making fun of her dream of being a couture shoe designer.

"Thank goodness I was outside on the patio talking to Mama," she spoke to herself as she normally did when finally left alone. "So lucky not to have seen it, and here I thought they were fighting over Flora again. I probably shouldn't have lost it and told Mama about the affair. I didn't have time to think about preparing her about Vlad. Who knew she'd find out about his death on Facebook, taking it so hard that she gave herself a fucking stroke." Oksana felt the familiar twinge of guilt creeping in, but she stopped the thought immediately. "No use blaming myself. Mama is old and sick."

Oksana took out her fake red-soled black booties, examining them with a critical eye. The shoes looked authentic enough, but the four-and-a-half inch heels were too thin and would surely get stuck in the grass. There was no way she would risk the damage knowing Vlad was going to be buried and not interned. Next, she thought of last season's resale boutique cobalt suede Sergio Rossi pumps, but she remembered that she had just worn them to a luncheon with the girls at the newly opened Waldorf Astoria in Beverly Hills. She took out the pretty silver-and-black Stuart Weitzman strappy sandals, but the medium-heeled sandal felt too American. She was beginning to feel that habitual dread. The Tory Birch two-tone spectator pump: too working girl. The Jimmy Choo platforms: too sexy. Maybe the Gucci's with the crazy curved heel?

She thought of the classic black-and-white spectator pumps she had drooled over at the Chanel boutique at the Winn Las Vegas and sighed with deep longing. Then it dawned on her: the Luciano Padovan peep-toe platforms. Of course, why not? No one had seen them yet. They would make just the right impression. As she got up to look for them, she remembered they were still in her mother's hallway closet, hidden among the Russian junk and rolls of paper products from Costco. Now she began to freak out for real, because she promised Maya that she would ride with her and the kids in the limo after the burial.

She took several deep yoga breaths and finished the content of her wine glass in a gulp. Someone had to run over to her mother's apartment and get them. She simply didn't have the time to get ready and drive over to West Side with the damn traffic.

Where was her husband when she needed him? Maybe she'd call Bozena and offer the caregiver extra money to bring the shoes right over, but who would sit with Mama? She was probably sleeping anyway. *Maybe I could call Bella for help*, she thought in desperation. *No, that sister-in-law of mine is too stuck-up and will only make fun of my passion for fashion. Intelligentsia, indeed: she's just a dentist, and as Mama says, not a real doctor. Who knew Yuri would turn out to be such a* podkobluchnik? She smiled at the word. *What a perfect description—a husband who literally lives under the heel of his wife's shoe. Well, I'll show her when my own designs are sold in Neiman's.*

All I need is for Maya to let me have the seed money and not charge her usual crazy interest. I know she would, if only Slava doesn't forbid her to loan me money. Who charges interest to family, anyway? No wonder people call her a fat bitch. The design drawings are ready, and they are hot, if I say so myself. I'll just have to be so good to her and help with everything now that's she's been left alone, without a man. She'll need me and feel obligated, and then I know I'll get the money for sure!

Maya was hungry. The longing for food was deeply seated in her belly, and it demanded immediate attention. It felt just like missing her parents and grandparents, like missing her homeland. The feelings of emptiness started in her gut and worked itself upward to her mouth. It ached, it nagged, it was stronger than her, and it always won. Half-awake, she had woken up after a few hours of dreamless sleep and slowly crawled out of bed. She didn't need to look at her cell screen to know it was still middle of the night. Keeping the lights off, she opened the bedroom door, making sure not to wake up Vlad, who wasn't snoring. If he'd wake up, he'd yell at her again about her "filthy" habit of night binging. She had learned to be as quiet as an army forward.

Maya entered the dark kitchen and opened the refrigerator. Oddly, it was empty of the usual goodies; then she remembered the Kiev Tort in the freezer and decided to thaw a slice in the microwave. She knew how to plug in more time than you need and then take the food out before the microwave would beep and wake up Vlad.

She struggled to slice a large enough piece. *Bliat,* she whispered to herself. They make ice-cream torts, don't they? She began to quickly swallow the sweet, creamy, frosty morsels, feeling both guilty and excited. The pleasure of it elated her mood.

Within seconds something went wrong. She had never experienced such a violent gut reaction, even during both pregnancies, which hadn't been exactly pleasant. Maya barely made it to the sink before she vomited the entire content of her stomach with such violence that she broke a sweat and almost passed out—and then it hit her. Vlad would never yell at her about her night eating again because he was dead. He was not sleeping off the latest hangover. He wasn't in bed at all. His body was being readied for the burial.

The kitchen lights went on, and Maya's best friend and boss, Svetlana, who was sleeping in the downstairs den, rushed in to help. Maya didn't have to ask for help when it came to Svetlana. She volunteered to help her get ready and ride along in the limo to the cemetery.

"*Bozhe Moi*, goodness, let me help you," Sveta pronounced loudly with a strong Eastern European accent. "You poor thing: why didn't you wake me up? I'd make you something to eat. You forgot you can't binge eat anymore. The balloon won't let you. I Can I make you some eggs? Maybe you'd better have some saltines and tea."

"I did forget," answered Maya, keeping her voice to a minimum. This was the big surprise she was holding on to until the cruise. While Vlad was away, she had a small balloon inflated in her stomach as an outpatient procedure. She wanted to prove to Vlad that this time she was serious about losing weight.

Maya had shared her decision with Oksana (who was her driver)—and of course Svetlana—because she had to take a few days off from work. The boys didn't notice, as they were preoccupied with their own lives. She'd already lost over fifteen pounds.

"Why are you whispering?"

"I don't know. I was starving and trying not to wake up Vlad," she moaned. She began to rock back and forth.

"My poor girl," Sveta wrapped her arms around Maya. Gently, she maneuvered her distraught friend toward the family room sofa.

"There, sit down—put your feet up and close your eyes. I'm putting the kettle on: ginger for gas or rose hips for nerves?"

Maya didn't answer, just shook her head in agreement. All at once, she came to and remembered the heartbreaking events of the last week. Normally, Jews—like Muslims—bury their dead quickly, but that was not possible.

It had taken a few days to get Vlad's body released because of the odd circumstances of his passing. Although he was pronounced dead on arrival (DOA), the head wound and the presence of a crapload of alcohol in his blood demanded further inquiry. The coroner insisted on a complete autopsy, including a chemical screening. The results were definitive: Vlad died of massive heart rupture; his blood alcohol was four times the legal limit. Maya suspected the tests would also show a presence of cocaine and some other party drugs he got into in Vegas. The worst of it was having to call the boys.

She was damn lucky to be surrounded by family and friends. Maya's brother, Slava, made the calls and met the boys at the hospital; unfortunately, they never got to see their father among the living again.

Slava pulled all the strings he could to get Vlad's body to the funeral home to prep for an open-casket viewing. Thank God she still had her brother. She didn't tell him too much, just enough to let him know about her plans.

For the first time in years, Maya refused to have anyone over to the house. Instead, she asked Oksana to make arrangements for a luncheon at her favorite, newly remodeled Russian/Armenian restaurant. She was done with the kitchen in more ways than one. She wished she could just disappear and mourn in private. She was angry at Vlad. She was enraged at his business partner Ken. She was infuriated with herself. She was scared. She was lost. She was finally free.

—⊗⊗⊗—

Jason didn't exactly enjoy working funerals, but when Sasha told him it would take place at the Hollywood Forever Cemetery, he told his mother he would gladly help with delivering and setting up.

The place was an absolute treasure of Hollywood history, just a few short blocks from famed Vine Street. Jason began to be obsessed with old Hollywood early on when his mom let him stay up late watching the Classic Movie channel, as they both waited for his dad to get back from another late night at work.

Like his mom, Jason loved classic movies—the perfect stars, the music, the choreography, the black-and-white moodiness, and of course, the fabulous décor and clothes. With his mother's encouragement, Jason began to take swing lessons and often met a few friends at the Lindy Loft. He was mad for the hundred-year-old building, the stunning views on the ninth floor, the artsy downtown scene. Who said LA didn't have a fresh cultural life to rival San Francisco, or even NYC? Well, maybe not yet, but it was moving in the right direction! All these hip new eateries had opened, not in snooty and tired Beverly Hills, but right smack in the middle of the Jewelry Mart and the Garment District.

The free monthly lessons were always followed by social dancing. The fun and camaraderie, the vintage cocktails and always the amazing, uplifting music made Jason both blissful and wistful for the glamour that was Hollywood. He was clearly born in the wrong time, but he was no longer alone as he had found his tribe. His friends teased him about inventing the time machine so he could go back. He dressed in vintage clothes he'd hunted down all the way south, in the funky city of Orange.

Jason attended concerts and joined in the expanding crowds at the cemetery's Movie Night. It was a bittersweet spot, too, because of memories of Avi—their "official" date and ensuing first romantic kiss. Too bad it was the last time he saw Avi in person. They texted back and forth a few times, made some vague plans, but nothing serious came out of it.

One good thing came out of his last fight with his grandfather. The old racist homophobe told him, dripping with venom, that Avi left LA and moved in with a "normal" woman he married. At least now, Jason understood it wasn't him, but what his mother wisely called "life circumstances."

Funny, it had taken so long for Jason to respond to Avi's advances, but once he committed to this new chapter of his personal life, he thought things would be different. Avi was a flirt all right, but he didn't discriminate between males and females, single or married, Israeli or not. The only positive thing that came out of the Avi fiasco as far as Jason was concerned was that he finally had it out with his grandfather, if you could even call him that, considering how he treated Sasha, the kindest, most loving, and the best of all people. In all fairness, Jason stopped thinking of Victor as family when he heard him scream at Sasha about being grateful that she was adopted and not his blood since she gave birth to him, a cock-sucking freak.

Jason still hadn't figured out how the old man found out, but at this point he didn't give a rat's ass, even though he knew the effect the terrible fight would have on his mother. It was about time that she stood up if not for herself, for her child.

The LA traffic was truly unexplainable. Jason was posting pics on Snap, tweeting and texting with friends, making plans to go dancing. Sasha was trying to stay calm, navigating the van filled with enough flower arrangements, heart-shaped easels, and plant-filled urns to decorate the entire section of the cemetery. Even with the air-conditioning turned to full blast, the floral scent was unbearable. Normally, she listened to classical KUSC or traffic updates, but not when Jason was around. She didn't want to distress him.

Within minutes of loading the van, she developed a piercing headache. Her eyes itched and watered, and she had a hard time not sneezing uncontrollably. By the time they made it through the usual nightmare of Santa Monica Boulevard traffic, she was praying to get the flowers out of her van.

It was only ten in the morning, but the line into Hollywood Memorial Park stretched way into the main drag, cutting through various ethnic sections. Here, Death herself didn't discriminate. There were Jewish and Eastern European Orthodox Christian sections and Thai communal burials. Several women tended to the heartbreaking work of picture-decorating the Armenian family plots. Of course, the tourists gathered around the old WASPY Hollywood crowd and the forever remembered luminaries.

The portraits on Cyrillic-marked granite or marble headstones were so realistic that one felt as if they were visiting a huge Russian nightclub party for the deceased. Some headstone monuments were marked with the names of the dead, buried back in the old country, as if the simple name acknowledgment could make up for the guilt of leaving their bones to turn into dust all alone.

Sasha made a quick right turn by the Thai section and parked in the designated spot near the main chapel. As if on cue, a rush of icy energy ran up and down her spine. She used to get distressed when the feeling hit, but by now it had become as normal as taking a deep breath. Although Sasha never said a word to anyone, she was able to feel the presence of a newly departed soul. In the beginning, she thought the answer was to avoid the cemetery, but after speaking to a psychic medium, who reassured her that she was safe, Sasha decided not to give up on that part of the flower business.

Sasha crossed herself again and said a little prayer, hoping she wouldn't feel Vlad's soul. *Come on,* she told herself, *it's time to pay both my respects and my debts.* It took a while to unload and set up the arrangements, but Sasha was a pro, and she had help from her son. She arranged for the music and placed a huge photograph of not-smiling Vlad right in front of his open casket. The beloved deceased looked damn good for a corpse; somehow his features appeared more refined without its usual alcohol- and drug-induced bloat, his complexion perfect instead of blotchy red.

Maya asked Oksana to choose his burial suit, and she chose a new gray-and-blue-checked obscenely expensive Zegna, still with the tags. Maya had never seen it, since apparently Vlad had an entire wardrobe of suits he never wore while with his family. He always told Maya and the kids that expensive clothes were just a waste of his hard-earned money. She had to practically force him to buy new underwear, let alone a four-thousand-dollar Italian suit! For some inexplicable reason seeing Vlad dressed in clothes that she hadn't bought enraged Maya even more than his sordid little affairs.

Just before the mourners began gathering outside, Sasha received a text asking her to meet Maya at the office. Since her job was done, she felt funny about staying for the service and the burial. She barely knew Vlad, and while her heart was aching for Maya and her children, she was aware of his sordid reputation and the painfully embarrassing situation with Flora. Sasha messaged her son to let him know she'd be a while. He responded immediately and told her to take her time because he wanted to visit his favorite Hollywood gravesite. Sasha remembered when Jason took her to see it: a serene, reflective pool and a marble resting place for the original movie stars, the Fairbanks—father and son, both named Douglas. She was still thinking of the Fairbanks graves when she walked to the cemetery office.

Maya sat in a dark leather chair, looking somehow smaller and encased in professional-widow black, from her comfort shoes and tights to the shapeless black frock and black head scarf. Her face was devoid of any makeup—not that she usually bothered with such nonsense. She looked composed.

"*Vot i ti Sashen'ka,* here you are," she addressed the florist who looked extremely uncomfortable as she approached the new widow.

"My condolences, dear," offered Sasha kindly as she kissed Maya's unlined cheek, her skin smooth and warm to the touch.

"*Spasibo,*" Maya responded, still looking down at her ring-free hands, habitually folded across her stomach. Sasha couldn't believe how Maya's body had shrunk.

"Everything is arranged, and it's just beautiful. In fact, it's perfect. The music will begin playing just after you and the boys enter the chapel. You asked me to choose, so I decided on Gregory Leps's 'A Peaceful Night, Gentlemen.' Is that all right with you? Jason will stay and supervise the flower transfer to the burial site," reported Sasha. "Of course, there won't be extra charges for any additional services."

"I'm sure you did your best, which is always perfect," said Maya blandly. She looked up and called out to Sveta, who stood quietly by the door. "Leps? That soul-sucker, ex-boozer—how fitting. Da, Vlad liked him. Leps is a *muzhik,* a real dude. I think I know the song." Maya began to hum softly off-key.

"The envelope with money is in your purse," she said, looked directly at Sveta. "I don't carry anything to the services," she explained to Sasha.

"Yes, I've got it right here," answered her friend as she brought the envelope over.

"Sasha, pull up the folding chair by the other door and sit next to me. We need to talk things over," ordered Maya. "Sveta, go outside first and make sure no one comes in," she continued with authority. "Please," she then added softly. Sveta smiled reassuringly and did as she was asked.

Wow, thought Sasha as she carried the folding chair over to Maya. *You'd think she owns this place. She's fortunate to have such a wonderful friend, especially during the bad days to come.*

"Look, I know we've never been friends," started Maya, still not looking at the visibly apprehensive Sasha, whose hands began to shake.

"Well, I don't know what to say, but . . ." Sasha began unconvincingly.

"Then just listen; don't talk," interrupted Maya. "I'll be blunt. You know I say it like it is. I don't understand you, but I respect you. Hell, I envy you with your gentle soul and your patience and your sunny spirit.

Hell, I envy you your husband. And I don't know how you've put up with your fucking evil old goat you call Father and your son being gay. Of course, you were adopted and have no idea about real family; it probably makes you a good American."

"Jason is not gay," spoke up Sasha. "And my father is moving to New York to be near his real son, Gary. I'm not going to stop him. I owe him a debt I can never repay for raising me, but I can't have him and Jason both in my life right now. And I love this country. It's given us freedom and safety." Sasha was deeply hurt by Maya's words, but not as hurt as she was by her last phone call with Papa, who told her with glee how grateful he was that Jason wasn't his blood.

"So, I'm getting on a plane and starting over. I'm not that old yet, right, Sasha?"

"No, Papa. Have a safe flight."

"Why shouldn't I have a safe flight? I could fly the plane by myself if I had to!"

"Of course, Papa."

"I guess I should tell you I'm going to miss you."

"You don't have to tell me anything you don't want to."

"*Horosho.* You're still a good girl, but that dirty cocksucker pedo son of yours is another story. Luckily, he's not any relation to my own grandchildren, Gary's kids."

"Stop! That's enough. I don't care about what you and Mama did for me—it doesn't give you the right to hate my child, who's been so good to you! We're finished. *Proschai.*" Papa had crossed the final line. If Sasha wouldn't stand up to him for herself, she would for her son, though Papa's leaving still hurt.

"Yes, yes, as you say. Look," Maya continued, speaking with a note of impatience, "I have only one thing to say. We're even. Your loan is paid in full as of right now. Here's some cash for delivering the flowers. And there's extra money, call it a service fee, for your son for helping and staying back to supervise."

"No . . . you're pulling my leg, right? Please don't joke. Are you sure?"

Sasha felt the heat of tears flowing freely, unable to contain her joy and shock. "*Spokoino*, Sasha. Relax. It's a done deal. You only had a few payments left anyway," explained the new widow.

Before Sasha could offer her profound gratitude, a loud noise outside made them both look toward the door.

A man pushed in, chased by a red-faced Sveta. It was Vlad's partner, Ken Bowman.

"You're a crazy commie bitch," he roared at Maya at the top of his lungs. "I'm going to destroy you and your fucking family. I'm calling the Feds. Who the hell do you think you are?"

Sasha was horrified and looked for a way out of the room. Maya merely sat there without blinking, looking straight ahead as he continued his diatribe, bending over her and spitting his saliva into the suddenly foul-smelling air.

"I would think before I speak, Kenchik," cautioned Maya, as Ken felt the barrel of a gun placed at the back of his head.

"*Spasibo, Svetik,*" she said. "Shh. *Spokoino.* Don't shoot yet. Let's give Ken a chance to calm down. I've been expecting him," Maya continued, eerily serene.

"Sit your sorry American ass down, Bowman," the widow ordered the stunned man. Sasha again tried to exit, but Sveta stopped her. "Stay and hear this. We need an unbiased witness," she said to the florist in Russian. Sasha didn't dare to disagree. "So, let's have a little chat before we bury the motherfucker," said Maya.

Ken, clearly taken aback by these unexpected developments, didn't respond. Sveta pushed the gun deeper into his scalp.

"Sit, dog!" Sveta commanded, showing her natural backbone. Sasha couldn't help but smile. This American had no idea what and who he was dealing with.

"Now you can speak!" spit out Maya.

"How dare you send your brother to Vegas and demand that I sell the business for pennies on the dollar?" Ken began, trying not to move his head.

"*Sell?* Who said anything about selling your business?" retorted Maya. "My brother's English is poor, and he has a heavy accent. You must have misunderstood."

"Oh, well . . . that's another story." The relieved man breathed out slowly so as not to trigger Sveta's gun. "I shouldn't have lost my temper. I'm sorry. It's been a hell of a few days."

"I'm glad you understand," said Maya, finally getting up. "As you see, despite having an accent, my English is perfect, since I came here knowing the proper British English and not your low-class dialect." Both Sveta and Sasha gasped. Maya continued, "Just so there's no misunderstanding, you will give my brother the entire Las Vegas operation, and I will allow you to keep 10 percent of the LA office, strictly out of respect to my dead husband."

"You're mad!"

"Perhaps."

"You'll never get away with this!"

"We'll see."

"I'll call the Feds. I'll call the State, you fucking, fat bitch. No wonder Vlad was getting ready to leave you! I'll file bankruptcy before you get your slimy fingers on my business! I'll make it my life's work to make sure you and your criminal family are deported. Go back to fucking Putin, where you belong, you dirty cunt!"

Ken was clearly unable to control his fury that this woman, a guest in *his* country, would dare to cross him. His threats and screams had an odd effect on the three women in the room.

Sasha, who abhorred violence and would do anything to avoid conflict, wished she and not Sveta held the gun. All the years of swallowing her pride for the sake of keeping the peace moved from her throat down to her hands as she clenched them into fists.

Sveta pulled back the trigger of the brand-new Taurus Curve 380. She was the only one with a legally obtained concealed weapons permit.

Only Maya remained composed. In fact, the more he threatened, the less she engaged. "You're repeating yourself, Kenchik. I'm getting bored. Shut him up, Svetochka, or we'll have an unsolved homicide on our hands. Look at poor Sasha: she's looks like she's about to blow him away all by her gentle self.

Sveta took her finger off her gun and bumped the back of Ken's head with its handle, hard enough to make him stop talking.

"Thank you! I tell you what. If you want to keep the entire LA business, since Vegas is not negotiable, let's say you pay me the money you owe, and we shake hands and part ways."

"I don't owe you anything. I paid Vlad every penny you loaned my wife plus the interest, which cost me plenty."

"Hah," Maya said, chuckling with such menace that shivers ran down Sasha's back. "Yes, you did pay off Flora's little loan, and I received the cash. The word is that the crap she gets shot up in her face really fucked her up. No, the money I'm talking about is a personal loan I made to your idiot son, Zack, to cover his gambling debts to the big boys. Let's say I collect two million US dollars in two days from you. Da, that should do it, although I prefer euros. Of course, I've got control of the business bank accounts, and my brother has already laid off all your hires. Guess you'll have to sell Flora's perfect house—hope she understands and loves you when you're broke. No worries, as you people like to say. This is America, after all—the land of opportunity where all your dreams can come true. You can always start again and get another piece of that disgusting apple pie. I hope you choke on it, along with your whore of a wife."

Ken was stunned. Thoughts rushed in and out of his head, but no words formed.

"No more name calling or threats? What? You don't believe me?"

Maya took out her phone and pushed the icon that saved her latest messages. The VMs started with a call from Zack asking Maya to tell her brother to get the creditors off his back. Several playbacks of messaages later, Ken's heart, already beating out of his chest, stopped as he heard his ass of a son beg "Aunty" Maya for a loan to cover his astronomical debt, swearing he would pay her back. The last message was addressed for Ken, and it read 9:00 a.m.

"Pops, I'm so sorry. I'm an idiot. I know. Please do as Auntie Maya says. They've got me. They will start cutting; I know they will. Please help me. I'll make it right, I swear. I'll work night and day to pay you back. I'll never step foot in another casino. Oh my God, you're not serious, no! Fuck! Daddy, they cut my ear. Oh fuck!" The voice message stopped abruptly.

Ken, as white as a sheet, began to cry into his hands. Maya got up slowly and approached him.

"Look, Bowman. I'm sorry it had to come to this, but it's the best thing for Zack. He won't ever forget this little incident, and he'll stay away from Vegas. It takes a true business mind and strong character to survive it. Think about my Vlad: you should have known him before. He was such a good boy, such a mensch. You think it was his heart that killed him? No. What did him in were you and your American dream. That's what killed him: the booze, the drugs, the whores, the gambling. You thought I didn't know about his lunacy with the fucking stripper?"

"No, I didn't know him then, and Flora didn't either. How could she have known about Vlad leaving you for a stripper? Her health became weak. The doctors said no stress. I couldn't tell her the truth about Vlad," said Ken bitterly, all his anger suddenly turned into hopeless despair.

"Of course you wouldn't upset Flora. That is the chief reason you still have a bit left of my respect: you're a devoted husband. Proper father, not so much. . . . Take control of your boy now, or next time it won't be a silly piece of his ear that's missing. I assume we have a deal?"

The distraught man felt Sveta remove the gun from the back of his neck and shook his head in the affirmative.

"What are you going to do about the baby?" Ken tried one last time to rattle Maya. He couldn't even get the satisfaction of that. She remained neutral.

"There is no baby. Looks like the dumb whore changed her mind about Vegas and went back to whatever Midwest village she crawled out of with a few bucks in her fake Hermes. Stupid bitch thought Vlad's gifts were real."

Ken just sat there, shaking his head. He was clearly outmaneuvered. *These Russian animals were professionals,* he thought.

"Dear, are you in there?" It was Flora. Maya gave a wordless signal to Sveta to open the door, giving Ken a few seconds to wipe his eyes and put on a strained smile to greet his wife.

"Yes, honey. I was just offering my condolences, and we got into some business talk. Sorry to take so long, sweetheart. Are you all right?" Addressing the young woman wearing jeans and a black blouse who followed behind Flora, he added, "Is she still dizzy, Liza?"

Maya whistled to herself and mumbled to Sasha in Russian, "Got to give it to him—he's a prince of a husband."

As Ken gave Flora a gentle hug, she looked directly at Maya with hate in her strangely sunken eyes. Always fit and augmented, today she looked skeletal and frail. Although her shiny red face was devoid of wrinkles, her recent illness made her look at least a decade older.

"Looks like you're feeling better. You look nice," Sasha complimented politely, trying to diffuse the palatable tension in the room.

"What the hell are you talking about? Are you blind? Look at me: I'm sick. I'm only here because I promised to support my husband," responded Flora, still dressed and accessorized to the hilt. "They think they're going to get away with crippling me and ruining my life? As soon as we find a good lawyer to take my case, we're suing the doctor for everything he's got! It's a conspiracy!"

Sasha and Sveta exchanged incredulous looks, and Maya rolled her eyes.

"She didn't want to stand with the mourners, and you were gone for too long, so I took her for a little walk to see the stars. We found the cartoon rabbit guy and Douglas Fairbanks!" interjected the young caregiver in heavily accented English. "You should see the Armenian section and all the pictures on the monuments. I cried when I saw those two poor young brothers," she said, sniffling and dabbing her overly made-up eyes. "I'm sorry for your loss," she said, turning to Maya. "He was so young, just like my papa." Repeating the most common Russian saying at funerals, she ended with, *"Zemlia emu pukhom."*

"Shut up, Leeza!" Flora barked at the girl. "You're not here to make friends. I need my pill and some alkaline water. I think we're done here. I have nothing more to say."

Not looking at Maya, Ken escorted his wife out.

The women were silent until the door closed. Maya took out her phone and texted someone for several minutes. After she was done, Sasha said, "I'm so sorry, Maya, but can I leave now?"

"Yes, you can go. I thank you for your service and loyalty," answered Maya. Sasha wanted to give her a customary kiss on both cheeks, but she couldn't make herself. She bowed her head and walked out into the blinding Southern California sunshine.

Sveta approached Maya and held her tight without a word, as Maya stared at the ceiling. Something in her broke. The tears had been shed; it was showtime.

"Let's go put that cocksucker into the dirt, and may he burn in hell," whispered Maya. "You know he was horrified of being in the ground. He wanted to be placed in the wall, with all the Hollywood stars yet."

'Don't say such horrible things, Mayechka. Forgive him. He's dead. He's paid his debt to this world. Let God and the saints judge him." Sveta shook her head, feeling Maya's pain and bitterness.

"Never!" Maya spit back emphatically. If I knew then what I know now, I'd have killed him with my own hands, better yet shot his balls off, just like Grandma Zina did to so many of her enemies.

"Forgive him. You're not doing it for Vlad. Forgive him for yourself and the boys . . ." pleaded Sveta, trying to talk some sense into her best friend and the love of her life.

"Not now—maybe not ever, and please don't ask me again. I appreciate everything you do for me, but not this. Back off."

"Okay, dear; I understand. Anything that helps you," Sveta agreed wisely. "Have you thought about going to Varna to my folk's beach flat with me? It wouldn't cost anything, just food. We'll go to Italy first, just as you always wanted and then take a few weeks and see how you like it there. I know how you love the Black Sea, and it's just a boat ride to Odessa. You'll love Bulgaria. You know I was born there, and then my father sent me to Moscow to study. It's so peaceful, and you can rest. The food is fresh, and I'll cook for you. You're losing so much weight so fast. You need extra vitamins to keep your strength up."

"I'm not hungry anymore," Maya said with a sense of wonderment. "Look, I can't leave with you right now. I mean, I don't know if I ever can. In any case, it will be a while. I must move us all to Vegas and set up the boys and my brother's family. I promised to back Oksana in her shoe design business. You know, she's great at it, and my brother can be such a stubborn mule. I think we'll make a fortune with her ideas." Maya took out a faded embroidered hanky from inside her bra and wiped her eyes. She was now her grandmother Zina, carrying old pieces of tear-stained cloth between her own breasts. "I'm sure there'll be some complications with Bowman. Vlad always warned me about American ex-military guys: lots of ego, very stupid. Wait till her majesty, Flora, finds out that her cushiony life is kaput. It will be a while, as I said."

"Of course, take your time. You know I'll never leave your side. I told everyone that you won't be back at the spa. Everyone sends their love, and they will miss you."

"Thank you again, but please don't count on me, Sveta. I can't promise you anything, let alone a life." Maya raised her eyebrows, looked in a framed mirror hanging on the office wall.

"I'll wait," Sveta responded quietly but firmly.

"Don't. I'm broken; he broke me, and now I must face them and pretend this cheating, disloyal piece of shit was the love of my life. You know I've known him since we were kids. I didn't like him at all; I should've gone with my first instinct. I've had it with being nice to these people who never had a kind word for me except when they needed to borrow money from Fat Maya or to sit at my table and pig out."

"I know. I ache for you."

"I know. Funny, I won't be Vlad's fat Maya anymore, but who will I be? *Nu idem*. That life has ended."

Sveta held out her hand to Maya and said, "Ne boisia. Don't be afraid. *Vse budet horosho*. Everything will work itself out. I'll wait for the new life to begin—for the both of us."

FINDING OKSANA

Six months later

THE SUMMER WAS long gone, Thanksgiving was just around the corner, but as usual, Southern California was experiencing an intense heat wave.

Oksana was choking. She thought her nose was probably broken, and her left eye was swollen shut. Her ribs hurt like hell, and her knuckles were scraped up. She had the presence of mind to spit out the blood quickly filling her mouth. The blood came out along with a broken tooth and a chunk of tissue.

Oksana raised her badly bruised hand to her face to see if there was more damage. A jolt of adrenalin prevented her from blacking out, but she was starting to shake as if she stood hatless in the middle of a Russian winter and not propped up against a furiously swaying palm tree. The Santa Ana winds had been blowing for days, and the air crackled with electricity. LA was bracing for a firestorm.

The only lucid thought in Oksana's mind was to find her phone and call Mama. Then she heard a ghastly scream. She wondered for a second who was screaming like a wounded cat. Recognizing her own voice, Oksana placed a blood-covered palm over her own mouth. Mama couldn't help her. Mama wasn't Mama anymore. Ever since her latest massive stroke a few months ago, Mama was stuck lying motionlessly in a state of suspended existence—not here and not there, as her father would say.

She thought of Yuri but remembered that he was supposed to have left for the desert. She didn't know exactly where—probably Palm Springs. Yuri was chasing after his wife, who had recently filed for a legal separation.

On a positive note, Oksana's brother's unexpected marital woes made her own challenges more bearable; although she still couldn't believe how her clever, cautious brother had gotten involved in a silly, Facebook flirtation with Bozena, their mother's former caregiver. Oksana suspected simple physical proximity was half the battle as far as the "other" woman was concerned. Bella was always busy at work or with her horses or whatever else she deemed more important than her husband, so Yuri had been spending a good deal of time at their mother's bedside, and Bozena took advantage of his devotion and Bella's absence.

It's not like Yuri and Bozena were having sex, but unfortunately there were some rather explicit photos. Bella was no fool. As soon as she saw the photos, she hired a forensic accountant, sold her dental practice for a great deal of money (all cash), and threw Yuri out of the house. At the moment Bella was on a writing sabbatical in the desert, and Yuri was trying to get his irate wife to forgive his foolishness and take him back.

Although on the surface Oksana was supportive, she was not optimistic. Bella was both stubborn and self-righteous. She was lucky to have such an amazing husband. Who in the hell would flip, considering the so-called unforgivable betrayal was a silly flirtation, a trifle of an inconsequential middle-age *romantika*?

Oksana couldn't very well turn to Maya, either. Considering what took place the last time they saw each other, Oksana had forbidden herself to even think about her monster of a sister-in-law. Based on what Oksana had seen with her own eyes, Avi was most likely dead. Come to think of it, she'd probably die as well—alone, murdered by her own legal spouse.

She began to feel faint and pinched herself hard to keep awake. Just then, she remembered that she had slid her second, "unofficial" phone inside one of her tall, over-the-knee boots she'd providentially put on that morning. It was a pocket-sized, reconditioned Alcatel GO flip phone she used exclusively to text Avi. Since it only cost her four bucks a month, the bill was paid out of Mama's checking account, meaning Slava couldn't snoop. The only problem with the flip model was that it didn't hold a charge; she prayed she had some battery time left. Avi was always yelling about her absentmindedness, and he was right. "If I get out of this situation alive, I'll change. I swear on my kids' health, I'll change," Oksana muttered to herself. She unzipped the gray suede Jimmy Choo boot. Despite the discomfort, she reached down, unfortunately smearing the beautiful satin lining with her blood. *"Bliat,"* she cursed out loud. *"Yob vashu mat!"* The stain on her newly purchased dream boots made her madder than the pain.

Miraculously, the little Alcatel was still there, although the battery only had 20 percent left. Oksana raked her spinning mind to come up with a name. She so wanted to call 911 and report that suka Slava to the police, but even in her state of shock, she knew better. She needed to calm down, try to reach her family, and only call the authorities as a last resort.

Bella, I'll text Bella. She will tell Yuri, and even if he's not there, she will get me help. She's not afraid of Slava or Maya. In the worst case, I'll ask her to call one of her doctor friends.

"Where am I?" she wondered out loud.

Gradually, Oksana got to her feet. Because she was dizzy, she had to use the trunk of a tree so she wouldn't fall. When her head stopped spinning, she looked around. The place was obviously a large neighborhood park. It was quiet because of the bad winds. Oksana noticed a scary-looking homeless woman sitting on a nearby bench. The vagrant was talking into thin air, rocking back and forth. She was clearly distressed, and she began hitting herself on the head, which was covered in a dirty rag.

Oh my God! What is she doing? Should I try and talk to her? Oksana stood still, gathering her strength. She tried not to take deep breaths but each intake hurt her rib cage. The wind was picking up, and she could swear she smelled something burning. Holding her right side with her left hand, she slowly made her way over to the bench. Not wanting to agitate the woman, she approached bit by bit. Once there, Oksana sat on the other side of the bench, not saying a word. She took a few more breaths, but kept silent, hoping the woman wouldn't freak out—at least not more than she already was. The two women, bearing a strange resemblance to each other, sat in silence for a while.

After time had passed—Oksana couldn't tell how long—a young Mexican girl approached, her thick, raven-black hair blowing in the wind. She was pushing a baby carriage up the considerable slope. As she walked past the bench, she deliberately avoided looking at the two women.

This was her chance, so Oksana called out to her in Spanish. Oksana was pretty good with languages, and since most of the LA's Garment District manufacturing workers were Hispanic, it made sense to focus on her conversational skills, rather than book Spanish. *"Hola, muchacha! Puedes ayudarme por favor?* Can you help me?" she added in English, just in case.

The girl looked back at Oksana in surprise and answered, "Si, senora." *"Habla Ingles?"*

"*Si.* I speak."

"*Bueno. I had el accidente. Donde estoy?*"

"We are in Elysian Park."

"Oh, thank God—near Dodgers' stadium?"

"*Si,* you can see it, if you want."

"*Gracias,* that's all I wanted to know. I'll get mi esposo to pick me up here."

"Okay." The girl shrugged her shoulders and walked away. Oksana took out the phone and sent a text to both her brother and Bella, all the time keeping her eyes on the woman sitting on the other side of the bench. "BDLY HURT SOS LA Elysian Park Bench, NEEED YOU," she typed quickly and then turned off the phone to save the remaining battery.

Suddenly the homeless woman got up, leaving behind a suspicious wet spot. Oksana was horrified and got ready to be attacked, but the poor soul walked away without giving her a glance. Oksana closed her eyes and began to pray she would be found alive. She hoped someone up there was listening.

—————— ❧ ——————

The late autumn day had started with fantastic news. The shoe production was going smoothly. It was beginning to look like Avi's hard work and connections would pay off in a big way. Oksana's whimsical and reasonably priced line was about to be picked up by a prominent TV shopping network. The message from the network asked Oksana and Avi to fly to the East Coast, where the pair would meet with management and arrange a premier show. If everything went according to plan, the premier would come just in time for their shoe promotion day in the upcoming spring season.

The friends and now business partners decided to celebrate with a nice early dinner at one of downtown LA's popular hipster restaurants, Redbird. Avi loved the location and the chicken pot pie. He also thought it was too funny to put an eating establishment inside the rectory of a former cathedral. LA was a weird place, all right.

Oksana couldn't care less about the trendy, "new" American dishes, but her shoes were exactly what the social media influencers who frequented Redbird, would tweet or post on Instagram. She took extra care to wear a pair that was both unique and in your face. Several times in the past, compliments had turned into posts. One time, a girl asked to be directed to her online store and bought three pairs of the same style in different colors!

Stupidly, Oksana made a huge mistake and texted her itinerary to the babysitter. She was on cloud nine and not thinking clearly. Avi wanted to use a ride-sharing company, but Oksana asked him to drive so he could drop her off at home after their little celebration.

Somehow, the information got back to Slava, and he intercepted the pair just as they left the office for the restaurant. Oksana couldn't believe her eyes when she recognized Slava's personal bodyguard/driver. *No wonder bad things happen in parking garages,* she thought just before all hell broke loose.

Kicking, biting, scratching, and making as much noise as she could, Oksana was still shoved into one of Slava's goons' SUVs. She put up quite a fuss, but unfortunately, it didn't make a difference when one of Slava's cocksuckers lost patience and threw a full-fisted punch, knocking her out.

In the meantime, Slava sat in the back seat of his Range Rover, observing his men doing the job he paid them to do. When he saw one of them hit Oksana in the face, he exited his vehicle before thinking. Slava didn't intend for his wayward wife to get physically hurt. His plan involved teaching a lesson by scaring Oksana out of her dim-witted head. He had given his men orders to drive her around and then drop her at a nearby park, where he could pick her up an hour or so later. His plans, however, did include getting rid of her "partner" once and for all.

It never occurred to Slava that Oksana would fight back. Her fucking Krav Mag training must have kicked in. That'd teach him a lesson. Never again would he lose control over what was rightfully his!

The Israeli saw Slava exiting the Rover and charged him, bloodied, his clothes torn, but with an expression on his face that would scare Batman. A jolt of adrenalin hit Slava so hard that he almost shit his pants. Slava's men—who were supposed to have pistol-whipped Avi into a pulp, were both left on their asses. Avi had fought them like a lion. Slava wasn't exactly a pussy, but the Krav Mag instructor posed a lethal threat. Slava barely had the chance to draw his weapon. He shot Avi at close range in the chest. Avi continued lunging at Slava, but eventually dropped to his knees and lost consciousness.

Back in the SUV, Oksana's arms and mouth were bound with duct tape. She was driven around and then dumped in a park, where exactly she didn't know. The tape was unceremoniously yanked off, and she was told in no uncertain terms that if she even thought about going to the police, she'd never see her children again. The goons drove off, leaving the bruised and terrified woman to fend for herself.

For the past year, Oksana had been working alongside Avi in downtown LA's historic garment district. Thanks to Maya loaning Oksana a fair amount of seed money, they were able to rent a small but well-furnished office in a multistory historical building. Oksana didn't need the entire office for her work, but Avi said they needed a proper place where they could meet and greet buyers and potential "angel" investors interested in their up-and-coming shoe manufacturing company.

Avi was right: Oksana's design ideas were gold. Deprived of her mother's crippling criticisms and put downs, Oksana blossomed not only professionally, but also personally. She met other designers and creative folks who accepted and admired her work. When she apologized for being a little late or acting "spacey," no one labeled her stupid or useless. In fact, everyone expected her creative brain to be, well, just different. She had found her tribe.

Step by step, one design at a time, Oksana took to the business with such a natural verve and so much passion that even her doubting husband was impressed. He was not so impressed with Oksana's newly discovered confidence. When he warned her to get rid of Avi or else, Oksana shocked him by refusing to follow his orders and instead asked for a divorce. Optimistic and high on her new possibilities, she flew to Las Vegas to plead her case before Maya. For once, Avi and Yuri agreed and tried to discourage the meeting.

Sitting alone in the park, Oksana began to cry, worried she'd never see either of them again. She went back in time, rehashing the Vegas trip and thinking what she did wrong to deserve such a terrible ending.

In all the years of marriage to Slava, Oksana never went anywhere by herself, let alone fly to Vegas. She asked Norma, her factory manager's wife, to watch the kids. Norma was an amazing mom, and she was happy to make the extra cash. Oksana dressed in skinny black Joe's Jeans, a velvet red-and-plum Drifter hoody, accessorized with her own brand, a newly manufactured pair of red-and-white booties lined in synthetic fur. The booties were not only chic, but so comfortable that Oksana was sure she could spend an entire day of travel without pain. Avi said it was as if Luciano Padovan and Ugg's had a kid, and he was right.

She put two pairs of hand-embroidered flats (a gift for Maya, who didn't wear heels) into her camo Lug. The bag was nice and light since it would most likely be just a day trip, but Oksana was prepared for an overnight visit too. She brought a change of clothes, a set of cute PJs, and a few personal items. Norma told her she'd stay overnight with the girls if need be.

The economy Jet Blue flight left Long Beach Airport right on time. Oksana planned on having lunch at Maya's new place. If Maya insisted, she'd change the flight. If not, she'd turn around and go back to LA that evening.

Avi was both worried and pissed off when Oksana told him that she was going alone, insisting that he at least drive her. They argued all the way down the south 405. Once on the plane, she had to turn off her phone, since Avi wouldn't stop his barrage of texts. He was scared for both of them.

Unbeknownst to Oksana, who was having a blast, drinking Pinot Grigio and chatting with another passenger, a fun-loving Arizona woman in the next seat, Avi called the Krav Mag studio. He needed a backup plan in case Oksana couldn't get through to her cunt of a sister-in-law. Avi had very little faith in Oksana's judgment. She was simply too stupid to see people clearly.

He wasn't about to walk away when his dream was so close; he could smell the Mediterranean air and taste the grilled octopus tapas. Still, he was a practical man with realistic expectations and many years of bad luck.

"Hey, it's me," he greeted the man on the other end of the line.

"Hey, yourself."

"Remember I told you I was expecting trouble from her family?"

"Yeah."

"Well, it's here, and I may need your help."

"Anything."

"Do you still have connections with your friend?"

"Affirmative."

"I want a meeting."

"Not a good idea."

"Then you are my point man."

"Affirmative."

"I have some valuable info about hubby and the business."

"I'm listening."

"I'm keeping it close to the vest, but I will use it if they come after me. I'm sending a package to you at the studio, just in case I'm, well, disabled in any way."

"I will receive it and do the right thing."

"*Toda, amigo.*"

"*Ze beseder, amigo.* It's OK."

After just an hour, including twenty minutes of gut-wrenching turbulence over the desert, Oksana's plane landed at McCarran International Airport. Oksana, still nauseous and upset by the last minutes of the flight, practically ran off the plane. She texted Maya while on the toilet. There was no response. She took her time leaving the terminal and then waited to be picked up. She sent two more texts, just in case Maya didn't get the message. Half an hour later, when Oksana was starting to panic, Maya responded. "*Vozmi* Uber. Red Rock Casino. Pool."

Oksana was perplexed, but not wanting to start the visit on a negative note, she answered, "*Vozmu* Uber. Can't wait. xoxoxoxo."

No matter what it took, Oksana made up her mind to talk with Maya without even the slight chance of running into Slava, so she flew to Vegas to meet her. She was sure once she opened up completely, including about the physical abuse, Maya would understand and take her side in the upcoming divorce, considering that Oksana had been both a devoted sister and a true friend to Maya, especially since Vlad's death. Of course, she didn't expect 100 percent support—just Maya's blessing. After all, she was a woman, and a woman who suffered in a bad marriage. She wouldn't allow scary thoughts to spoil the visit, plus she knew Maya had no place for weakness.

Maya lounged comfortably in one of the nineteen private poolside cabanas at the Red Rock, sipping on a tall tequila and soda with mint and lime. The red décor wasn't entirely to her liking, but privacy was.

Her hair was damp and her angular face makeup free. (Sometimes, catching her own reflection in a store window, Maya would cringe, not recognizing her features.) She had just finished several exotic spa treatments, including a hot stone massage at the Red Rock Spa. Previously never one to pay a penny for beauty treatments, Maya had now become a spa-aholic. The massive post-surgical weight loss changed how she felt about her body, and not in a positive way. Even at her highest weight, Maya liked her smooth, plump skin, free of stretch marks, and her full breasts, now sadly deflated. No one had told her about that!

She was informed of possible hair loss, a sagging face, and bad runs. Always pragmatic, Maya dealt with those issues head-on. She even contacted Flora's fancy dermatologist for some injections to restore some of the loss of volume around her mouth. She had Sveta cut her formally lustrous hair into a sassy Kaneki Ken style and began to use expensive hair-growth products.

There was one more thing on her mind. The gastro surgeon neglected to give Maya a heads-up about the possibility of a diminished sex drive. Maybe it didn't matter to others who'd given up on fucking long ago, but sex was always a priority with Maya. Hell, she lost her virginity during the summer before she turned fourteen and never looked back. She was one of the lucky ones—her first lover, a first-year Odessa University student from West Africa, was as gorgeous as he was tender, and first-time sex was spectacular. Maya was proud to have crossed the threshold from girl to woman and proudly shared her experience with her grandmother.

Well, that was then, as she told Sveta. Not that she hadn't tried—several months after Vlad's death, Maya went to bed with one of her new Vegas employees, a great-looking hunk of a local contractor turned Maya's personal driver. She had always fantasized about Latin lovers, and Esteban didn't disappoint. It was Maya who couldn't relax. For the first time in her life, Maya, who used to pop like a firecracker just by squeezing her thighs, didn't orgasm, and it bothered her more than she would even admit to herself. She used to make fun of women like her: skinny and frigid.

So, until the pounds of excess skin was cut off her body and her breasts lifted, spa treatments would have to do. She needed to be touched and not judged for what she looked like under her clothing. Vegas was a perfect place to indulge her new obsession. She was barely out of the official mourning period and not even thinking of having regular sex, but a little light action in the sack would be much appreciated.

Dressed comfortably, Maya wore a long, flowing silk dress by Australian designer Camilla, and Hermes flip-flops. The dress and silly shoes were both a gift from Sveta. Maya no longer needed to cover her fat, but the massive amount of loose skin bothered her enough to schedule a full body lift. The surgery would take place back in LA. The plan was for Maya to recover near her doctor, who recommended a live-in nursing staff. Once the plastic surgeon gave her the green light, Maya agreed to finally take a proper vacation, possibly to Europe. She decided to be accompanied by her sons, maybe the boys' girlfriends, and her beloved brother, Slava.

Sveta was not invited. She was becoming a nuisance, always telling Maya what's right and what's wrong, who to forgive, and hovering, hovering, hovering. Maya had put up with enough crap from her husband. There was no way in hell she would repeat the same mistakes—and with a woman yet.

Oksana wasn't going to Europe either; she had been on Maya's shit list for months. In fact, Maya refused to let Oksana near the Las Vegas family house.

The house was located outside of the Vegas strip in Summerlin, at the edge of the stunning Red Rock National Conservation Area. Once the messy business with Ken was over, Maya ended up spending half of her time in Las Vegas. She also sold her LA home, where Vlad took his last breath, and bought a large, airy condominium on the border of Beverly Hills and West Hollywood so the boys would still have a place for their friends.

Maya fell in love with the Vegas house from the day she first saw the models. The over-four-thousand-square feet of beautifully designed space overlooked the Las Vegas Valley to the east, meaning she could enjoy a glorious sunrise along with the city lights. Maya single-handedly chose all the luxury upgrades to the six bedrooms and six bathrooms, thinking she would probably sell the place and make a nice little profit. *Hell,* she thought, *it was cheap, the price of a one-bedroom condo in West LA, so why not go for it?*

The biggest change, though, wasn't the house itself, but the fact that everything inside and outside was hers and hers alone. She didn't have to please Vlad or take anyone else's needs into consideration. For the very first time in her life, she was completely free to do as she pleased. She even felt different—reenergized and relaxed. If only her old life would let her be, particularly her brother's marital problems. She worried about Slava and his temper, which had gotten him into a shitload of trouble in the past. If he lost control with Avi, who knew if he could stay in the States.

When Oksana insisted on seeing her face-to-face, Maya was not happy. She tried hard to get out of it. Slava and the kids were her priority, not this viper who dared to test Maya's loyalty to her own blood. Unfortunately, Oksana wouldn't let go and kept pestering her. When Maya complained to Slava about it, he said his wife was just being a drama queen. Maya finally agreed to a quick lunch on neutral ground, but nothing more. Never one to care about hurt feelings, Maya made it clear to Oksana that she was not welcome until she fired Avi, became a better wife and mother, and put thoughts of divorce out of her head.

When Maya saw the smiling, overdressed Oksana, her stomach turned, and she muttered under her breath, "Fake cunt."

"Here you are! I found you!" Oksana chirped loudly in English. "You look gorgeous! New dress?" she continued, after giving Maya an awkward hug and kissing her on both cheeks.

"*Privet,*" Maya replied, uncharacteristically cold.

"*Skuchala!* We all sure miss you!" Oksana said, not missing a beat.

"Sure, well . . . I have to be here with all the business interests and to keep an eye on Ken's friends."

"Of course! We understand. Still, I miss coming for coffee and your cakes and those cream puffs. Yummy!"

"I don't bake anymore. In fact, I'm not in the kitchen much at all anymore," Maya responded with clear irritation.

"So, how are the boys?" Oksana wisely changed the subject.

"Fine. Cut the crap, Oksana. Why make a trip, and by yourself, too— surely not for my cream puffs?"

"*Mayechka!* Why are you angry with me? What wrong have I done? I've always been devoted to you!" Oksana began to tear up.

"Stop with the crocodile tears. What do you want? I'm not inclined to make any more investments in your business until you come to your senses."

"I don't want money," Oksana said, bristling, and then softened her tone of voice. "I mean, thank you for believing in us, but as a matter of fact, the company is doing fantastic. We've been working day and night, and our shoes are about to be sold on TV! Avi's connections are paying off! Isn't that amazing?"

"TV shopping, hey? Avi's connections, you say? Well, I'm glad he's good for something other than causing problems. It looks like you'll be able to repay my outlay sooner rather than later. So, if it's not the money that put you on the plane, then what?" Maya's tone darkened.

Terrified, Oksana swallowed hard, and for a brief second, she considered making up some excuse, but she knew of no other way but forward. She looked down at her hands and took a deep breath. It was now or never.

"I don't want to upset you or worry you, but it's not the business that's hurting me; it's your brother. He won't let me go," she spit out in one breath.

"Go? Where you going?" Maya said menacingly.

"You know what I mean. You know Slava . . . we've been having problems. He's so mean to me."

"All marriages have problems."

"Yes, but you should understand more than anyone how painful it is to be married to a . . ."

"Married to a what? Are you saying something derogative about my dead husband? I wouldn't if I were you," Maya responded blandly, taking a large sip out of her tumbler.

"Of course not! I was just remembering everything you went through with him."

"Precisely my point: went through, not abandoned my responsibilities or turned to another man, let alone a man with—how shall I say it—an untraditional sexual orientation." Maya began lecturing Oksana. "You should wash my brother's feet and drink the water for the way he puts up with your shoes drivel. And now, when you finally can bring some profit to the family, you want your freedom? You must be not only dense, but crazy. I suggest you think and come to your senses. Do you want to lose your children?"

"Avi is not his sexual preferences. He is a wonderful human being. He is my business partner and my best friend! I would rather give up the business than do it without him, and I'm not going to lose my children!" Oksana said with newfound assertiveness.

"*Aga,* I see how it is. Slava was right—you are whoring around behind his back."

"How can you say that after all we've been through? Forget it! You know what? I'm going to divorce your fucking nightmare of a brother with or without your blessing. I've retained an attorney—an American attorney, and he is not afraid of you low-life criminals! I have pictures to prove Slava's been beating me, and I have doctors' records too! I wanted to divorce him nicely. Everyone told me about you people, but I chose not to believe them. My bad. Maybe I am stupid, but I'm not crazy. I will not stay with a criminal and an abuser!" Oksana didn't wait for Maya to respond. She jumped to her feet, spilling her water, and stormed off.

Maya shook her head, pursed her lips, and reached for the phone. *"Eto ya."*

"Something's up?"

"Possibly."

"Who?"

"I'm at the Red Rock. Your spoiled whore of a wife just stormed off."

"What the fuck? She flew to Vegas to see you?"

"Yep. I think she was afraid of running into you. She was also trying to manipulate my feelings. Well, she was barking at the wrong militiaman. When I didn't bite, she left in a huff."

"So, what do you think I should do?"

"Nothing too drastic, but she and that fag pedo need to be taught respect. Nothing drastic, though, you hear me, Slava?"

"Da, I heard you."

"I love you. You are my blood. Remember what babushka Zina taught us: it's just you and me against them all."

"I remember."

<hr />

The Santa Ana winds wouldn't die down; if anything, they had strengthened. The air smelled like dried beech wood and negative ions. Some time had passed, but Oksana couldn't tell precisely how long. She didn't have the strength to get up, so she continued to sit on the bench, listening to the howling winds rustling through the trees and feeling the ions brush against her sensitive-to-the-touch skin. Eventually she began to drift off.

"Hey, sleeping beauty, time to wake up! *Davai!"* Oksana felt a hand shaking her awake. Her head hurt worse than before, and she was sick to her stomach again. She forced herself to focus on the dark shadow blocking the sun. Here it is, she thought. Death.

A jolt of adrenalin did the trick, and she screamed.

"Ti shto, dura? Ohuela?" The shadow cursed in Russian. "It's me, Svetlana. Maya's friend. I was sent to pick you up and take you home."

"Svetlana?"

"Da."

"Did she send you to finish me off?"

"Who?"

"Maya!"

"You're crazy: of course not! Slava called and said he and your dick wand Avi got into a fight, and you freaked out and ran."

"I don't understand. How did she know where I was?"

"You really are as stupid as everyone says. Slava put a tracer on you. He's always kept an eye on what's belongs to him. He called Maya and told him where you were. Since she won't be back in LA until the weekend, she called me and asked me to pick you up and drive you home. Slava is waiting."

Oksana put her head down on her lap and began to scream. There were no tears left.

"Up you go," Sveta said, managing to pull Oksana to her feet. "I don't have all day. Some of us work for a living, not play with colored pencils. Let's get you home."

"No, stop! I want to see Avi!" Oksana finally came alive. "Take me to the police station. I want to make a statement! There's been a murder and kidnapping!"

"What murder? What kidnapping? You're fine. Who told you to fight Slava's co-workers? They were just trying to help you. Your Jew is fine, too—just a little bruised. Don't pretend that you didn't know he was wearing a vest. You should be worrying about your husband! Your fucking boyfriend attacked him. You're lucky he was carrying. If something happened to Slava, Maya would make sure that you and your pimp would die a slow and painful death."

"I don't believe a word out of your lying lips. It was Slava and his goons who attacked us! Let me go, you bitch!" Oksana mustered just enough strength to slap Sveta, narrowly missing her eye. "I demand to call Avi!"

"As a matter of fact, I have a message from your Avi. You are not to contact him again. As soon as it can be arranged, he'll be on his way to

Europe: Spain or somewhere like that. He and Maya came to an agreement. Amazing what money can do . . ."

"I don't believe you. Avi would never abandon me and the business. This is our dream."

"Dream, hey? Well, dreams change—just ask me."

"Help, help! Call the police!" Oksana began to scream at the top of her lungs, thrashing about like a fish running out of oxygen.

"Oh no, you don't!" Sveta didn't want to resort to violence, and she had prepared for potential resistance by bringing with her a small syringe filled with a mild tranquilizer. Sveta, the taller of the two women, grabbed Oksana and quickly gave her a shot on the side of her neck. It took just a few seconds for the smaller woman to calm down. Seeing that she couldn't walk without assistance, Sveta used her considerable strength to drag her back to the car. She buckled Oksana in the passenger seat. Not wanting to take a chance, Sveta also tied her hands together. "You're going to sit next to me, so I can keep an eye on you, and if you even think of moving, I'll use something stronger than a little valium."

Oksana didn't respond, the trauma of being physically hurt, scared, and drugged finally taking the last drop of fight out of her. She closed her eyes and fell into a dreamless state, hoping to never wake up.

"Finally. That's a good girl, "Sveta took a relieved breath and dialed Maya. *"Vse. Ona so mnoi,"* she reassured Maya.

"Good. Glad it went well. *Spasibo.*"

"No thanks necessary. You know I'll do anything for you."

THE BLUE TATAR

YURI DETESTED THE Southern California desert. He hated the dry heat, the dry winds, and the never-ending summer. He suspected that was the exact reason his estranged wife chose to lease a house in Indian Wells. The drive from West Los Angeles was taking too long, thanks to the fucking winds. He was expecting traffic, but in addition to cars, Interstate 10 was jammed with trucks on their way to Arizona or New Mexico or somewhere back east.

Yuri longed for summer rain or early winter snow or the St. Petersburg fog that would soothe his skin. He dreamed of being enveloped by the sea mist that reminded him of being wrapped in his mother's fine Siberian shawl—anything but these dry fire winds. His skin itched and his eyes were running. He needed to pull over and take his allergy meds.

Funny, he never had any problems growing up in the North. It didn't matter how much of his life was spent in sunburned California; it would never be home. It simply didn't smell right. He remembered reading something similar to the grand ballet diva, Galina Ulanova, said. She had been forced to move to Moscow, leaving her beloved St. Petersburg, then Leningrad, behind. Even after forty years, she said she never got used to not smelling her city. Maybe that had been the problem with him all along, being married to a more successful, domineering mate. He was a Northerner through and through, self-contained, subdued, while Bella was all explosive Southern emotion and drama. Still, he couldn't imagine life without her.

Bella, always a class act, didn't share details with their daughters, but somehow, they found out about his asinine flirtation with Bozena. They were firmly on the side of their mother, calling him out on what they said was even worse than drunken sex with a stranger—an "emotional affair," something unforgivable. Yuri wasn't exactly surprised, but their reaction hurt like hell.

If Bella takes me back, I'll take her on that Scandinavian cruise she'd been talking about for a long while. Let Oksana take care of Mama for once. I swear I don't care how much it'll cost me, if only she'll take me back. She must. I know she still loves me! And what did I do that is so unforgivable? I never cheated on her. Damn her neurotic demands and her obsession with absolute loyalty. Like Papa always said, "Woman, if you want fidelity, get a dog." Christ, I hope it's not too late. It can't be. I will make her understand.

The traffic went from bad to worse. Yuri barely had a second to slam on the brakes. When he looked down at his traffic phone app, he saw indications of a dead stop ahead. What now? He looked around and noticed smoke rising over the hills to his left. The winds had picked up to the point that they were affecting visibility. He considered exiting the freeway, but there were too many big trucks attempting to do the same because it was now just too dangerous for high-profile vehicles.

That must be it. They're rerouting the entire freeway. Yuri began to laugh. *Maybe it's for the best I don't see her until she comes to her senses,* he thought; then stopped himself from being a coward. *No. I must go get her. If I turn back now, she will be right about us ending. It's been too long as it is. It's now or never.* He reached out for his phone and sent a message to his sister.

"OMW to Bella. Trf. Nightmare. Take care of Mama for me. Back with Bella."

Over two nerve-wracking hours later, starving and badly needing to urinate, Yuri finally made it past Palm Springs. The windswept Coachella Valley spread out in front of him, covered with as much sand and desert vegetation as the ever-encroaching residential communities with their golf courses and unsightly strip malls.

Cathedral City, Rancho Mirage, and Palm Desert rolled by. Finally, about fifteen minutes later, Yuri exited I-10 at Washington. Slightly familiar with the area, having had several business-related tennis matches at Tennis Gardens, the Indian Wells premier facility, Yuri turned off his phone. He drove straight toward the mountains surrounding the area. Oddly, the winds calmed down and the air cleared well enough that he could see the stunning beauty of the Santa Rosa and neighboring San Jacinto ranges in the setting sunlight.

Years ago, he tried to work with an older American dentist who belonged to the ritzy Indian Wells Golf Club with its host of famous and not-so-famous "rich" millionaires or "poor" billionaires. The dentist made him feel like a loser. He insisted on name-dropping and showing off "the" golf club to Yuri, who frankly had no interest in either golf or the fucking old rich guys who spent their remaining days on the greens and at the bar.

Predictably, since it was Bella who made the introductions, Yuri told his wife to butt out and let him find his own clients. They fought and then, after days of not speaking, had wild sex in the bathroom while his mother was taking a nap.

He stopped at the gas station to use the restroom and get an iced frappuccino, not knowing if and how he would be greeted by his wife. His stomach was in knots and his mouth was dry. Yuri was self-righteous and determined. Yuri was desperate.

He turned on his phone and pulled up the info. Getting Bella's new address from their daughter, Polina, took a lot of persistence, including some emotional blackmail, and only after he swore he wouldn't reveal his source.

He made a right turn into the residential neighborhood and was immediately taken aback by its charm. *Hmm . . . a one-story with no security gates, no fancy clubhouse or communal pool? No cookie-cutter Mediterranean architecture? What is she up to now? Maybe Polina is playing a trick on me? No, this is the correct address. There's her Tesla in the side carport, and it's plugged in.*

Yuri parked on the street, slightly across from the unimpressive, one-story gray-and-white L-shaped house, although there was plenty of space on the faded flagstone-trimmed two-car driveway. The house wasn't even a hip mid-century bungalow, and it probably hadn't been remodeled since Nixon. *Clearly Bella must be having money problems.* Taking a relieved breath out, he allowed himself to feel more hopeful than he had for months.

Opening the car door, Yuri's senses were overwhelmed by the sweet scent of honeysuckle and refreshing citrus. Bella's rental was covered by out-of-control multicolored bougainvillea, lemon trees, various species of mature cacti, and huge yellow rosebushes, still in full bloom. Two gently swaying date palms completed the unexpected picture. So unlike their

172 | THE BLUE TATAR

glamorous, perfectly landscaped house, this property was a complete mess—a glorious, romantic mess—and Yuri felt rare tears burn his eyes and his throat.

He opened the trunk and took out a large, refrigerated shopper. He couldn't very well show up empty-handed. Inside was a box of Ukrainian chocolates, Bella's favorite childhood treat. Since there were no Russian stores in the area, Yuri also thought Bella would enjoy something comforting and had purchased two bags of frozen dumplings—one, veal and chicken *pelmeni*, and the other, sour kraut-filled *vareniki*. Country cheese and sour cream, along with a small package of fresh dill, completed his gifts. He probably should have brought flowers, but he couldn't bring himself to spend money on something that would wilt in the desert heat.

The front door was located at the end of a long walkway, behind a rusty, no longer white iron gate. To his utter amazement, the gate wasn't locked, so Yuri pushed it open and let it close by itself. Bella was a fanatic about security. Something must have made her lose her mind, and it wasn't him. She refused to see him face-to-face. All communications were done by email, openly copied to her attorney. To Bella's chagrin, Yuri refused to hire his own attorney. What he saw as not giving up on their marriage, she saw as not taking her seriously. Several months dragged by until Yuri made up his mind to put an end to their separation once and for all.

He rang the bell. An older Asian woman, possibly of Philippine origin, opened the door. Yuri cringed. No more employing hot young Eastern European women. It was yet another reminder.

"Hello, I am Doctor Bella's husband," he said carefully with a shadow of a tense, if polite, smile.

"Hello," the woman answered, smiling back at him, revealing a wide gap between her two front teeth. The day was getting weirder by the minute. Bella would never allow anyone in her employment to have bad teeth—it was bad for business.

"Is my wife at home?" he asked the woman.

"No. Lady doctor is riding, but Dora is home."

"You mean Bella's mother?" Yuri was surprised yet again. Just then he heard his mother-in-law's voice ask the woman who was at the door.

"It's me, Yuri," he raised his voice so she'd hear him. "Can I come in?" he added in Russian.

"*Yurochka!* Come in! Of course, come right in, my boy."

Yuri took a deep breath. Relieved she didn't tell him to get lost, he entered the front room, rubbing his eyes. The contrast between the brightness outside and the dimness inside blurred his vision. The space was much bigger than he expected. It was a long room divided into two distinct spaces. He could barely see the outside, but it looked like the property faced golf greens.

When his eyes adjusted, Yuri couldn't believe what he saw. An Arclight Billiards table! He'd been drooling over one for years. Bella placed it right in the middle of the living space. The customized table had all the bells and whistles, including dark-lacquered trim and aqua-colored cloth. The table was gently lit by a skylight. It was clearly a man cave of a playroom. On the big wall, his astonishing wife had hung a forest-green, pub-style dartboard—right above a funky fifties' diner-style jukebox and a small card table with two club chairs. The entire front room was decorated like an English pub with horse prints and a gray-and-blue swordfish, clearly a fishing trophy, mounted on the opposite wall. Yuri's jaw dropped. *What is this? She has a man. Who lives here with her? Am I too late?* Yuri felt sick to his stomach, a rush of adrenalin hitting him right where it hurt.

He steeled himself and continued toward the actual living room, where Bella's mother sat on an overstuffed cream-and-forest green recliner, a stack of manuscript pages stapled together on her lap. The elderly woman's feet were slightly elevated, and one foot was clearly injured, dressed in bandages.

"*Yurochka!* I'm so happy to see you, my boy! What are you doing here?" she cried out, setting aside whatever she was reading, but not before turning it over.

"How are you, Dora Osipovna?" Yuri asked formally, ignoring her question, wondering what was written on those pages.

"No need for such formality, my boy," assured Bella's mother. Yuri felt bad, but he simply couldn't bring himself to call her Mama.

"You look well—no, better than well," he said. "In fact, you're glowing," he added, amazed at his mother-in-law's appearance. The last time he saw her, just before the breakup, she was bedridden, listless, and in pain. Here she was, lightly tan, her light colored hair cut and styled, and wearing a most becoming dress. *Wait a minute, was she wearing lipstick?*

"Oh, you were always a charmer . . . all these compliments. As you see,

I am feeling wonderful, although I must attend physical therapy because I sprained my ankle. Bellachka and Estelle are taking such good care of me. Estelle is a doctor with years of experience from the Philippines. I know I have to return to my own apartment, but I really don't want to."

"Well, that's good to hear. I'm glad you are doing so well."

"Come, come sit down on the sofa. Make yourself comfortable. How about some tea? Have you eaten?"

"No need to bother. I'm here on business, so I thought I would stop by for a visit, have a bite, and then get back to LA."

"Ah, well, I understand. Too bad *Bellachka* is riding and won't be back until after dinner. I must say, you were always such a bad liar," she said with her peculiar smile, both kind and ironic. When Yuri didn't respond, she continued gently, "Listen, I don't know all the details; you know my daughter—she is forever protecting my nerves—but I want you to know that I still care about you and will always think of you as a part of our family. You are *Polinochka's* father."

Estelle entered the room, thankfully interrupting the uncomfortable moment. Yuri paid no attention to the caregiver. He was preoccupied, wondering how his wife had gotten to the stables since the Tesla was here.

"Time to go, Missy, the caregiver chirped with a heavy, sing-song accent. "We'll be late."

"Oh, we've got plenty of time, dear. I'm already dressed, plus I'm enjoying catching up with my son-in-law. Have you two met?"

"Please don't mind me. I'll go," Yuri mumbled, hoping he would be asked to stay. He breathed a sigh of relief when Dora Osipovna insisted that he stay and wait for Bella.

"It's really quite perfect: I have PT and then a show at the senior center. You two can talk things over without interruptions."

"Thank you, *Mamasha*," this was the first time he ever called her anything close to Mother. Yuri helped Dora to her feet and kissed her small, soft hand. She smiled again, kissed him on the shoulder, and whispered, bringing startling tears to his sore eyes, "I'm rooting for you. Especially since you finally stopped calling me by my name and patronyms."

After a bit of fussing and teasing each other, the two women left through the garage, leaving Yuri alone. Though he felt like an absolute cad, he couldn't help himself and decided to snoop around. A jolt of guilt mixed with excitement and the fear of getting caught made his heart beat faster. What in the world did this woman do to him, considering that one of the paramount character traits he admired in himself was his insistence on personal space?

Still uncomfortable, if resigned, Yuri used the small half bath near the kitchen, noting the plain white sink and neutral décor, so unlike what Bella usually preferred. He couldn't fight the urge to see her bedroom. The house had dual master suites, with the one on the left clearly Bella's. Again, the furnishings were rather plain—what she'd call uninspired. The only familiar items were Frette luxury linens and her favorite Anichini cashmere blanket, but there was no sign of a man. He noticed several volumes of poetry casually strewn on the small bedroom chair's ottoman. *Hmm,* he thought, looking to see what she was reading, *Joseph Brodsky and a bio of Walt Whitman. How Bella of her . . . except that Brodsky's book was not his Nobel Prize-winning poetry, but a collection of essays on grief and reason. And why Whitman?* Yuri wasn't aware that she was a fan. Somehow, not knowing this made him feel out of sorts.

Yuri put the books back and picked up Bella's reading blanket. She must be cold in the air-conditioning, he thought. He picked up the blanket and buried his face in the whisper-soft wool, smelling his wife's fragrance; the perfume was the same—he saw the bottle near the nightstand, but something was different. And not only the blanket, come to think of it—the entire space had a subtle leather and cut-grass scent. His stomach flipped, and his heart skipped a beat. *Enough is enough—stop torturing yourself. Just wait until she returns before you freak out.*

He left the bedroom, went into the kitchen with its oak cabinets and granite counters. He found an apple to snack on and a bottle of great Pinot. Thank goodness, that was familiar. He gulped the wine quickly and poured himself another glass, starting to relax.

Yuri took out his phone, turned it on (he had turned it off to show Bella he was serious about making changes). *Not again, what's now?* He saw yet another hysterical text from his sister. *Oh no, you don't. Not this time!* He turned the phone off again, determined to let Oksana finally take responsibility for her own life. It was time that he did the same.

Yuri went over and sat on the couch. A manuscript caught his eye. Compelled beyond his control, he reached for it, took his readers out of his shirt pocket, and read the title page: *The Blue Tatar* by Izzy Ginsburg. *Izzy? I've never heard her call herself by a nickname. And her maiden* name—am I too late? Intrigued and surprised by Bella's choice of pen name, he turned the page and read the first several paragraphs.

I was born with what the Irish call the gift of blarney. Of course, at the time, I knew zilch of blarney or the Irish. When I was small, but never a child, I lived with my young, beautiful, rather eccentric parents in a small communal flat in Odessa, the Black Sea port in Ukraine. Odessa, commonly crowned "the pearl by the sea" by its obsessively adoring citizenry at the time, was mostly a Russian-speaking town; Ukrainian was spoken only in school as a "second" language or by folks who lived in the surrounding countryside.

Just as the universe revolved around the Earth for pre-Galileo Europeans, for Odessa natives, the world revolved around their city, as it still does today. Thousands of words have been written exalting its classic Baroque architecture and cobblestone streets. Songs have been sung celebrating mackerel-full barges (yes, the Black Sea was full of fish before the ecological Armageddon). I've yet to taste anything better than our sun-ripened produce creatively displayed and aggressively lauded at the city's generous farmer markets, called bazaars. Nostalgia, you say; you may be right, but I invite you to take a little culinary tour and see for yourself!

Our "pearl" proudly claimed as its own a dozen or so world-famous pianists, violinists, writers, comedians, and satirists, as well as academicians. We were also equally swollen with self-importance thanks to Odessa's world-renowned Filatov Eye Institute and my own personal favorites, Odessa's brash and colorful gangsters.

The Eye Institute, with its optimistic motto—"Everyone Should See the Sun!"—was founded back in the 1930s and is beautifully situated on the French Boulevard. Thank God for the Institute; otherwise, my own father would have been blind in one eye. When Papa was just a boy, he injured his eye so badly that my grandparents were convinced he would be forever branded as an invalid. Lucky for us, the great eye surgeon Filatov was among the first in the world to successfully perform a cornea transplant. After WWII, so many were blinded that the Institute was packed with folks looking for miracles, and many did indeed regain their sight! I used to love walking past the elegant, neoclassical compound, grateful and daydreaming about being a famous eye doctor myself.

Damn, if we didn't develop our own linguistic traditions since the Russian language became too static for our entrepreneurial heads. In fact, I recently read of a Japanese philanthropist who was about to sponsor a scholarly publication of the Odessa lingo. How about that? No wonder my adorable, barely-out-of-their-teens parents weren't surprised when they produced me: a walking, talking encyclopedia of anything at all, especially useless trivia. In fact, once I started talking, they couldn't shut me up. As they say: some things never change.

Yuri shook his head and laughed out loud at Bella's descriptions. He wanted to read on, but first he decided to go outside and check out the scenery.

The rental house, although not large, opened to a fairway with a grouping of sand traps on its right. The fairway ended at the very bottom of the small mountain range. He could see more houses on the opposite side. Yuri whistled, appreciating the stunning colors and textures spread out before his eyes. *I see why you want to be here*, he thought silently, turning his attention to the backyard. Although the flagstone patio was quite narrow, there was plenty of space for a black-bottom infinity pool and a small spa, both designed in tropical style, more appropriate to the islands than the lower desert.

He took out a pack of cigarettes, a nasty old habit he knew Bella wouldn't approve of and lit one, turning his body against the wind. Whoever owned this property must have bought it for a song; the Indian Wells location alone pointed to its tremendous potential value in terms of a complete gut. Why, if Bella asked him for advice, he'd recommend offering at least $800,000, if not more, since it seemed to be at least a quarter of an acre. He took a few hits before deciding to finish his cigarette later. He still missed his mortgage business: all the wheeling and dealing, huge profits and the respect he garnered from his grateful clients.

Before getting back to Bella's manuscript, Yuri checked to see if there were any more messages from Oksana. There were none, so he picked up right where he left off, but not before filling a tumbler with ice and two fingers of fine Scotch.

My lovely, glamorous mama loved dressing me up in frilly dresses and lacy socks. She'd pin a big white nylon bow on top of my scanty hair, and we'd take the trolley to the Odessa center square, just us girls. Because I started to talk in sentences before I was two (yes, everyone in the family can confirm that this is true!), folks thought I was a small person—what they called a "Lilliput" in those politically incorrect days. Our fellow trolley passengers would hear me chatter, pointing to this or that, especially to nicely dressed women. Curious, they would then see how small I really was, gasp, and offer their sincere condolences to my mama. It went something like this: "Poor child, such a pretty face and so communicative; too bad she's defective." In response to such insolence, my mama, who never held her tongue, would snap back, "You are a complete idiot. She's not a Lilliput—she's only a few months pass her first birthday!"

A few years later, my propensity for showing off went further. Although I could've stayed more conventional road to easily charm grown-ups with my numerous recitations of popular children's poetry or entertain them by play-acting entire scripts of popular films and cartoons, my personal all-time favorite subjects were those that I decided were most interesting to adult males. No, it didn't involve even a whisper of sex. In those splendidly righteous days, the noble Soviet man wasn't interested in sex . . . unless he was rather pervy, like in the West. (Incidentally, as soon as we turned five years old, our grannies sat us down and warned us about so-called uncles who liked "special" hugs or promised "special" candy, if you get my drift.)

By the time I attended kindergarten, our entire circle—family, friends, and neighbors—knew of my curious gift of answering questions on demand; in other words, entertaining grown men with my deep and profound knowledge of two subjects proper little girls should know nothing of: politics and sports. To be more precise, my knowledge storefront involved the names and affiliation of all the Communist Party leaders and local soccer players. (A bit later I became interested in the space race too.) Funny enough, I wasn't that special—just a bit ahead of my time. Nowadays, my folks would display me on YouTube or put me on a popular Russian show, *Better Than All*, where little kids astonish the public by what they know and what they can do. Isn't it always the case: wrong time, wrong place . . . especially in my personal experience.

At any given get-together, or vecherinka, my "genius"—or what my paternal grandmother called goldenkampein—manifested itself in a kind of trivial pursuit hand-to-hand combat, with small amounts of cash being wagered either for or against me. Of course, my maternal grandmother, who disagreed with anything coming from my paternal grandmother, thought nothing good could ever come from my mental calisthenics.

She chided me regularly for not "controlling that hanged tongue," which one day—"and you will remember that day"—would "undoubtedly" bring on the wrath of "them" (meaning the authorities) on our entire family!

Customarily, after the eating portion of the evening get-together, the women would retreat to either the kitchen for cleaning duties, or to the sleeping area of the room (back then most of us didn't have a separate bedroom). There, they'd fuss and coo over any given infant parked on top of visiting fur coats, often spitting on the swaddled pink kid for good luck and to block the ubiquitous "black eye." It seemed that evil was ever-present everywhere, or so the women told themselves.

Inevitably, I'd end up sitting on top of Granddad's round oak table covered with an immaculately ironed white linen tablecloth. Despite the pristine appearance, one could also enjoy a line of cut crystal ashtrays overflowing with the noxious remains of Turkish cigarettes. No filters, please!

There, surrounded by both of my grandfathers, older cousins, uncles, great-uncles, and communal flat neighbors I'd be subjected to their boisterous, rigorous examination; which by the way, I found exhilarating.

Yes, even at such a vulnerable age, I loved showing off my intellectual superiority to men. Little kids and women who slobbered over them, exchanging "battle lore" about their mysterious "female troubles," forced me to chew my nails until my delicate cuticles bled from sheer anxiety. Their syrupy, estrogenic fog obscured the innate vision of inner calm I so desperately needed to be able to think. In other words, the women and children gave me tummy aches and constipation. I still do not truly understand why they're the first to be saved in case of maritime emergencies.

Yuri roared with laughter. He was beginning to enjoy these pages more than he'd expected.

"And who is Tito, Belka?" Uncle Yosif would start the game with a slight twitch in his deeply set left eye framed by a heavy black-and-gray brow.

"Marshall Tito, Josip Broz, our one-time friend and ally, the greatest leader of the anti- fascist partisans is the president of the People's Republic of Yugoslavia."

"Whose friend is he now?" Uncle Garik continued the interrogation, trying to trip me up.

"Currently, President Tito is allied with Chairman Mao Tse-tung, the undisputed father of the Chinese revolution and head of the CP, the Communist Party of the People's Republic of China." And so, it would go on for a while.

"And what is the motto of the Warsaw Pact of the Socialist Nations?" our upstairs neighbor, one-eyed Uncle Semyon, himself a heroic partisan and resistance fighter, threw in for good measure.

"Oh, that's too easy: it's 'Union of Peace and Socialism,'" I'd answer with a sarcastic smirk. "Now ask me something really hard. How about: Tell me the name of the American Speaker of the House or ask me who the Prime Minister of Israel is."

"My God, Izzy. *Shah!* Close your mouth, stupid girl! Do you want to get us all picked up by the black car?"

"Izzy, hey? That's where she got the name," Yuri said out loud.

Interesting, he thought, *she never mentioned this to me. I kind of like it: Izzy. Let's see what else she never told me.* Yuri went back to the story more intrigued than when he started.

The uncles would shush in unison at merely an allusion to Israel. In those days, even the walls had ears. One day you make a little joke among what you considered family or friends, and the very next morning, the black car would take you somewhere you wouldn't send your worst enemy.

"Stop yelling at her, blockheads! Where do you think she gets this stuff? You with your stupid politics! Why can't you all be normal men and ask her about football?" Finally, my father would chip in without turning his undivided attention away from the tiniest of black-and-white screens, my grandparents' first television set. Since color wouldn't be available for years to come, all I can recall were the fairylike figures of footballers running up and down the gray-looking field.

Without turning his mane of a head, Papa would ask: "Come on, my little bird, why don't you tell them about our beloved Chernomorets."

"*Net!* I don't want to tell them! I hate them. Papa, give me a knife!" I'd rebel loudly. "And stop calling me Izzy the squirrel (*squirrel* in Russian is *belka*). My name is Bella! Mama says it means beauty in Italian!" I'd yell at the uncles who enjoyed torturing me by calling me by my dead great-grandfather Isaac's nickname. I still believe they secretly enjoyed pushing my buttons to see my legendary temper run red-hot. For some inexplicable reason, seeing an out-of-control little girl asking for a knife made them laugh. Even now, I cringe when I think of those old dudes.

I lovingly remember our football (soccer) team, the Chernomorets (Black Seaman). It was an old franchise, founded back on March 26, 1936. I'm so glad they changed their name from the original Dynamo. Even their black-and-blue uniforms bring a smile to my face: so wonderfully exotic! I still grin when I see them play on YouTube.

Back in the old USSR, Kiev had their Dynamo; Moscow had their Spartak; there was the Army team from Rostov and Zenith from the chilly Leningrad. But for us, there was nothing more important, no one who could compare with our guys! Even their nicknames were as outlandish as the imported palm trees flourishing at our favorite beach parks. Of course, the entire Jewish Odessa burst with pride at the sight of the great Boris Razinsky, the goalkeeper and striker during the magic 1963 season.

When I was small, our team included the famous "Chicken" and the "Beak Man"—and my dad's personal hero, the "Blue Tatar." Eventually, my deep love and respect for the Blue Tatar would betray me, just as Marshall Tito betrayed Comrade Stalin and the Leninist Revolution.

At the time, I didn't go to school just yet and couldn't have known the "traitorous nature" of the Tatars. (The classification was given to the entire Tatar nation by the Soviets in order to "justify" ethnic cleansing. As they say, history is written by the winners, all the way back to the Bible. Of course, we all know you can pretty much revise anything. You can fabricate documents, deny facts, and erase entire events from the history books. You'd think that events clearly documented and supported by photographic and film evidence, such as the Armenian Genocide or the Holocaust, could not be disputed by anyone with a smidgen of logic. Emotion above evidence—that's the prevailing historical trend, unfortunate as it is.

But back to my Tatars: as history would record, 1944 was a banner year for the Great Mustached One, our beloved leader, Comrade Stalin. The previous year brought the miracle of the victory at Stalingrad. (If you're truly interested in the mind-blowing mysteries associated with the Battle for Stalingrad, look it up for yourself. All I can say is that you must suspend your logic—something we Russians do much better than the Germans). After the destruction of the previously unstoppable Wehrmacht army, it was only a matter of months until the glorious Red Army would march into Berlin. Twice in the previous five years, Time magazine crowned Stalin "Man of the Year" as the hearts of the Hollywood communists and their sympathizers swelled with pride.

Having withstood the fascist blitz of '41 and successfully aligned with the Capitalist West, Stalin was now willing and able to deal with the internal enemies of the Great Socialist Motherland. The poor Crimean Tatars, they had it coming.

The Top-Secret Decree No.5859ss proclaimed the entire Tatar nation guilty. Guilty of the most heinous crimes against the Motherland: betrayal, desertion, active collaboration with the Germans, and "savage reprisals against Soviet partisans."

There she blows! Yuri put down the pages, rubbing his forehead. He truly enjoyed the family recollections. *But why did she have to put all that history nonsense in? Who cares about Stalin and Khrushchev? Well, that American lady was right: since the story has zero chance of being published anyway and if it makes Bella feel better, why not?* He decided to continue reading, hoping to gain some insight into his wife's convoluted brain.

The verdict was clear: the Tatars were judged and convicted as "spies" and "saboteurs." Having made a pact with the German Devil, they would now pay dearly for betting on a losing team. Not a whiff of independence would be allowed for the Muslim Tatars, the descendants of Genghis Khan himself, despite the inconvenient fact they'd been living in the area for centuries. If you don't believe me, check out the Big Khan

Mosque built in 1532! Crimea would remain Russian, as it had been since Catherine the Great and her one-eyed lover, Potemkin, annexed this contentious piece of real estate from the Turks, almost two centuries earlier. (Frankly, I don't blame anyone trying to hold on to this paradise: the climate is positively balmy; the Black Sea is deliciously inviting, and the sun shines over the lush sub-Mediterranean landscape. Have you ever spent a dreary, endless winter in Moscow or St. Petersburg or froze your balls off in Murmansk or Novosibirsk? Brrrrr.)

And so, with a much-practiced signature, the Tatar Nation's collective Fate was sealed by Comrade Stalin, a native of the neighboring Christian Georgia. That weaselly Comrade Beria, head of the dreaded NKVD (the Interior Ministry), a predecessor of the much more "civilized," yet equally brutal KGB, was instructed to supervise the following orders: total confiscation of property and banishment into far-off Uzbekistan for the Crimean Tatars. Here was a fine example of en masse ethnic cleansing long before anyone in the West was aware of the term. Comrade Stalin was always on the cutting edge of nation building and genocide. Let's face it—the unfortunate Tatars were just too ethnically and religiously different to be allowed to live in comfort, basking in the warm Black Sea sunshine.

Of course, even now, we observe much brouhaha and puffed-up emotion surrounding the fate of the prized Crimean Peninsula after Russia's current tsar took a well-calculated gamble that the Americans would sit on their hands, severing Crimea from the West-allied Ukraine in one greedy bite. From Comrade Vladimir Lenin to Mr. Vladimir Putin—at least you can applaud our panache for consistency.

What I find amusing is the ongoing commotion and personal attacks between my Ukrainian and Russian FB friends. For instance, no one can agree how Ukraine ended up with such a geopolitical prize in the first place.

That would be an easily answered question since Comrade Khrushchev, as my English friends would say, was not only awfully fond of Ukraine, but looked to geography and economic expedience rather than history. Plus, who could have foreseen the coming disintegration of the USSR, the "Evil Empire" itself, or as he saw it, "the greatest, the most humanitarian and just nation in the history of the planet? Not him.

Poor Nikita, by 1992 his" generosity" toward Ukraine was called treason and theft by the post-communist Russians. Of course, it took decades and the complete incompetence of the Ukrainian authorities for the new Russian tsar to manipulate the populace and take back Khrushchev's gift to his beloved Ukrainian Cossacks.

Poor Russian-speaking Ukrainian citizens being forced to conduct their lives in the language many don't even think of as a "legit" language, but merely a Russian dialect! Poor Ukraine with its troubled past, disrespected and exploited by competing empires while considering themselves the "true" cultural and religious descendants of the Great Kiev Rus! Poor Jews, stuck between the Russians and the Ukrainians—first being blamed for the horrific 1930s Soviet-era famines by the pro-Nazi Ukrainian nationalists, then called Ukrainian allies by the Russians! Poor everyone! I hear the new history books have arrived there and the neofascists are marching in the streets. I hear they're blacklisting any performers who dare to work in now Russian-occupied Crimea. I find it fascinating that the Central Intelligence Agency has had a long history of supporting the UPA, the Ukrainian Insurgent Army, although the UPA and other factions of the Ukrainian opposition fought for the Nazis against the USSR. I guess the old "enemy of my enemy is my friend" saying holds true in this case. Poor CIA!

Curiously, the dubious Khrushchev transfer of Crimea to the Ukrainian Socialist Republic took place on the 26th of April, 1954, or so we were taught in school. Do you think it's odd to remember the exact date? At first glance, yes; however, I think it would be odder to forget your own wedding anniversary!

OK, I can hear you: "Enough with all this boring history crap. I thought this was about sports and food. I don't care about my own American history that much," you say. "Why care about yours?" Have a little patience, I say, as we return to me and my traitorous Blue Tatar goalkeeper.

"Exactly!" Yuri cried out. Still, he couldn't keep from reading on. He got up and stretched his neck side to side before turning to the next page.

As far as my own family experience went, the food shortages, or "deficits," during Soviet times were not nearly as they'd be twenty years later, just before the shocking collapse of USSR. Still, even during the good old 1960s—dubbed the "Thaw"—getting your children fed was a major undertaking, to say the least. After the carnage and horror, the devastating loss of millions of lives, the Revolution, the Civil War, the Stalin purges, ethnic cleansings, and WWII, the time of liberalization and cultural openness was, if not a gift from above, then at least a gift from Comrade Khrushchev.

I still hear my mama's voice, accusing me of being a picky eater. "How can you be so unspeakably ungrateful and refuse the cauliflower and meat fat soup, when your mama and papa were lucky to eat dry black bread crumbs and potato peels?" You'd think she was exaggerating or being manipulative. It was an absolute fact, though. This is why, even as a severe diabetic with outrageously high blood pressure, my father never ate anything but tasteless fluffy white bread, sneaking handfuls of nauseatingly sweet hard candy, and snacking on dry Italian salami . . . even in the end.

Yuri noticed a handwritten note from Bella to herself in the side margins, making him feel closer to her than in years.

Come to think of it, I'd better ask Yuri to get Mama something fun to eat at the Russian Deli and tell Holly, my office manager, to have Alexandra of the Valley deliver fresh flowers to her flat. Mama loves fresh flowers, especially hydrangeas. They remind her of so many wonderful Crimean holidays with Papa.

When I dream of the past, I can still hear my grandmother's shocked voice imprinted in my brain when I send back an inedible veal chop in a two-star Michelin restaurant. So sorry, but it reminds me of the foul texture of my childhood meals. Quelle horror! Such guilt! What chutzpa!

Ah, this I know. Yuri smiled and nodded.

To be fair, it's not that I didn't eat, for how else would you explain being diagnosed with an "obesity of the second degree" by age six? I just made it a challenge. When I was four, I was deemed too thin and sickly and so, my mother, always an energetic overachiever and a perfectionist, decided to take matters into her own hands by making me her own science experiment.

She came up—mind you, on her own—with a devious eating plan. Anytime I refused to swallow another bite, holding the muck inside my ever-expanding cheeks, she'd ask me questions. I, as well-trained as a Pavlovian puppy, had no choice but to swallow the gook in order to answer.

First, Mama would ask political questions, and then, when I finally caught on and refused to answer, she came up with sports-related ones, calling out erroneous names and corresponding positions of our soccer team players and leaving me no choice at all but to correct her.

Within several months or so, her brilliant strategy began to pay off. My scratchy brown wool stockings no longer hung around my scrawny knees, my inner thighs began to chafe, thick copper hair grew below my waist and all the little old ladies in the park couldn't pass by without painfully squeezing my pale cheeks. Mama was delighted by the well-earned compliments and praises as her status in the family began to supersede her own mother's.

Being a Leo, I'm usually slow to recognize profound betrayal coming from those I love. It took me a while to catch on and begin to deal with weighty emotional conflict. Like the proverbial Danish prince before me, a question of the most life-altering kind began to interfere with my sleep. Who was I and what was my place on Earth? Will I be judged by society as fat but smart, or skinny but stupid? I believe this is when I had to ask my first existential question: "Do thin thighs equal low IQ?"

Yuri snorted at his wife's wittiness.

The conflict came to an ugly head one fateful, late winter afternoon with my mother doing her absolute best to weave her web of deception. While still hungry, I continued to play along, dutifully swallowing the dreaded lukewarm cauliflower liquid studded with bits of jellied cow fat while responding to Mama's queries. Unfortunately, the temperature in our flat's communal kitchen began to drop as the furnace ran out of coal, and the soup congealed into an inedible mass. I took a spoonful and refused to swallow despite all her pleading and the ensuing manipulations. Finally, frustrated she remembered about my obsession with my favorite footballer, the wicked Blue Tatar.

"Ah, now you'll have to swallow one last bite and finish your torture of me," she exclaimed with certitude. "Daughter! Who is our goal keeper?

Answer me this minute! I've got borsht on the Primus stove and ironing and visiting. The goalie's nickname, I'm telling you, give me his name!"

Of course, I knew that it was he himself, the dreaded Blue Tatar. He was doubly traitorous, for his name usually took two spoons. I still don't know what provoked my rebellion, but then and there I made up my mind. I wouldn't swallow the last bite, no matter what—and once I make up my mind, as everyone can tell you, I'm as immovable as the fabled Armenian mountain Ararat.

"Who minds the goal," politely whispered Mama, changing her strategy.

"Mmm-mm," I responded, shaking my head from side to side.

"C'mon, you know his name! Just say it!" she said, raising her voice.

"Hmm," I responded, shaking my head with a firm no. I took slow, deep breaths through my nose for fear of swallowing. I had lots of practice holding my breath.

"Daughter, I swear by Comrade Lenin, you will tell me his name. I must know his name."

Firmly I stood, I still holding on to my convictions, squaring my chin. Then, copying my paternal grandmother, I folded my chubby hands (with their made-for-fortepiano fingers and chewed-up nail beds) across a shabby apron dress in categorical defiance.

Poor Mother, she was starting to lose it. Surprisingly, instead of feeling guilty or scared, I was beginning to feel much better. Within seconds, the top blew, the cork popped, and she truly careened out of control, hollering at me at the top of her powerful young lungs, "Who minded the goal gate? Who is the goalkeeper?"

Just at that moment, the communal flat neighbors began to tiptoe into the kitchen to see what was causing the entire ruckus. The scene that lay before them must have been too surreal to describe, unless you've been raised on Fellini's cinema.

What they must have seen was my mother standing close to the edge of the old wooden table holding an empty soup plate and screaming at me while I sat on the table with an angelic smile and puffed-up cheeks full of food.

"If you don't answer my question right this second, I will have a heart attack and die!" she pleaded, while tears ran down her unlined cheeks, smearing her pretty rouge. Oh-oh, now she was getting to me.

I loved my mama and didn't want to be sent to the orphanage. I was beginning to weaken as my cheeks went numb.

But, as it often happens, the fates smiled, and my luck held. My salvation arrived in the form of fat Baba Zina, a big-bosomed, plain-spoken, visibly mustached neighbor. She resided in a two-room flat, two doors down our narrow communal hall, sharing the kitchen with two more families in addition to us. According to her, she was a long-time war widow and the grandmother of Maya and Slava, who lived in far-off, cold, snowy Moscow. The much-adored, can-do-no-wrong siblings would visit Odessa in the summers to fortify themselves for the next winter. They arrived the first week in June and left a few days before September, accompanied by freshly pickled local dilled tomatoes and many tears. Maya and Slava were older than I was, and they refused to let me into their sacred "sibling" circle.

When she heard Mama's tirade, Baba Zina couldn't just stand by. "Leave the girl alone! Let her be!" She interfered bravely, putting her manly, un-manicured hand on Mama's shoulder.

"What? How is this any of your business?" responded shocked Mama. "I'm just trying to feed her," she said, attempting to explain her strategy and trying to remain well-mannered in the face of such rudeness.

The neighbor woman wasn't at all worried about being uncouth. "What's wrong with you, citizen? You're acting like a complete idiot, not a proper Soviet mother. Even I don't know the name of the fucking goalkeeper! Give a child some food without conditions. What is she, a circus monkey?"

My mother finally took her eye off me and swung around to turn her attention on the nosy old Zina.

Oh my God! Maya's crazy mob grandmother. Bella wasn't kidding me when she told me that story.

"I am an idiot? It's you who's a blockhead! I am trying to feed her." The two women began to hurl insults at each other, bringing up old grievances and stifled feelings—something about a dirty Primus stove, a cut-off ear, bandits, and dirty money.

I was left sitting on the table, unable to get down by myself, but luckily close enough to the soup plate to spit out the offending liquid.

"Tphew!" I spit three times into the plate, cursing the damn soup in perfect imitation of my maternal grandmother's habitually practiced spitting technique.

As the fighting went on, yet another neighbor joined in, frightened by the sound of an unusually shrill "cat" fight. I called the second woman Auntie Anya. She was nice, and I liked her last name, Kanevskaya, meaning "horse woman." (I loved horses with such passion that I would have gladly joined the Soviet Cavalry—if I were a boy, of course.) I spent hours daydreaming about riding, sitting surrounded by pillows on the windowsill and watching the huge metal cisterns of sweet, grass-tasting raw milk brought up from the surrounding countryside in horse-drawn carriages. How fortunate for me to live right above a milk distribution center. Once in a great while, an adult would take pity on me and allow me to offer a horse a bit of a carrot. (Apples were too precious and expensive to share with the animals, but carrots were easily grown and plentiful.)

Auntie Anya was an agonizingly thin young woman without a husband or family. She was the sole ethnic Russian among us, and originally from a small town near Moscow. She took a lot of flak from the other neighbors who teased her about not having enough meat on her bones to please a man. She never went anywhere without her son, and there he was in his pale blue pajamas, a sniffling creature with awful red hair bundled up in a brightly colored Ukrainian shawl. He was about the same age as Maya and Slava, but they wouldn't play with him either. He was always trying to get near Maya, who'd finally lose patience and hit him on the back of his head. If he still wouldn't let her be, she usually asked Slava to save her from the vile boy's constant pestering.

This is about Vlad? Yuri shook his head and rubbed his forehead—he was getting a dull headache.

"Girls, women, comrades, please let's try and be logical," chimed in the usually quiet Anya. She was a highly educated, dainty sort who despised violence among the fairer Soviet sex. "I don't know who the goalkeeper is either, but it's almost suppertime and if you just control your emotions for a bit, the men will be returning from the factory. I am sure one of them, if not several, will know his name," she said with an amiable smile. This time, my mama truly lost it. "Dumb asses! Have you both lost your minds? I was just trying to get her to answer so she would swallow her soup."

The two neighbor women couldn't have looked more perplexed. Zina shook her head and asked respectfully, "She must tell you the goalie's name before she can eat? Good God, if there's such a thing, I bow to you. You truly are a strong disciplinarian."

The other neighbor picked up her son, Vladimir, and said to him quietly through pursed lips, "See, Vladik? Your mama is thrilled when you eat your supper. This poor girl must pass a rigorous exam before she can swallow even one spoonful!"

I could see steam rising from Mama's head and murder in her eyes. Just then Papa strolled in, rubbing his hands together from the cold. Always my hero, he came in just in time to save the neighbor women from being beaten over the head with a metal borscht ladle. My mama was fierce!

Go Dora Osipovna! Yuri smiled, thinking fondly of his mother-in-law.

"*Nu,* what's wrong now?" Papa demanded sternly, winking at me, as Mama practically flew into his arms. "She . . . she . . . she wouldn't tell me; she just sat there and tortured me with her eyes!"

"Who?"

"Your daughter, that's who; I ask her to tell me the nickname of the goalie and she won't tell!"

"Is that all? "Papa asked, rubbing his hands up and down Mama's shoulders. "I never forgot his calming touch. "It's the Blue Tatar, silly. Couldn't you have waited until I got home?"

At this moment, Mama finally gave up and burst into laughter, the kind of tearful, hysterical laughter that cleanses both your soul and your bladder. Papa and I joined in, holding our stomachs as the horrified neighbors stood by in silence until fat Zina finally understood and joined in. In fact, she laughed so hard, she peed right on the freshly scrubbed linoleum floor. That made old Zina and my parents laugh even harder.

Auntie Anya grabbed her sniffling boy's hand, turned on her heels, and gave a toss of her top-braided pale wheat hair.

"Let's go back to our room, Vladik! We are living in a psychiatric hospital, not a communal apartment." With those prophetic words, she walked out of the kitchen.

"Ha ha," Yuri roared, nearly doubling over. "Brava, my girl! You made me laugh. Maybe you are a writer after all . . ."

I learned two valuable lessons on that historic day: always make Mama laugh and she won't punish me, and second, better not let the others know everything you know, for one day they will use your knowledge against you, so help you God, if there is such a thing.

Yuri put the pages down and took a deep breath. He was touched and proud and even more upset by the possibility that he had truly hurt this precious girl with his asinine disloyalty. He then noticed Bella scribbled something in Russian on the back of the last page, her handwriting sloppy and childlike. It was a little reminder to herself to change everyone's names if she decides to let anyone read the story. Yuri whistled and said, "Oh yeah, I would."

⌾

"What the hell do you think you're doing? How dare you?" Bella rushed into the living room, grabbing the manuscript and holding the pages to her chest. "Who gave you my story? Why are you here?" she screamed at the top of her lungs, tears pouring down her cheeks.

Yuri was beside himself. "I came to see you, and your mom left me here to wait for you. I'm sorry. I didn't think. I just wanted to see what you've been working on. It's wonderful, my heart. It's truly wonderful."

"You never think! You're not welcome here! Get out!" Bella wouldn't stop her tantrum, but Yuri didn't mind her screaming. He was terrified of her silence.

"I'm sorry, baby. I'm so sorry. I get it now: the pain, the disloyalty. You had every right to feel betrayed." Yuri bridged the distance between them and fell to his knees, holding on to Bella's waist. "Please forgive me. I'm stupid and selfish and stubborn and unworthy of washing your feet and drinking the water."

Bella was in shock. She was filled with rage and a strange feeling she used to confuse with love. Now she wasn't so sure. She felt betrayed—no, worse than betrayed; she felt violated. She hated that he had read her childhood recollections without waiting for her to give him permission; yet at the same time, she felt the familiar deep longing for him to understand her. *Damn that man,* she thought, *from the very first time I went to bed with him, he's had a ridiculous effect on my hormones.* It was a pattern. He fucked up, she put her foot down, they had wild sex, and she forgave him. Just like that. Well, this time was different.

Bella used all her strength to break free from Yuri's grip and succeeded, leaving him kneeling. She went into the kitchen and poured herself a glass of water. What she craved was an entire bottle of freshly opened Chardonnay, but she needed to keep her wits about her.

She gulped down the water and squeezed her eyes shut. She felt his energy envelop her; she smelled his passion, mixed with something she could only think was fear. He smelled amazing. *Son of a bitch...*

Yuri didn't get up until Bella left the kitchen and went into the bedroom to hide the manuscript. He followed her. She turned around and gave him a look of such confusion and longing that he got an instant erection. Come to think of it, he had been semi-hard while driving. That hadn't happened to his cock in years!

"Leave! Why don't you just let me be?" Bella whispered, not knowing what to do. She went to stand in front of the French doors leading to the backyard. She could see two neighbors—an elderly couple—across the narrow airway, having their daily four o'clock happy hour cocktails in anticipation of sunset. She always thought that would be Yuri and her until it was time to take their final breath.

"I just can't give up on us. I love you, and I am truly sorry." Yuri came up behind her, standing close enough to smell her, but not daring to touch her. Yuri noticed the same muskiness he first smelled when he was snooping around. Was she actually sweaty? Come to think of it, her entire appearance was odd: high-waisted Levis, a wrinkled denim shirt and scuffed up short boots—not at all her usual glammed-up riding outfit. Her hair was pulled back into a loose bun. They stood without talking for longer than he expected. Usually he couldn't shut her up when they were quarreling.

"I'm tired of us. I've been so peaceful away from you," Bella said finally.

"I don't blame you."

"But I blame you," she replied. "Although Mama thinks I must share the blame."

Yuri swallowed hard and hung his head. What he wanted was contact.

"Mama says I've been too strong and too successful, and I made you feel less of a man."

"Well, you should listen to Mama," Yuri quipped.

When he noticed Bella wincing, he backed down. "I'm just kidding. It doesn't matter who's to blame. We have to fix it—for Polina and her future kids."

"Polina will be fine. She's fine now. And who knows if she'll ever have kids anyway. Your daughter is making more money with her insipid Instagram posts than you've made in years! Why don't you talk too her, instead of judging? I refuse to stand by and see you treat her like you treat Oksana!"

"What are you saying? I love Polina and my financial failures don't mean I'm not trying. I've never thought of you as being cruel. Stop, I beg of you, before it's too late, and I will talk to our daughter about her ruining her future!"

"That's what I'm trying to tell you. It is too late . . ."

A feeling of desperation hit Yuri in the center of his gut, and his pulse jumped. He realized talking wouldn't do any good. He turned Bella around and cupped her tear-stained face. Thank God! He was still able to reach her. He shook his head and reached for her lips, her cheeks, her eyes, and her forehead. He showered her with soft kisses until he couldn't control his hormones. Finally, he stuck his tongue deep into her mouth. She whimpered and softened. Without saying a word, Yuri grabbed on to her butt and brought her close to his crotch to show her how much he needed to be inside her.

She responded by throwing her head back and exposing her throat. Yuri used his tongue and teeth to assure himself of her response. She didn't push him away, but she remained still.

"No?"

"No," she finally said.

"I can't make love to you?"

"Are you asking?"

"No, I'm taking." Still kissing her, Yuri lifted her body, noting how much lighter she'd become. His heart fell.

Gently and slowly, he placed Bella on the bed and lay next to her, just stroking her hair and kissing away that line between her brows, that annoying wrinkle she was always trying to get rid of, the wrinkle he loved. She didn't move. Her eyes were closed. Yuri noticed a spray of freckles around the bridge of her nose and thought of that clever little girl in her story. He picked up her hand with her short, unpainted nails and kissed it. She still wore her wedding band. Tears filled his eyes, tears of longing and guilt and something not exactly comfortable, something new—a sense of dread, of possibly losing her love. "I'm going to explode," he whispered in her ear as he nibbled it just the way she liked it.

Bella moaned and opened her eyes. The storm of raw need he saw in her accusing eyes pushed him over the edge of all constraint. He unzipped her jeans and pulled them along with her underwear all the way down to her ankles, leaving her exposed to his view. She was much thinner, more defined, more muscular than he recalled. She was also deeply tan. She looked and smelled different—and if he was honest, he'd have to admit that these changes were to his liking. She was the same and she was someone else.

Bella continued to make little noises as he put his lips near her wet, dripping center and began his assault. He could have counted on one hand the times she was relaxed enough about her body to let him go down on her. (It was usually she who performed oral sex.) A bit uncomfortable, but fully grateful that his wife exploded in just a few minutes, Yuri stripped off his own clothes and plunged inside her with such a force that Bella cried out. She didn't reach out for him with her hands or her mouth, but that's not what he wanted anyway.

He began to move frantically, trying to get ahold of his madness, but to no avail. He was used to a good deal of movement from his wife, but Bella was motionless with her eyes closed, making soft little moans without moving her hips. The more he banged around, changing from one position to the next; turning her to her side, flipping her onto her stomach, the less she responded. Her lack of sexual response was both maddening and exciting. Finally, Yuri lost all control and came so hard that his teeth chattered. It had been a long time between orgasms. He almost blacked out, as he fell, full-body, on her, eliciting a small "Ouch."

"Sorry . . . sorry, baby. God, it was so good." Yuri dragged himself off of Bella and fell into a stupor.

Bella remained on her back, feeling sore and sticky. She looked over at Yuri who was snoring softly and reached out to touch his shoulder. He was out cold. Normally, just about now, she'd feel relieved, full of love and hope; enjoying the make-up sex. This was different. She came hard before intercourse, but even the orgasm didn't relax her nerves. Not that sex wasn't great; Yuri was a fantastic lay, both in terms of his size and technique. Still, something was amiss. Bella got up, took a quick shower, threw on her favorite robe, and went to the kitchen. She was usually famished after sex, but not today. She poured a glass of wine and scrambled to find something to eat that didn't involve carbs or sugar. She found half a chicken breast and took a bite. It tasted like a cardboard. Dropping the leftover bird in the trash, she decided to check her phone. As she expected, there was a recent text from Steve asking if she made it home safely. Although she thought about it twice, she dialed his number.

"Hi, it's me."

"Hi, me. Home safe?" Bella liked Steve's pleasant, unaccented voice. In fact, she thought he sounded twenty years younger on the phone. She also liked that, unlike Yuri's, Steve's voice didn't make her nerves jump either.

"Yes, thanks. I mean, thanks for checking on me."

"Of course, hon. Traffic is crazy this time of day. Leo and I miss you already. How about I drive up and take you and your mom to a nice supper at the golf club?"

"No, please don't."

"Did I do something wrong? Are you mad at me?"

"No." Bella took a big gulp of wine. She was never a good liar, and Steve was too good to her to be lied to. "I miss Leo too."

"Just Leo?"

Bella felt a jab of guilt when she couldn't respond to Steve's fishing for something she wasn't able to offer. "Look, I have to tell you something."

"Alright, shoot."

"Yuri, my husband, drove up to see me. He was waiting for me here, at your house." "Ouch."

"I'm not going to lie to you. He wants us to get back together."

There was a long pause on the other end of the line. "And what do you want?" "Honestly?"

"With me—always."

"I don't know what I want."

"I understand. It's not easy to break those ties, and you have Polina to think of."

Bella felt the heat of tears filling her eyes. Steve was so nice, so understanding, and she truly was fond of him, but Yuri had been her life for so long. Steve was so much more than Leo's trainer, yet so much less than her infuriating husband. The last time they saw each other for what was supposed to have been Leo's strategy session, she ended up at his place. She had too much to drink and was on the rebound, but still she was glad they ended up in bed. Surprisingly, and despite her fears, Bella liked Steve even more once she finally allowed herself to stop comparing him to Yuri. Steve was fit, short and stocky, with very little body hair. He was also well-endowed. Attentive and lighthearted, Steve made her feel beautiful, even though she knew she wasn't at her best. He kept thanking her for making love with him! Sex wasn't intense or transforming, but it was comforting and relaxing. She even had a gentle, rolling orgasm.

They lounged for a bit, and then he grilled some steaks and shrimp for them. Bella thought she could get used to a man taking care of her needs for once. Now, here she was going to bed with yet another man, albeit her husband. She was overwhelmed by guilt and maybe a bit of sexual thrill.

"Thank you for telling me about your husband, Isabel. Clearly, you've got some thinking to do. I tell you what: I'll ask Lisa, the ranch owner, to meet you at the stables; that way you can visit with Leo, and I'll see you some other time. You have a nice evening, Isabel."

"Steve, please don't go. I'm sorry. I didn't mean to hurt you."

"Stop worrying about my feelings. I'm a big boy. It's fine. You were being up front with me. We'll talk some other time, but for now I don't want to bring you more stress. You've got enough on your shoulders."

"Oh, Steve, I really like you, but you're right, of course. I'm the one who's to blame for all this mess. Please try to hang in there, and I promise I'll call you tomorrow," Bella said, not at all happy with herself.

"Are you talking to Polina?" Yuri staggered into the kitchen, still sleepy and not wearing a stitch of clothes. Bella shook her head. "Getting familiar already, hey?"

"*Da,* why wouldn't I be? You're my wife. We've just had great sex. We're back together." Yuri scratched his balls and grabbed Bella's hand. "Look, I'm still hard. You want another shot before it goes away?" He smiled with that half-crooked grin that used to melt her heart. It didn't anymore; if anything, Bella felt pissed at his casual attitude and his complete disregard for her needs. Nothing would ever change between them.

There and then, she decided to move into new territory. If he thought one roll in the hay would bring her back, he was mistaken!

"No, it wasn't Polinochka. It was Steve. Steve is my new rescue's trainer.

"You bought a new horse?"

"I rescued him. Leo is an amazing former champion. He is the most beautiful boy I've ever ridden. He was so weak and thin, and he had parasites. They over-bred him and dumped him, hoping he would die, but he didn't! He's simply gorgeous, and Steve is helping to return him to his past glory. I'm going to jump with this horse." Bella couldn't stop herself.

"Well, OK, I guess that's fine. It's your money."

"That's right. It's my money!"

"Hey, hey, let's not fight about money. We've just made up. Is your horse all right?" Yuri asked in a conciliatory voice.

"Leo is fine. I always call Steve when I get back to the desert. He's my landlord here as well."

Something in Bella's tone sounded an alarm. Yuri narrowed his eyes and suddenly became painfully aware of his nudity and his now-limp cock.

"Let me get dressed, and then you can tell me all about that new horse of yours and Steve."

"Why bother dressing? It's not like you care about offending my sensibilities."

"Wow, sarcastic, aren't we? What's gotten into you?" Without waiting for yet another caustic reply, Yuri turned around and went into the bedroom. Bella heard him turn on the water. For some stupid reason, that alone made her blood boil. He didn't even ask if he could use her shower.

To calm her nerves, she refilled the wine glass and took it outside. She turned on the spa and sat in the corner with her feet in the swirling water. The sun was going down, and the mountain range in front of her was bathed in that magical desert light, as if someone switched on HD. She didn't want to think about her marriage. Come to think of it, she didn't want to think about anything. She just wanted a swim and the mountains and to be able to ride Leo first thing tomorrow morning.

"Are you sleeping with Steve?" Yuri asked coolly, standing in the doorway. He was dressed and freshly shaven.

"That's none of your business. We've been separated for months." Bella chickened out.

"You're sleeping with him," Yuri said quietly.

"It's not that simple. You don't understand."

"So, explain."

"Why bother? You're not going to believe me anyway. All you care about is who has access to my vagina."

"Try me, Izzy."

"I don't trust you. And don't call me Izzy!"

"I understand. Still, you owe me this."

Yuri went over to the spa and sat next to Bella. She hung her head and began to cry. He reached out and put his arm around her shoulder.

"Talk to me. Please give it a try."

"You're not angry?"

"Of course, I'm angry, but I also know I'm the one to blame. Even if we don't reconcile, we need to make peace with this—for our future and for our daughter."

Bella wiped her face and nodded her head in agreement. She began to talk quickly as if she were running out of air. She was prepared for interruptions, but none came. She talked about her pain and how embarrassed she was when she found out about Bozena and the pictures. She talked of never feeling comfortable with being more successful than her husband. She cried about lost pregnancies and having to practically throw herself at him to get him to make love to her. She talked about how tired she was of dealing with people's dental problems and how much courage it took to sell her practice and try to launch a full-time writing career so late in life. She told him her fears about her mother dying and leaving her an orphan, and she talked about how she always felt intimidated by his enormous intellect, how she was tired of trying to keep up with him.

Yuri listened without offering excuses or explanations. "And Steve?" he finally asked when she stopped.

"He is a friend. He's been there for me, and we have so much in common."

"Do you love him?" Yuri didn't want to know, but he had no choice.

"No, I love you. I've always been in love with you."

"Thank God. I love you too!"

"God? You don't believe in anything other than yourself, and I don't

THE BLUE TATAR | 199

want your love, Yurochka. The thing is, I want peace and companionship and life with a man who focuses on me and not on making lots of money to prove he's a real man. Because Steve comes from a prominent family, he has nothing but respect for my achievements. He doesn't compete with me, and I don't have to look perfect either to get a compliment or two.

"I see. You finally found your rich American. A real fucking John Wayne. Well, fuck him and fuck you, too—and for the record, I never asked for you to be perfect! You're the one with that overblown ego!" Yuri spit out, suddenly so bitter he could taste bile in the back of his throat.

"See? I knew you wouldn't understand," Bella concluded, resigned.

Yuri's phone rang. He didn't know why he picked it up, but it seemed like something to do. "I'm listening," he said in Russian. Bella heard a woman screaming. It was Oksana. Yuri listened for a several minutes and then hung up.

"What's wrong? Is it your mother?"

"No, Mama is the same. It's Oksana; she's at the condo. Slava is threatening to take away the kids if she doesn't break it off with Avi. I have to go. Something happened. I didn't really understand her. Something about divorce and being kidnapped and Maya, and she also said she's been hurt. I have to go."

"Oh no! She sent me a text about needing to be picked up at some park, but I thought she was just being dramatic. I'm so sorry. I've been preoccupied. I feel like shit. Yurik, please drive carefully. If you need help, I'll come."

"No need to come with me. If I need help, I'll call the cops. These criminal animals are about to get what's coming to them."

Bella was filled with dread, but she stopped herself from telling Yuri what she thought. "Please text me; I'll wait. As late as you need to. We're still family, and I care about your safety.

"Bella, I'm angry and jealous and hurt, but if you think we're done, you are the one who doesn't understand." With those words, Yuri rushed off, leaving Bella alone.

POSTMORTEM

ANOTHER BORING DAY, another worthless life over and done. The electromagnetic entity that used to be Vladimir Sergeevich Konevsky was stuck, drifting over a freshly dug half-filled gravesite, prepared to be completely covered with worm-infested dirt. Sometimes he was aware of sights and sounds, and sometimes he was not aware of anything at all. He didn't know how he had gotten here—one moment he was hot and thirsty, looking inside his refrigerator, and the very next moment he was trapped, not able to do what he wanted. Once in a while, he saw a blinding light at the end of a dimly lit tunnel.

Strange, he didn't recall seeing any tunnel before when making his many visits to Hollywood Forever Cemetary. A few times he saw, or perhaps imagined, a face—a thin, pale face that reminded him of his mother, albeit a lot younger. The face, with its delicate features and wretched smile, drifted out of the mist and looked at him with such sorrow that he felt somehow scared. Sometimes she wasn't alone, accompanied by a man with a shaved head, wearing a pre-war military uniform and filthy boots, one eye—a gaping black hole.

Once Vlad almost reached the woman, but some force pulled him back. He saw his own shadowy image reflected back from a shiny, polished granite headstone, at first not recognizing it for what it was: a preteen Vladik, bone-thin with sunken eyes, wrapped in his mother's shawl.

Most of the time, if what he experienced was in fact time, he just hung around, hoping to make himself less bored. He didn't really enjoy listening to all that screaming and cursing and crying and carrying on. The old Russian women wearing head-to-toe black were especially annoying. Eventually, in a moment of stunning clarity, a frightening thought came to him. This place must be his own final destination—his private prison, his Gulag.

Vlad seemed to be forever hanging around in the hope of seeing someone he knew before, someone who could help him make sense of what really happened, but up until now, the faces were unfamiliar. Where was Maya, his wife, and their two sons, the fucking morons? Where was Slava? And who the fuck was this old, white-haired hag in a wheelchair, crying and crying out his name? Why was she wearing a surgical mask? Was she contagious?

Flora was cold. The fire-breathing winds whipped around her fragile body, pulling on her long dress and rattling the wheelchair. She wore a mask to help breathe better, since the winds stirred up so much dust and pollen.

Flora wasn't having one of her good days. Her pulse was weak, and the constant pain and needle-sticking sensations on the top of her head caused her a good deal of discomfort. She shouldn't have been outdoors; the crazy winds made the stabbing pain worse. However, ever since she woke up, she got it in her head that this was *the* day she'd visit Vladimir's gravesite. Convinced she wouldn't be at peace until she'd offered her prayers for Vlad's soul and sincerely asked for forgiveness, she pulled herself together for this life-changing event.

She couldn't believe it had been over a year since she attended Vlad's funeral; for her, it had been a year of ill health and physical suffering, but also a year of miraculous spiritual redemption. After days of contemplation and guidance from her spiritual advisor, Reverend Mike, Flora made up her mind that distant prayers weren't enough. She had a sacred Christian duty to offer her prayers and apologies in person. She asked her stepson, Zack, to bring her here to say her goodbyes to both Vlad and Los Angeles. She also asked the young man not to mention the visit to his father. There was no need. Flora promised Zack it would be a short visit, although Zack felt the need to remind her that they needed to get to Union Station at least an hour before the train. (She suffered from terrible brain fog.)

The train trip to the Midwest would take almost two days instead of just under four hours; unfortunately, Flora still couldn't fly. Several times, she had tried to make the short flight to Vegas, when Ken was still trying to save his part of the business, but her breathing was affected by the altitude and she suffered massive panic attacks—one bad enough to cause her to be taken straight from the airport to the ER.

Flora and Zack were scheduled to board the famous Southwest Chief at 6:00 p.m. Zack was excited. He read and reread the itinerary out loud.

"Say, Mom," Zack told Flora just that morning. The two had been getting closer and closer, especially the last few weeks. "Did you know that we're going to see eight different states? We'll see the Red Rock and the Santa Fe Trail and even the Continental Divide. Too bad you're not feeling all that good; I mean, not yet," he added gently without trying to make Flora feel guilty. "Otherwise we could've seen the Grand Canyon! There's a bus at Williams that takes passengers on an antique train. You know—cowboys and old-fashioned musicians, even a train robbery!"

Flora smiled. "God willing, one day, when I'm all well, and you get back from your tour, we'll all take a fun vacation," she reassured Zack. "You know, honey, I rode the Grand Siberian Express with my own dad when I was a schoolgirl—all the way from Moscow to Vladivostok!"

Zack was impressed.

"I'd love you to see Lake Baikal for the first time: it's the oldest and deepest fresh-water lake on the entire planet, near the Mongolian border. In some places free of pollution, the water is so clear, you can see your own face like in a mirror! Some say the fight for Lake Baikal brought down the entire Soviet system—all that industrial waste from mining and toxic runoff. I'm proud to tell you, my dearest father was one of the most vocal environmentalists, being a hydraulic engineer, a true specialist!"

Zack was doubly impressed. "What is hydraulic?" he inquired, trying to learn more about his stepmom's background.

"You really want to know?"

"Sure!"

"Father worked at a hydropower station—you know, like a Hoover Dam. He was in charge of a good deal of heavy machinery using water instead of gas."

"You know what I think, Mom?" Zack said.

"What do you think?" Flora asked, smiling at him, reaching up to smooth his hair.

"I think as soon as you're well, you need to go back to school so you can teach little kids! You're so good at making boring science stuff fun and easy to understand."

Touched by Zack's obvious admiration, Flora wiped unexpected tears from her eyes.

Zack knew his dad would be waiting for their arrival in Chicago. All three would then drive a few hours west of the Windy City to their new home in Galena, a delightful three-bedroom Victorian with a large yard and a gazebo. The house was mortgage-free since it had been in the family for nearly a century.

Flora had never been to Illinois, but Ken sent her daily video updates, and she was charmed by its cobblestone streets and old-fashioned inns. She especially loved the little town's traditional Russian name, Galena, and of course, the grand Mississippi River. This was the fresh start she'd been praying for. Ken promised she could bring her mom over from Russia to stay as long as her visa would allow.

Her thoughtful spouse has gone ahead several weeks before to get the house ready, leaving Flora in the care of Zack and an ever-changing rotation of Russian-speaking caregivers. After the big house was sold to pay off Maya, the couple rented a small apartment in Culver City. In a way, Flora was glad she had plenty of time to think and adjust; time spent getting ready to simplify their lives by moving to a small old-fashioned town in the American Midwest, to the real America and not this California nightmare.

Flora could walk on her own, but Zack decided to use the wheelchair since it was a large cemetery and he didn't want to tire her out before the trip. Zack understood Flora's need for privacy, so he told her to take her time and just text him when she'd finished.

As the young man wandered off, Flora sat by Vlad's burial site. She was shocked at its poor condition. There was no bronze upright monument, no granite statue, not even a flat grass headstone—just a simple marker with his name. In fact, they had a hard time locating it in the first place. They only found it after Zack went to the office to get its exact location. The place stuck out because of its terrible condition, loads of palm fronds, rotted leaves, sticks, and dirt.

They almost didn't see the large easel with Vlad's picture from the memorial service. The photo, faded and cracked, showed a much younger and thinner Vlad grinning down on his remains. The entire scene gave Flora the chills. She thought she recognized the year-old dried-out flower arrangements, still decorated with funeral ribbons. She forced herself to bend down to clean the grave and then placed a small pot of succulents right where Vlad's heart would be. *Why was this allowed to happen? Clearly, Vlad's family has not been around at all!*

"Shame on you, Maya!" Flora cried out. "No one deserves to be treated like an animal! Vladimir, I've come to ask for your forgiveness. I'm so sorry for everything. I had no right to love you and try to take you away from your family." Flora choked up. "May you find peace in Jesus' care, and may your soul rest, knowing that you are remembered and prayed for."

She opened her Bible to an earmarked, tear-stained page and began to read in English, her voice weak and her breathing labored. "Repent, then, and turn to God so that your sins may be wiped out, that times of refreshing may come from the Lord." As she finished, she felt an icy breath on her back. She gasped and crossed herself three times, whispering in Russian, "God save me and have mercy."

Vlad had just about had enough of Flora's bullshit. What sins, what God? She must be mad, not just old and ugly. He put all his energy forth, trying to get her attention. "Hey, baba Yaga, why don't you shut the fuck up, take your Bible and leave me alone!" She did remind him of the old witch from the Russian folk tales used to frighten little kids.

Flora didn't hear him, although he had a distinct impression that she felt something. Still, she had more to say.

"I am leaving this cursed place, but I will never forget you, and I will include you in my daily prayers. Here is something from Ephesians. I hope you can hear me, my soul." If Vlad could have vomited, he would. "*Sterva*, why don't you just die, and I will show you just how much I love you." He focused on her head, and sure enough, she cried out in distress, but continued to read.

"*Florachka*, are you all right?" Flora's prayers were interrupted. Startled, she let the book drop to the ground. Although the voice seemed familiar, Flora didn't recognize the person speaking. She looked closely. A shape of a woman was blocking the sun, her shadow falling on Vlad's gravesite.

Alexandra (Sasha) the florist was delivering an arrangement for yet another memorial service when she ran into Zack. She recognized him from several pre-wedding meetings before Vlad's tragic death, so she said hello.

Although it took a minute for Zack to recall their last meeting, he greeted her warmly. When she inquired about his stepmother, Zack kindly pointed Sasha toward Vlad's grave.

"It's Sasha, do you remember me? Sasha, the florist, from Alexandra of the Valley—next to the Nail Spa?" Sasha asked the almost-unrecognizable Flora.

"Ah, *Sashenka! Da-da.* Of course, I remember you. You look wonderful!"

"As do you," Sasha said, trying not to gasp at Flora's much-changed appearance. "How are you, my dear, and how is your health?"

"Oh, I'm good; better than that—I'm fine, as you can see for yourself. In fact, I'm getting better every day with God's help. And may I ask after your father's health? How is he?"

Based on what she saw with her own eyes, Sasha didn't believe the fragile woman was well. Based on what Sasha heard, Flora did seem at least nicer. Even her tone of voice was gentler. Her appearance was very different: Flora's habitually shiny, wrinkle-free face looked as if it had deflated. Her skin was covered with a light cobweb of wrinkles, not at all unbecoming. The snow-white hair complimented her skin, so it looked like she was lit from within. In all the time Sasha had dealings with Flora, the woman never asked about anything personal, let alone inquired after Sasha's father's health.

"Thank you for asking about Father," Sasha said. "Unfortunately, he has passed on. Let's see . . . it's been half a year now."

"Heavenly kingdom to him," Flora said, offering a traditional condolence and crossing herself in the Orthodox manner. "And may the earth be like a featherbed to him," she added for good measure.

Although Flora didn't ask for details, Sasha found herself having a hard time continuing the conversation. She couldn't quite place it, but for some reason she felt an odd sense of discomfort around the woman. It was as if some energy was enveloping her energy field, sapping her strength and listening in. Sasha shivered.

"Actually, Papa Victor died in New York. I don't know if you knew, but he found his blood son, Gary, and decided to move there to be closer to his real family. You see, Papa lost so many years with Gary after the divorce."

"What do you mean 'real family'? You were his real family! I never saw a blood daughter take better care of her father," Flora cried out. Sasha was touched. With tears in her eyes, the florist gave Flora a spontaneous hug. "Thank you for saying that. I still feel guilty for letting him go alone, but he was not very nice to my son, Jason, and I had to take a stand."

"What happened in New York?" asked Flora, more polite than curious. "Of course, you don't have to tell me if it's too distressing for you."

Sasha was flabbergasted by Flora's newfound sensitivity.

"It was a fatal heart attack, following a stroke. Papa hadn't been taking his blood pressure medication, and he had too much alcohol on the plane. No one met him when he got there, so he got very upset. He never told Gary that he was coming to meet him, and Gary was out of town. Apparently, Papa had a stroke in the cab."

"Well, what did he expect—for his son to just open his arms and forgive all the years Victor neglected him?"

"It's not that simple. There were extenuating circumstances. Gary's mother took him away from Papa."

"She probably had her reasons. He was an alcoholic, right?"

"He drank. In any case, Papa would have died right then, but the taxi driver spoke Russian, and he was able to take Papa straight to the ER."

"They couldn't do anything for him?"

"They did all they could, but it was a massive stroke. He stayed in the hospital for several weeks, and then they moved him to a nursing facility, where he finally passed away."

"It must have been a shock."

"Not, really, *Florachka*." Sasha rubbed her hands together and sighed. "I knew the trip was too much for him—all that excitement and stress. The hospital contacted both Gary and me, but since Papa couldn't survive the move, I had to fly in to arrange his care."

"What about his blood son? Did he even lift a finger to help you?"

"It wasn't like that. Gary is a retired physician—very understanding, but since he didn't even remember Papa, the entire meeting between us was awkward. He seemed nice, but I felt he had no connection to us."

"Yes, life is very strange, isn't it, Sashenka?"

"Gary did help with the funeral expenses, though. Papa was cremated, and I've got his ashes with me. Jason says we should use the Neptune Society and scatter them at sea, but I want to buy him a spot here."

"You were a wonderful daughter. I know the cost here is very high, and you work so hard. Perhaps your son is right."

"Perhaps. But I also know they weren't speaking in the end because Papa hated Jason being gay. He also blamed me for making Jason gay."

"No one can make anyone gay."

"Yes, of course, I know that in my head. Still, I love my son, and I worry a little. He has moved to San Diego to be near his boyfriend."

"You must miss him very much."

"I do miss him terribly. He was such a comfort to me, especially when Papa left, but he has his own life."

"How are you managing the business alone?"

"Actually, I'm not alone. My husband Lee is now working with me. We're busy, thank God."

"You deserve all the success! You are very talented and honest!" Flora said, which made Sasha feel uncomfortable since normally Flora had had nothing but complaints about her work.

"Thank you. I appreciate your kind words, but what are you doing here?" Sasha stirred the conversation away from herself by changing the subject.

"I've come to say farewell to Vladimir and ask for his forgiveness. You know, we were very much in love. He was going to leave his family for me. I've since repented, and through my suffering, I've become closer to the Lord. I hope God has forgiven him as well and taken him into his care, but I worry about his soul. He was not only a Jew, but an atheist."

"I see. I'm glad you've found comfort in your religion. It must make your illness easier to bear."

"God is not a religion. God is the way—the only truth—and without his grace, there is no healing. Yes, Sasha, I'm a completely different person now," Flora went on, using her new "instructional" voice. "I'm so blessed to get a second chance in life, both with my own husband, who is a saint, and with the Lord himself. I don't even blame Maya, that evil incarnate, for being so jealous of me that she destroyed our lives. She will have to pay for her sins—she and her wicked family. On second thought, I hope God strikes her dead. Did you hear what happened to her sister-in-law when she tried to escape?"

"What do you mean?"

"They say, Fat Maya ordered a hit on Oksana's business partner: luckily the man was able to escape, leaving the poor girl to fend for herself. Considering her own family doesn't have the right connections, she's lucky to be alive. Slava is now in complete control of her business, meaning she'll never escape his claws, not while he and his sister are alive.

Sasha was surprised by Flora's story. She also heard a few rumors about Oksana having marital problems, but nothing as shocking as what she had just heard.

"Ken and I are leaving California—our own paradise lost. This is no longer our home," Flora said with resolve, lifting her chin.

"Where will you go?"

"Oh, we're going back to Ken's family home in Illinois."

"I don't believe it!"

"Yes, Christ is full of miracles. Ken has inherited an old family house where his mother grew up. You would love it! It's charming and we won't have a mortgage. After all the troubles, Zack, our son, has just gotten married and enlisted in the Marines, so we're off to Chicago and then on to Galena. Can you believe the name? Galena was my grandmother's blessed name. It was meant to be, don't you think? In a few weeks, Zack will be leaving for basic training back East and then he hopes to join the fight in Afghanistan, but his bride will live with us."

"Meant to be…" Sasha sighed. "I wish for you only what you wish for yourself. But you must be upset about Zack."

"Why would I be upset about him? He's doing great!"

"I meant worried about him joining the military."

"We are proud of our Zack. He's following his father and grandfather into the Marine Corps! Here you go, you liberals putting down our military. Someone has to defend your son's right to marry a man!"

"Oh no, please don't be angry with me, dear. I didn't mean to offend you in any way. Of course, we are proud of the military. I'm so happy for your new life. I know your health will get better, and Zack will be safe."

"I accept your apology," Flora said coolly. "But this is exactly the kind of unpatriotic attitude about defending our freedoms we're fleeing."

"Of course; again, I didn't mean to upset you. Let's keep in touch!" Sasha offered.

"Yes, I will find you on Facebook. Maybe one day you can come and visit. It's so peaceful. It's the way I always imagined America would be, not this horrible place full of drugged-out homeless, illegals, criminals! Typhoid fever!"

"Well, people have problems. It's very expensive, but it's not that bad," Sasha disagreed diplomatically.

"It *is* that bad and getting worse every day!" Flora cried, forgetting all about her newfound "sainthood." One day, you'll have to leave as well. All they want to do here is rob honest-working Americans and give it away to the freaks."

Sasha didn't like what she heard, but she didn't respond. Instead she softly made her excuses, saying she needed to get back to work. The two women hugged. Sasha offered to push Flora's wheelchair toward the office where Zack was waiting near the car. Flora agreed, and after crossing herself one more time and blowing an air kiss to Vlad's grave, the two women left.

Finally, good riddance to bad rubbish! Vlad was pissed, having to listen to this stupid conversation between the two dim-witted women. The florist was all right, just boring, while Flora—well, that bitch was another story. Imagine the hypocrisy! She was praying for his soul and asking God to forgive him! As if there was such a thing. There was life, and there was this—being trapped, bored, and unable to do as one pleased.

The winds were picking up again. Several burials around Vlad's part of the cemetery ended quickly as the winds blew the dirt around and messed up the flower arrangements. The mourners, rubbing their eyes from dust, hurried to get into their cars and leave for parts unknown.

Yeah, you can't wait to get back to your own lives, Vlad thought. *I wonder how fast you'll forget your so-called beloved departed.*

Vlad was beginning to drift off when he noticed something. At first, he couldn't register the oddity. All around him, huge, floppy snowflakes were coming down in force. In the blink of an eye, the flakes covered the road, the grass, the open gravesites, and the headstones. *What the fuck?* Vlad was taken aback. *Snow in LA?* Then he remembered something. He recalled a conversation with his mother. Sadly, it was their very last phone call, just before she died—alone, back in Ukraine.

"We will never see each other again on this earth," she said uncharacteristically sure of herself.

"Stop being a drama queen," Vlad said, feeling annoyed. "Of course, we will see each other. I'll send for you. You'll see. You'll like coming to LA."

"One day I shall come to LA, but only when it will snow."

"Don't be juvenile, Mama! It never snows in LA!" Vlad had laughed at the old woman. Mama loved the snow. Being born and raised in the Northern city of Tver, she never had enough of it. Vlad remembered how she used to awaken him in the middle of the night, bundling him up to go outside and play, since by morning the snow would melt. He remembered how much she loved visiting him and Maya in Moscow when they first got married. He remembered kissing beautiful young Maya, who wore a fluffy red fox hat over her luscious black hair, softened by the silvery white flakes.

And now it was snowing in Los Angeles! Maybe he could go into that light tunnel, where he saw Mama's face. Vlad felt a jab of something in the middle of what used to be his heart. He didn't know what. Was it hope? Perhaps there was some other force greater than himself, and perhaps that force could offer salvation. Maybe he could be free to see Mama again.

Above Sunset Boulevard, wind-driven fires were moving up the hills with such fury that the local battalion chief texted furiously, giving orders to abandon the fire lines and get out ASAP. Even the fire retardant-dropping planes were ordered to leave the area. A seasoned professional, the man was nevertheless terrified as he witnessed the living flames, mixed with ash, dust and smoke creating their own tornado. The tornado swirled, twisting and spinning up higher than he'd ever seen, way over 15,000 feet to his estimation. This was the fire Armageddon he feared all his professional life. The last *I love you* text went out to his wife and sons.

The air was thick with stench and smoke, and the normally packed 101 Freeway was eerily free of traffic. Huge toxic ash was falling over the city, blanketing everything in sight, including the famed cemetery. Azrael, the Angel of Death, God's own helper, his wings glowing crimson, flew over the hills prepared to do his job.

Hollywood was burning.

To be continued in *The Red Mongol* . . .

ACKNOWLEDGMENTS

I HAVE TO start by thanking the late Professor Allingham-Dale, who assigned a one thousand-word essay in my very first English Literature class at a local community college. Imagine my surprise, when not only did I receive an A, but I also got invited to have coffee with her Laguna Beach weekly writer's group, where she read it out loud. After she edited the essay, she suggested that I expand it into a short story worthy to be entered in a writing contest (which I also won). And so, *The Blue Tatar* would never have happened without her unending belief that I have a real passion for her native tongue, English, which is not even my second language!

I would be remiss not to extend my sincere gratitude to the team at Union Square Publishing, especially Scott Frishman, who has been nothing but supportive and professional.

Many thanks to my rock star of an editor, Claudia Volkman. My appreciation also goes to Sandra Harding for her direction and, of course, to my publicist, Darcie Rowan, for her sage advice, humor, and patience!

Last, but not least, I must thank my husband, Cary, who has always believed that I can turn a few paragraphs of immigrant stories, philosophical musings, history, and memories into a genuine American novel.

ABOUT THE AUTHOR

Born and raised in the former Soviet Union, L.N. Gruer is an internationally recognized wellness expert, blogger, and entrepreneur. A healer, prize-winning poet, amateur competitive ballroom dancer, and world traveler, she holds a master's degree in Eastern European Studies from UCLA, along with a PhD in Holistic Nutrition. L.N. Gruer has published nonfiction works on therapeutic nutrition, including her groundbreaking book on pediatric mineral deficiencies. *The Blue Tatar*, however, is her debut novel. When not at her desk, she can be found at her piano, gardening, or playing baseball with her two grandchildren. Dr. Gruer lives with her husband and an adorable Maltese, Pasha, in Southern California.

BOOK CLUB STUDY QUESTIONS

How did the book make you feel?

Which character did you identify with the most?

Which character did you understand the least?

What themes did you detect?

What is your impression of the author?

What are some differences between modern immigrant women and immigrant women of the past?

How is the notion of class different among the Russian-speaking community and American society?

What did you think about the male characters?

Did you find any change or growth in the characters from the start to finish?

If this book became a film, who would you cast?

Do you believe in forgiveness and redemption?

Printed in the USA
CPSIA information can be obtained
at www.ICGtesting.com
JSHW082325060324
58585JS00003B/72